GHOSTS

of

LILAC LANE

A compilation of short stories from:

The People Upstairs—2012

Cobwebs—2013

Scarecrows And Sentinels—2013

Redemption, Revenge, and Renewal—2014

DAVE LOPARDO

Cover: The "Ghosts" of Lilac Lane; John McGowan, David McGowan, Caden Riley DeFeo, and Eric Dean, photographed on July 20th, 2019.

TABLE OF CONTENTS

THE PEOPLE UPSTAIRS

COBWEBS

SCARECROWS AND SENTINELS

REDEMPTION, REVENGE, AND RENEWAL

FOREWORD

This collection of stories from my first four books is an attempt to keep them alive, of sorts, even though they have gone out of print. My fifth collection, *Sundown Serenade,* is thriving quite nicely, however.

Lilac Lane is the fictitious name of the hill I grew up on. There were twenty or so of us who inhabited that childhood world. Even those who lived on two parallel hills and side streets seemed *drawn* to Lilac Lane. It was our epicenter. All of us who lived in that magical world are gone now, of course. At least seven are no longer alive.

What was once a neighborhood full of raucous yelling, happy shouting, and good-natured cursing is now eerily quiet. No one replaced us. Lilac Lane has become a drive-through museum of our youth.

I have chosen, therefore, stories that feature young people, alone or in their friendship groups, struggling to cope, engaged in all sorts of activities, unaware of the timer that will all-too-soon run out. (One story features three grown siblings, but they are as foolish and immature as young children.)

The boys on the front cover at the top of modern-day Lilac Lane (three of my grandsons and their friend) are not ghosts at all. They are merely a representation.

The boys on the back cover, atop a 1960's Lilac Lane, enjoying their idyllic youth, *are* Ghosts of Lilac Lane.

I, too, am a Ghost of Lilac Lane.

Dave Lopardo
October, 2019

"THE TEN OF SPADES"
1993

"Dad, this isn't the way, where are we going?" asked ten-year-old Paul Virras, leaning over the front seat of his father's 1940 Chevy. Russell Virras exchanged a knowing smile with his wife Nancy, sitting beside him on the bench seat of the six-year-old sedan.

"Where do you think we're going?" he said.

"I thought we were going to see the bomber factory at Willow Run."

"There's nothing to see there any more since the war ended, Paul."

"I give up, then," Paul said good-naturedly. His father usually took him to fun or exciting places on Sunday afternoons when they headed out of the city. The Detroit area was full of great things to see, especially if you loved airplanes.

In reality, he *liked* airplanes, he *loved* bombers. They had a vitality you didn't find in other planes. With the colorful names and designs, it seemed to Paul they had a life of their own.

It was obvious that his parents weren't going to reveal the surprise destination. He decided to take another guess. "Dad, isn't this the way you go to work?"

"It's Sunday, Paul. No one out there today."

"Well, how much longer..." Paul stopped in mid-sentence and struggled to comprehend what his eyes were seeing. Rounding a turn, they were passing a large open field used for carnivals, an occasional circus, and other such events. The field itself could hardly be seen. From end to end were the olive-drab and silver bodies of airplanes--bombers.

"Dad, look! Stop the car!" Paul was frantic. His parents smiled as his father pulled into the entryway of the field.

"Good surprise, huh Paul?" asked his mother. "Your father found out at work that there would be bombers here for a while, so we hid the newspapers and told your aunt not to mention it."

"Were these the extra ones they made?" asked Paul, as his father guided the car into the makeshift parking lot by some small wooden buildings at the front of the field.

"No, Paul," replied Russell. "Every one of these birds was in combat. I was told they still have all their guns on board, too."

"Can we go right up to them?"

"Better than that. You can go inside."

"This is the greatest! I'm heading for the top turret of one of these babies!"

Paul zigged and zagged his way among the many B-17's and B-24's lined up on the dusty surface of the old fairgrounds as his parents tried to keep up. The day was hot, approaching ninety, and the sky cloudless. Russell and Nancy's futile efforts at staying with their son were matched by his frustration. Every plane had several kids *and* adults entrenched in the pilot's seat or the gun turrets. When Paul eventually found them, much of the luster of the surprise had been dimmed.

"Dad, can we come back another day? There's too many people around."

"Paul, Sunday's my only day off since we got so busy at work." Russell, an executive with *Wayne County Contractors,* was overburdened with the post-war housing boom.

Walking back toward the buildings and parking lot, Paul noticed another plane parked off to the side, its silver finish reflecting the bright summer sun. He correctly identified it as a B-17G. He had overlooked it in his initial enthusiasm. Apparently, so had everyone else. It seemed to be deserted, except for one of the maintenance crew that were stationed among the planes. Paul could not believe his good luck, and sprinted ahead of his parents and up to the man.

"Can people go inside this one, too?" he asked.

"It's all yours."

Even in his hurry, Paul couldn't help taking a closer look at the man. He was about twenty, Paul supposed. His face was an explosion of freckles surrounding bright blue eyes. Paul could see a trace of red hair beneath the cap. It was as though Huck Finn had joined the Army Air Corps.

"How come this plane is way over here?" he asked.

"It was the last plane in, and there wasn't any room left on the field, so we had to put it here."

Paul noticed the stripes on the plane's nose that identified it as a squadron commander's aircraft. It was named the "Ten of Spades," and had a large playing card of the same name on the side, under the pilot's compartment.

While his parents remained outside to let him fully enjoy the experience, Paul had the entire bomber to himself. He made a beeline for his favorite spot, the top turret, just behind the pilot. Paul squeezed into the gunner's seat, and was overwhelmed not only by what he saw and felt, but what he could *smell*. Plexiglass, gun oil, rubber and plastic combined with the heat to create one magical smell that Paul knew was ordinarily reserved for the men who manned these guns.

He squinted through the gunsights, found the manual traverse lever, and revolved around, sweeping the blue skies clean of imaginary enemy planes. No other moment in his life could ever be as special and magical as this.

From the moment they got into the car to drive the thirty-one miles back to Detroit, Paul was begging his parents to return the following Sunday. By Tuesday, he had gotten a 'we'll see,' which usually meant 'yes.' By Thursday, it *was* a yes, depending on the weather. Paul prayed for clear skies.

Sunday arrived, and while it wasn't as hot, it was partially cloudy, the air thick and heavy. In church, Paul's mother complained of feeling ill. When they arrived home, she went into the bedroom to lie down while Paul helped his father with a makeshift Sunday dinner.

After eating, Paul knocked on the bedroom door and asked her if they were still going.

"You and Dad can go if you want. I'll be all right. I just need to rest. I couldn't take riding in the car the way I feel."

After being reassured by his wife, Russell and Paul got in the Chevy and headed west, toward Ypsilanti and the old fairgrounds.

Paul's restlessness and squirming indicated to Russell more than anticipation. "Paul, two things. Hit the restroom when we get there, and don't be disappointed this time if there are other kids in all the airplanes. That's what they're there for."

"Dad, it's not the same," Paul insisted. "You can't pretend what you want when people you don't know are around."

When they arrived, they discovered that the cloudy, humid weather had held the crowd down somewhat. After parking the car, Paul and Russell went inside and used the bathroom. They found an information counter there, with bulletin board displays of the exact planes on the grounds, group photos of their crews, and other memorabilia.

"Paul, a lot of the planes look empty. You can take your pick."

Paul shook his head. "I'm going straight for *my* plane, the Ten of Spades."

Russell thought this a bit odd, but assumed it might make perfect sense to a ten-year-old with a vivid imagination. Perhaps Paul didn't want to "transfer" to a new crew after flying several missions with his imaginary comrades on the Ten of Spades. He decided to indulge his son and wander around for a while.

Paul dashed over to the Ten of Spades. He was surprised to find the same maintenance man. "Anybody in there?" he asked.

The young man smiled. "Nope, all yours again."

Paul climbed inside and took his position in the top turret. Moments later, as he was pretending to enter German air space, he sensed movement in his peripherals. Looking down, he found the young man who had been standing by the plane. His coveralls were gone, replaced by a Seventh Army Air Corps uniform, a red and white star on the shoulder patch. Paul stared at him in surprise.

"Mind if I join you in my old spot?" he asked.

"*You* were the top turret gunner on this plane?" Paul gasped.

"That's right. Seventeen mission."

Paul continued to stare in admiration and astonishment.

"Lane Thomas, Seventh Army Air Corps," said the man, as he pointed to a name patch over a breast pocket.

"You get to travel around with your old plane?"

"For now. So, you like being a turret gunner, huh? You stay there, I'll squeeze in up here." He settled into a position next to Paul. "What's your name, son?"

"Paul Virras. Did you shoot down any Germans?"

"I guess so."

"How many?"

"I don't know. It's not important, now."

"*That* must have been neat, seeing those Kraut planes dropping out of the sky."

"Paul," Thomas said, "they were Germans, not Krauts, and they were just like me, young and scared.

There wasn't anything *neat* about it." His bright smile had disappeared.

Paul was embarrassed, but regained his composure and continued his conversation with Airman Thomas. He learned that Thomas was twenty-two, from Billings, Montana, and had gotten engaged before the war. Paul already knew he was touchy about things Paul considered fun and exciting. Other than that, he seemed open and friendly. It was almost like having an older brother.

Thomas delighted in telling Paul stories about England, where he had been stationed, and some of the men he served with. Paul's favorite was how some bomber crews took containers of ice cream up with them, because the vibrations and freezing at high altitude made it taste so good.

Paul happened to look out the turret and saw his father waiting for him. "That's my father standing there, Mr. Thomas." Paul waved, and felt the Airman lean over and wave, also. Russell returned the wave, then pointed to his watch. "I guess we gotta go now," Paul said, disappointment filling his voice. "How much longer will these planes be here?"

"I think another week should do it," replied Thomas.

"Do what, Mr. Thomas?"

"It's just an old Air Corps saying, Paul."

Before they had reached the car, Paul was campaigning for a third excursion to the fairgrounds. "Dad, you know that man we saw by the plane last week? He was the top turret gunner on the Ten of Spades. He came inside in uniform and told me about the plane and their missions and stuff."

Russell looked at his son with puzzlement. "What man by the plane, Paul?"

"The one in the turret with me."

Russell stopped walking and looked at his son closely. "Paul, your mother and I didn't see anyone by that plane last week, and there wasn't anyone in the turret with you just now. You were alone." There was a hint of concern in his voice now.

"Dad, the young guy. With the red hair and freckles. Lane Thomas. He came *in* the plane. You *waved* at us, Dad."

"Paul, I waved at *you.*" The tone and expression had gone from concerned to stern, approaching a warning. "You've had a lot of excitement today, and I think you're letting your imagination get the better of you." He softened his expression. "I'm glad you had fun today, Paul, but you're old enough to know when to pull back on the old throttle."

"But Dad, he was *there!*"

"That's *enough*, Paul. I don't want to hear any more about some man with red hair in the turret with you. Let's go home."

. . .

"Is Paul still in his room, Nan?"

"Yes, he is. What *happened* out there? I haven't seen him this upset in ages."

"He spent the entire time in that one plane he went in last week. Everything seemed fine. On the way back to the car he comes out with a story about some man with red hair and freckles standing by that airplane last week."

Nancy searched her memory of that moment. "There wasn't *anyone* by that plane, Russell. That's what was so odd. It was deserted."

"Wait, there's more. He tells me the same man came in the plane later, introduced himself as the top turret gunner, and told him all about his experiences in the war.

He capped it off by having the man wave to me from the gun turret."

Nancy exhaled in disgust. "Is *that* what this is about? Russell, you know Paul was just pretending. You're the one that's always encouraging him to use his imagination."

"Nan, you don't understand. He can pretend *Hitler* was in the turret with him for all I care, but he should know where this stuff is supposed to stop. He was acting like he believed his own story. You can't encourage *that* in a ten-year-old."

Nancy was still not convinced this was serious. "What are you going to do, Russell, punish him for pretending?"

"No, Nancy. Paul has to learn to take responsibility for what he says. On my way home from work tomorrow, I'm going to check out his story."

. . .

Twelve miles from *Wayne County Contractors,* Russell Virras took a left into the parking lot of the old fairgrounds. A handful of people were browsing among the planes. As he headed for the information building, Russell took a quick glance over at the Ten of Spades. There was no one near it.

He went to the information counter, laid his briefcase down, and waited until a heavyset man with dark, slicked-back hair and a small moustache came over to him. The name badge on his blazer said *Ginsberg.*

"May I help you, sir?"

"I was wondering if any of the crew members from those planes accompanied them here."

"None that I know of. There are a few ground crew, though."

"Would one of them be a young red-haired man named Lane Thomas?"

"I'll check. I have a list right here." He looked up and down one of the papers in a nearby pile. "There's nothing even close to that name, sir. Sorry."
Ginsberg gave him a puzzled look and went back to his paperwork.

Russell walked aimlessly towards the display boards on his way out. Paul had made him up, but why? He glanced at the photos of the bomber crews and started reading about the Ten of Spades. The crew, it said, had selected the name because there were ten of them, and they wanted to pay Hitler back "in spades." Although the autographed photo of the crew was in black and white, it was obvious the man on the far right had red hair and freckles. His signature read *Lane W. Thomas.* Russell checked the caption. For a brief moment, he thought he owed Paul an apology. Near the bottom of the printing it said, "Far right, Lane Thomas, top turret gunner." Anger and disappointment returned as he read the last line. In parenthesis were the words, "Killed in Action, 1945."

. . .

It was the longest thirty-one miles Russell had ever driven. He concluded that Paul had gone back inside on that second visit and seen the photo. That explained how he knew the man's name and appearance. Why had he used a man whose death could so easily be checked? Paul could be as naïve as any ten-year-old, but he wasn't stupid. He did have a tendency to fantasize. Maybe he couldn't bear the thought of his favorite bomber's top turret gunner being dead. Maybe Paul wanted the man alive so badly that he *made* him alive, and got carried away. Russell wanted to give his son the benefit of the doubt, but there was no excuse for this, and it was up to him to correct it.

After dinner, Paul's parents sat him down in the living room. He sensed that this was serious. Russell explained about his side trip to the fairgrounds, and his discovery about turret gunner Lane Thomas.

Paul was overwhelmed with grief and confusion. His father was trying to remain calm, but there was an undercurrent of punishment or consequence in his manner. Paul sensed that to deny he made this up would only make things worse. He wanted one more visit to the fairgrounds, as this weekend would be the last time the planes would be on display. He hung his head and nodded in all the right places during his father's speech about fantasizing, respect for war dead, and truthfulness. His father did not rule out a last visit, but made it clear that it would be under "controlled conditions."

In the solitude of his room later, Paul tried to put the pieces together. He *knew* he had seen Lane Thomas. Why wouldn't his father believe him? What was this really about?

. . .

On the way to the fairgrounds, Russell put these conditions on the visit. First, Paul must read the photo caption that documented the death of Airman Thomas. Second, Russell would accompany him inside the Ten of Spades. Third, this would be the last visit, even though the planes were going to be held over for an extra week. Paul agreed, and resolved that he would tell his father whatever he wanted to hear.

When they arrived, they went inside to the display boards. Paul read the short bio on the Ten of Spades, and looked at the photo and caption. He knew his father had not been *lying,* but *he* hadn't been lying either. He could not understand this, but kept quiet as his father took him to the counter where Mr. Ginsberg stood.

"Mr. Ginsberg," Russell asked, "would there happen to be a young red-haired man here as a ground crew or flight crew member?"

Ginsberg recognized the man *and* the question from a few days ago. With raised eyebrows, he answered, "No, sir, there is *no* one here by that description."

"Thank you very much."

It had been a long three weeks for Arnold Ginsberg, kids running and yelling all around the usually quiet fairgrounds.

"You see, Paul," said Russell, as they walked out toward the Ten of Spades, "the man is dead, and no one even resembling him has been here."

"Okay, Dad." Paul climbed aboard the Ten of Spades, and instinctively got into the turret gunner's seat, his father still beside him.

"Paul, I didn't see anyone standing outside this plane, did you?"

"No."

"Is there anyone else inside with us now?"

"No, Dad, there isn't." This was the price, then, Paul thought. His father, the man he most admired, would not believe him, and didn't trust him not to start "telling stories" the minute they got here. He knew a lecture was coming, one that was supposed to make him feel ashamed.

"Paul, a lot of good men like Lane Thomas died so that we could be free. I don't think that's something we should make a game of, do you?"

"No, Dad." There would probably be a pause while his father thought of something else to add. Paul waited, his expression a blend of sadness and hurt.

Russell sensed how diminished Paul's spirit was. He loved his son's curiosity and exuberance. He did not wish to press the matter further. "If I walk around for a while, will you be all right by yourself?"

Paul recognized the peace offering from his father, and managed a smile. "I'll be fine, Dad."

Within two minutes Paul sat looking at the other planes and people, including his father, about twenty yards away. There was no joy left in pretending to be a turret gunner. He sat and thought about Lane Thomas, a man whom one reality claimed was dead, while some other reality insisted was still alive.

"Glad you made it back, Paul."

The boy jumped involuntarily. Lane Thomas was crouched beside him, in uniform. There was a sense of relief, but Paul was confused. There were questions here. Paul was sure this was his last chance for answers.

He returned the wave of his father, who now left his spot to walk around, as promised. "My dad can't see you, can he?"

"He's not part of this, Paul."

"What are you, Mr. Thomas?"

"I'm a turret gunner, Paul. Isn't it *neat* being a turret gunner?" The voice was heavy, had lost all its former sparkle and flow.

Paul felt a sudden hitch in his chest, his eyes started to well up. He was sure Airman Thomas was here for him alone, that there was some message for him in all this. "Am I the only one who sees you?"

"That's the plan, Paul."

"What plan?"

"Some of us got sent back. This is my last mission, my most important one. I have to convince someone like you that we can't have this stuff any more." He swept an arm in the direction of the field.

"No more *airplanes?*"

"Airplanes, Paul, but none with bombs on them, or turret gunners."

Paul could feel his chest getting tight, his breathing labored.

"When you're convinced, Paul, I want you to pass it on to another young person like yourself, one that thinks all this is *neat*. Ask them to do the same. Maybe someday we can put an end to all this."

For the first time, Paul felt an eerie sense of discomfort in the turret gunner seat. It occurred to him that Lane Thomas probably died there. "I don't think I'll be coming back here again," Paul whispered.

Lane Thomas smiled, the freckles, red hair, and blue eyes combining in an unforgettable look. "I don't think I will either. It's about time I moved on."

"Mr. Thomas, can I ever get my father to believe I didn't make this up?"

"People have to have faith and trust, Paul. That's what it's all about." He winked. "But I'll see what I can do." Thomas climbed down. Paul did the same and extended his hand. Thomas shook his head. "Sorry, Paul, can't do that." He straightened and saluted.

Paul tried to speak, but found his throat closing on him. He returned the salute, looking down to make sure his body was militarily correct. When he looked up he was alone. He held the salute for half a minute before leaving.

Paul was quiet on the ride home, and Russell wanted to break the tension. He felt the boy had learned an important lesson, and wished to compliment him. "Paul, I know I was tough on you today, but you took it like a man. They're going to have the planes here an extra week. We can come back again next Sunday."

"No thanks, Dad. I've seen enough."

Russell was surprised, and felt guilty, thinking he had ruined the boy's love of planes by rubbing his nose in reality that afternoon. They rode in silence for a while.

"Dad, do you have faith in me?" Paul asked, without warning.

Russell was caught off guard. "Of course Paul, why wouldn't I?"

"Do you trust me, Dad?"

"I certainly do. You've always been very honest about--" He stopped and looked over at Paul, staring out the window. Russell scolded himself. Paul had not mentioned the bomber or Lane Thomas. He was just now making the connection between his son's questions and the fantasizing problem. "Why do you ask, Paul?"

"Just wanted to know."

They didn't speak for the rest of the drive, but Russell could not help feeling he'd been suckered by a ten-year-old.

. . .

Russell Virras had no intention of stopping by the fairgrounds the next day on his way home from work, but here he was again. Furthermore, he had no idea *why,* but he felt that Faith and Trust were involved somehow.

He found himself at the display boards, and wandered over to the information counter, where Arnold Ginsberg stood, feeling as though he had been trapped in a bad play rehearsal. They had done this scene twice, and apparently were going to have to do it until they got it right.

"Please, mister, there's *no* young man here with red hair."

"I know, it's okay," said Russell. "I'm here for my son." Ginsberg was looking on either side of Russell, attempting to find the son he was here for. Russell identified the man's confusion. "He's not here now, I . . . never mind." Ginsberg put his hand on his forehead and looked down. "Mind if I leave my briefcase on the counter? I wanted to take a quick look by the window."

"That's fine, sir. I'll be in back if you need me." He walked off, looking at the ceiling.

Russell drifted over to the large plate glass, staring at the Ten of Spades. "Faith and Trust," he murmured, "are you on board somewhere?" He fixated on the top turret, almost willing himself to see someone. His heart leaped momentarily. Someone *was* in the turret. He moved slightly, then realized that the late afternoon sun, the window, and turret bubble had combined to create an illusion. He shrugged and walked back to the counter to retrieve his briefcase, which by company policy, was not to be left unattended.

He was about to lift it when an alarm went off in his head. The two metal buckles had been undone. Russell *never* left it like that. Someone had opened it while he was at the window. He could feel himself breaking into a sweat. Inside were contracts, bids on prospective jobs, and other confidential papers. He did a quick inventory, found all the folders there, and opened each one to check their individual contents. Nothing was missing. As he was reminding himself to be more careful, he noticed, under the bottom folder, a small rectangular object. It was a card, bearing the Seventh Army Air Corps insignia. He turned it over, and two more discoveries had him perspiring again. It was a playing card, *the ten of spades.* In the right-hand margin, was the signature, *Lane W. Thomas.*

It could not have been there before he got to the fairgrounds. The briefcase had been with him the entire time. He latched it and picked it up. Holding the card in his other hand, he walked over to the crew photo of the Ten of Spades. He stared at the boyish, freckled face of Lane Thomas, whose signature exactly matched the one on the playing card. The smiling face seemed to be mocking him.

"Why?" he whispered. "Why Paul?"

On the drive home, Russell realized that Messrs. Faith and Trust *had* been out at the fairgrounds, and had left their calling card as a reminder of how he had unintentionally wronged his son.

He was a man who dealt with real things in a real world, but in his shirt pocket was evidence of something *unreal.* He pulled the card from his pocket, looked again at the signature. It was real.

He debated with himself the entire drive home. Should he matter-of-factly tell Paul he now believed him and leave it at that, or would a wounded ten-year-old need something more concrete, more *real?*

Pulling into his driveway, he was still undecided. Paul was in the yard, and came trotting over, his rich smile giving no indication of the breach of trust he had been forced to endure this past week. Russell half-expected him to shy away, retreat into his room.

He got out of the car and watched him, the most valuable thing in his life, simple ten-year old adoration on his face.

"Carry your briefcase, Dad?" he asked.

Russell handed him the briefcase with his left hand, while with his right hand, which had begun to tremble, he reached into his shirt pocket.

"PERFECT FOR PACKING"
1994

It was Saturday, December 21st, the first day of Christmas vacation, and the snow pouring down from the northern Michigan sky was perfect for packing.

Maybe you've heard of me. I was mentioned in the book *Gruesome Coverups of Ordinary Crimes*. They won't let me have a copy here. That's okay for now. I'm a patient person if I have to be. The past thirteen years is proof of that.

On that Saturday morning in question, my older brother Alan and I were walking home from the YMCA. I'd been taking swim lessons, he was hanging out with friends. I was eight years old, Alan was fourteen.

We cut across Holdridge Park as a shortcut, although we probably lost time wading through the fourteen inches of wet, heavy snow that had fallen in the last three hours. We get some blockbuster snowfalls here in the Upper Peninsula.

We had nearly crossed the park to Gates Avenue when we came upon a weird-looking snowman. It had a cylinder shape, but the walls seemed to have been pushed in all around. It was shaped more like a tree trunk. It reminded me of the snow castles we would build around kids, in a tower shape. This snowman looked something like one of the snow towers, but much thicker. The top was decorated with rocks for eyes, nose, and mouth. It was a sort of hybrid snow tower-snowman.

Alan was a few feet in front of me, trying to climb over the huge snowbank. I could hear his grunts, along with the sounds of snowplows in the distance, and the warning beeps of sand trucks backing up. There was one other, nearly inaudible sound from just behind me, a muffled, half groan, half cry. I turned. The odd-looking snowman was all I saw.

There was a thud behind me. I turned to see Alan's head rise from the other side of the snowbank. He cursed and brushed snow off himself.

"Let's go, Christopher!" he shouted.

As his words died away I was almost positive I heard yet another sound behind me, more like loud exhaling. I looked back again, positive the sound came from the snowman. I scrambled over the bank, landing on my hands and knees, looking up at Alan. "The snowman! It made sounds!"

Before I knew it, he had grabbed the end of my long maroon scarf and was running up Gates Avenue, dragging me on all fours like a stubborn dog, stopping only after I fell onto my stomach. I got up and held my sore neck. "You idiot! That *hurt!*"

"Too bad! We still got a half mile to go in this stuff. We gotta *move!*"

"Alan, I told you, I heard—"

"I don't have time for your make-believe crap. Now *move,* or I'll drag you the rest of the way."

I didn't say anything else on the way home. Every so often, though, Alan would look sideways at me and mutter, "Stupid jerk."

We were half frozen by the time we reached home. I was terrified by what I thought I heard, but I kept quiet because of Alan. When Dad's office let him out early, we helped clear our sidewalk and driveway. The temperature was down to zero by then, and the chunks of snow we dredged up felt like concrete.

Dinner was the usual affair; pleasant, but subdued. Dad liked it that way. Alan excused himself when he was finished, whistling "Frosty the Snowman" under his breath. I shuddered. Mom and Dad smiled in appreciation of what they thought was his pleasant Christmas spirit.

That was the first of many tortures he inflicted on me that Christmas.

I was too uncomfortable and afraid to talk about the snowman to my parents, but I wanted to avoid Alan, so I hung out in the living room with them and watched TV all night. At eleven, when the local news came on, I was on my way to bed, but the lead story stopped me in my tracks.

Two boys, Brady Matthews, age 8, and Lewis Tranker, age 9, were missing. They had been on their way to a friend's house that afternoon, but never showed. The police had no reason to believe they were runaways. They were exploring the possibility of kidnapping or other foul play.

Dad shook his head slowly, Mom covered her mouth. The TV screen flashed their pictures, side by side. I didn't recognize Lewis Tranker, although he went to my school. Brady Matthews I did know, just by sight.

It was scary to think that something like that could happen to kids I went to school with, which made me think of the sounds I was sure I'd heard from the snowman. The two fears kind of ran together, and before I knew it, my mind was conjuring up images of one of those kids *inside* the snowman, calling for help.

Then it occurred to me. What if one of them *was* trapped inside, and by saying nothing all these hours I had helped kill him? Wouldn't that make me a murderer? I nervously excused myself and went to my room.

As I crashed down on my bed, it made the usual thump on the wall between my room and Alan's. I heard him moving around, then the slapping sound of a record being dropped onto his stereo turntable. There was a scratching sound as he lifted the needle. Then came the unmistakable musical intro to "Frosty the Snowman," from the *Beach Boys Christmas Album*. I buried my head under the pillow and quietly cried myself into a restless sleep.

The next three days seemed like a blur to me. Temperatures hovered between minus ten and zero. I was confined to the yard because of the missing boys, and Alan hounded me with the humming, whistling, and singing of "Frosty the Snowman."

On Tuesday afternoon, while rummaging around under my bed for a game I could play solitaire, I heard sounds outside my window. Pulling up the shade, I found a proud Alan putting the finishing touches on a snowman, just two feet from the window. He had gone to great lengths to dig out chunks of the frozen snow, and had spray-painted eyes, nose, and a gruesome scowl. Seeing me at the window, he gave the neighborhood his loudest rendition of "Frosty the Snowman," laughing and pointing at me as he sang.

I pulled the shade and jumped onto my bed, more haunted than ever by the snowman in Holdridge Park, and the pictures of Lewis Tranker and Brady Matthews on the TV screen.

On Christmas Day, the cold abated long enough for eight more inches of snow off Lake Superior, followed by more sub-zero cold. The two boys were still missing, and Alan continued his covert torture of me. Both awake and asleep, I was beset by haunting images of snowmen. In my dreams they groaned, growled, lunged at me. By daylight they seemed to me grotesque parodies of death.

And by now, of course, I convinced myself I had killed the missing boys by my silence. At some point in that turmoil, Christmas presents were opened. I don't even remember what I got. I opened box after box, not really seeing what was inside. "Just what I wanted!" I yelled.

. . .

Death is a magnet. I had to get to Holdridge Park. I asked Mom if I could go the day after Christmas, assuring her that lots of my friends would be there. She reluctantly agreed.

The capricious weather had done another turnaround. December 26th was balmy by contrast. The sky was clear, and a warm winter sun drove the temperature to nearly forty by noon, when I set out for the park, carrying my sled as a decoy. The warmth had penetrated the outer crust of snow. You could skim off an inch or two in round, mini-pellet shapes. It was perfect for packing, if that's what you had in mind.

There were a few kids in the park when I got there, and some adults, no doubt still mindful of the missing boys. No one was near the snowman, who had been left undisturbed, covered with a few more inches of snow.

I threw my sled over the bank and climbed into the park. I approached the snowman cautiously, as though expecting it might *know* it was me again. Working up what little courage I had, I walked up to it and listened. It was quiet, for normal background sounds of kids shouting at each other in the distance.

Encouraged, I removed the stones that had served as eyes, nose, and mouth. Faceless now, it didn't seem frightening at all. Further emboldened, I poked my finger where one of the eyes had been, drilling in an inch or so, scolding myself for ever having so much as lost my composure over this preposterous chunk of snow. I became nearly flippant about it. I knocked on the head. "Anybody home? Anybody in there?" I asked jokingly.

I picked up a nearby stick and drilled farther into the hole until it seemed to reach a hollow center, then swished it around several times, making it wider. "Peek-a-boo," I said, sticking my eye up to the hole.

There was another eye looking back at me. It was blue, half-closed, and spotted with ice crystals.

Everyone in the park, even those at the far reaches of it, eighty yards away, claimed later their ears were pierced by my scream. They saw a small boy, me, run toward the embankment, trip and fall over something, (my sled) and not so much *climb* the snowbank as *vault* over it.

I never stopped running, even when I reached home. I tore around to the back of the house and threw myself at Alan's hideous snowman, knocking it down and smashing it to powder and crystals. I crept into the house, shaking as I entered the living room, where Mom was tidying up. She looked at me with surprise and concern.

"Christopher, you look terrible. Did you get a chill?"

I nodded.

"Well, take off those wet clothes and hang them over the shower rod in the bathroom."

I nodded again.

"You go lie down after that."

"Okay."

I did as Mom asked and crumpled down on my bed. I tried to sort through the terror and guilt. Did anyone see me run away? Would I get blamed? Then it all seemed to wash over me in a sea of black and gray.

I slept until 4:30, when Mom awoke me and took my temperature. "One degree high," she said. "Not too bad."

I wish I'd stayed awake those three-and-a-half hours that afternoon. When you're awake you can brace yourself, make a plan. Asleep, your mind seeks its own level, and then *sets*. Maybe for good.

Dinner with my parents was mercifully uneventful. Alan was at a special all-night Christmas party fundraiser sponsored by the high school, and would not be coming home. I picked at Mom's homemade stew, then asked to be excused. She usually made a fuss when I didn't finish, but perceived me as "coming down with something," and allowed me to go back to my room.

I lay there for hours, tortured by thoughts of snowmen, dead bodies, and what might be done to me if— no *when* my part in the death was discovered. I finally fell asleep at about 8:30.

I dreamt I was on trial for murder. Alan was the judge. Brady Matthews and Lewis Tranker sat at the prosecution table, dripping wet, staring at me with anger and betrayal. The jury was made up of twelve identical snowmen, all clones of Alan's hideous model.

I was shaken awake at that point, and looked into the concerned face of my father. Mom stood behind him, her eyes red. "Christopher," Dad said, "were you at Holdridge Park this afternoon?"

I nodded sleepily.

He produced my maroon scarf. "Were you wearing this?"

"I guess so." I didn't understand.

"What did you find in the park, Christopher?"

I sat up in bed, petrified. I didn't know what to say.

"Christopher, we were just watching the late news."

I glanced at the clock, which read 11:10.

The lead story had been the discovery of the bodies of Brady Matthews and Lewis Tranker, missing since the 21st. Matthews had been discovered in Holdridge Park by some kids and their parents, who heard a boy scream loudly and then run. He was reportedly wearing a long maroon scarf, and left his sled behind. The adults investigated, and found that the column of snow the boy was near when he fled contained the frozen, suffocated body of Brady Matthews.

Police were called, and searched the nearby area. Under the snowbank bordering Gates Avenue, only twenty feet away, they found Lewis Tranker. He had died of head and internal injuries.

No one knew how the tragedy occurred, but police were going on the theory that Tranker had built a snow tower around Matthews in such a manner that he could not move to free himself. Tranker was subsequently hit by a car or snowplow during the ongoing storm, and was covered up in the snowbank. The additional snow and freezing temperatures concealed his body, while nearby, his friend suffocated and froze.

I had indeed, heard sounds from the snowman, Brady Matthews' last cries for help. Alan and I had probably climbed right over Lewis Tranker getting to Gates Avenue.

"Christopher," Dad was saying, "that was you those people saw in the park, wasn't it?"

I looked away, shaking, my eyes filling up.

"Why didn't you tell your mother when you got home?" he asked gently.

I threw my arms around his neck, letting the sobs loose. "I couldn't, Dad," I blubbered. "I was so afraid."

"Christopher," Mom said, "don't worry now. It's all over, honey." They consoled me as I cried some more, mostly out of relief that they weren't angry.

Something occurred to me. Neither one of them mentioned anything about my *first* encounter in the park. They obviously had no knowledge of it. That didn't change the fact that I had actually *heard* Brady's cries for help. In my mind I was still to blame for his death.

So, despite my mother's comforting words, it *wasn't* over. I knew I would still be traumatized by the sight of snowmen and Holdridge Park. But my brother Alan was my biggest worry. He might not only continue to spook me, but might let it slip that I had claimed the snowman in Holdridge Park made sounds that day. I wished with all my eight-year-old might that there would be some way that he would remain silent.

That very night, I got my wish, but it didn't come cheap.

Here's what happened. I can't prove it, but I know it's true. My parents and I had gone to bed. Alan had grown tired of the Christmas fundraiser, and had come home at some point. Everyone was asleep. He snuck into my room, apparently feeling the need to deliver one more stunning torture. He crawled under my bed, the bastard, and started whisper-singing "Frosty the Snowman."

In my half-asleep, guilt-filled mind, I was positive Brady Matthews was next to me, to take me to the hereafter with him for failing to save his life. I rushed screaming from the bed and down the hallway to my parents' room, babbling about snowmen, Brady Matthews, and dying. They had been expecting long bouts of nightmares from me, and immediately began to reassure me.

Alan popped in a few minutes later, having taken the time to get into his pajamas and mess his hair. "What's going on?" he asked.

Mom and Dad filled him in on the day's events. He put on his most convincing sympathetic older brother face. "Gee, that's tough, Chris, you findin' that kid. You gonna be all right?"

I was still shaking and sobbing into my mother's shoulder. But I recognized his voice as the one I heard singing. It *hadn't* been a nightmare, or Brady Matthews' ghost. I didn't dare tell on him. After all, I was terrified still that he would tell on *me*.

How did I know that it was Alan under my bed, and not a nightmare? The next day I looked under there. My games and baseball glove had been pushed over to the opposite side. Two or three game boxes had indentations, as though someone's leg or elbow had come down on them.

I knew he would never admit it, especially not after what that little prank of his caused.

I was one screwed-up kid after that. I had to have all kinds of counseling. Not that it did much good.

I may have been the only eight-year-old in the world who was scared of snowmen. I nearly fainted when I heard "Frosty" played. Yes, I was afraid of snowmen, but I was *more* afraid of what might be *inside.* Someone could be trapped in there, dying. I couldn't let that happen again.

I began to destroy every snowman I saw, whether it was on school grounds, in a neighbor's yard, or on stranger's property in another part of town. I got in quite a bit of trouble for it over the years. My parents had to keep explaining to people what was behind it. Or should I say, what was *inside* it?

From April through October, when there was rarely any snow, I seemed okay to everyone, but I wasn't. I knew they would be back. The snowmen, that is. They always came back, and I had to knock them down to make sure no one was trapped inside. Regardless of the weather, I couldn't pass Holdridge Park without flipping out a little.

Alan knew enough not to tease me any more. He played the All-American boy in front of Mom and Dad, but to me he was a vicious, cruel bastard who had driven me insane.

Yes, insane. What else would explain why I'm here at the Northern Michigan Institute for the Criminally Disturbed?

I bided my time with Alan, but one winter night seven years ago, it was just too much for me. Too much snow. Too many snowmen. There was no end to them. The snowmen, that is. Mom and Dad were on vacation in the Bahamas. I was not considered a danger to anyone.

Merry Christmas, Alan! I won't go into the gory details, except to say that I killed him in his bed, as he had killed part of me in my bed that December night six years earlier.

Then, in our spacious, snow-filled back yard, the fun began. I turned on the floodlights so I could see better. That was my big mistake. The neighbors all knew by now that I was pretty whacked. When they heard laughing and shouting late that night, and saw twenty-seven snowmen illuminated in our back yard, they called the police.

There was enough blood on the snow for them to conduct an on-the-spot investigation. I didn't help my own cause any, continuing to build snowmen as I answered their questions with whatever came to mind. I couldn't waste the opportunity, though. The snow was perfect for packing. Within minutes they made me stop, and began toppling my snowman society. I offered to help. After all, who was better qualified?

They found Alan in a snowman leaning against the corner formed by our stone wall and stockade fence. All that work for nothing, as it turned out.

. . .

I've spent the last seven years in places like this, playing the game, continuing my education, impressing the psychologists and social workers with my answers to their trick questions.

Recently, they put me in a room alone and played "Frosty the Snowman" repeatedly. Your tax dollars at work! I'm sure there was a two-way mirror or hidden camera somewhere. What did they think I would do, cover my ears and scream 'Stop it!' at the top of my lungs?

I merely suppressed all my rage and fear and sat there, quietly.

Now, the state of Michigan has determined that I, Christopher LeCoutre, am fit to re-enter society.

True, I have been *trained* and *prepared* to live a normal life. But the only definitive experiences I have had outside these walls are with snowmen: making them, knocking them down, discovering dead bodies inside them, and *placing* dead bodies inside them.

I'll *try* it their way, but I'm positive that it won't be long before I gravitate back to them. The snowmen, that is.

And whose bright idea was it to release me in the middle of February? There's nearly two feet of snow on the ground. The kind that's *perfect* for packing.

"CRAWLY STICK"
1995

D. J. Galley looked at the new apartments from his perch in the old tree fort, some thirty feet above the pine needle carpet.

He was paying closer attention these days to what his father called "external influences." He still wasn't sure what the words meant, but he knew they were bad. Dad had said so. It had to do with what he called "Northern trash movin' down here and takin' our jobs."

Last night, the *South Sullivan Daily* had an article about the new apartments, and how they were being filled by workers from a bankrupt plant in upstate New York. At dinner, Dad and Mom had discussed it.

"You read the article, Mel?"

"Yeah. Damn shame, that's what it is."

"Them people needs jobs, too, Mel."

"Then let 'um have their jobs up North. There ain't enough to go around no more, Linda."

"Their union was pretty smart, havin' a relocation clause in the contract."

"Pretty smart, all right. There's word goin' around that some of *us* might get bumped 'cause of *them.*"

D. J. took a last look at the apartments before settling down to the pile of Dad's comic books he was allowed to bring to the tree fort since turning nine last month. He had been watching to see if there were any kids his age. It could get lonely on the outskirts of South Sullivan.

The only kids he had seen were the pesty four to six-year olds, the kind of kids that could ruin a guy's secret hideaway. "External influences," he muttered.

For a while D. J. was lost in the comic book world of a generation past. A crunching sound snapped him back to reality. Looking down, he spied a small boy, about five, wandering at the wood's edge, a hundred feet away. He wore a faded red T-shirt and blue shorts.

D. J. squinted hatred through hazel eyes. What if he told the other pests what great woods these were? They would overrun the place in no time. His one sanctuary would be ruined. Dad was right. These Northerners brought nothin' but trouble.

He kept an eye on the boy as he descended the wooden rungs. *Got to get rid of him,* he thought. He *could* just bully him into leaving. But the kid might tell his parents. No. He had to think of something that would make *all* of them *want* to stay away. Maybe even move back North, and save his dad's job.

As he made his way down, he caught sight of the pond fifty yards farther into the woods. He had been warned about it ever since his dad helped him build the treehouse. Even now, he never even *considered* going near it. He reached the ground and got his bearings, looking for the boy. Noticing a patch of red behind some bushes, he approached, smiling.

"Hey," he said, startling the youngster, "watcha all doin' here?"

"Nothin.' Just lookin' around."

Plan 'A', D. J. thought. "You shouldn't be here, ya know. There's lots of dangerous wild animals."

The boy's eyes widened, but an excited smile accompanied them. "There are? Can we see some?"

D. J. swallowed his own smile. If anything, he had made the woods *more* attractive to him. "What's your name, kid?"

"Todd. What's yours?"

"Harold. How come you ain't ascared of the wild animals?"

I can't have none 'cause we live in a 'partment now. There's *lots* of kids, but no animals."

"Don't remind me," D. J. mumbled

"These are nice woods," Todd said. "I'm gonna come here from now on."

Plan 'B', D. J. thought. "The woods are okay, but the pond over yonder is even *better*. That's where all the wild animals hide."

Todd's head sank in further disappointment. "I guess I won't be seein' them, then. I ain't allowed to go near water. I can't swim."

Damn it all, D. J. said to himself. *I ain't even GOT a Plan 'C' yet.*

"Todd!" called a woman's voice in the distance. The boy snapped to attention, looking guilty and scared.

"I gotta go."

"Don't tell nobody about the woods, okay?" D. J. said. The boy didn't answer, continuing to run until he was out of sight. D. J. headed back to the tree fort. He had time to read a few more comic books. *And* think of a Plan 'C'.

. . .

The brown paper sack beside him in the tree fort held three small bottles of paint, paint thinner, brushes, and a dozen foot-long wooden sticks, formerly logs in D. J.'s construction set. He still used the set, but had decided to sacrifice the logs.

He placed the sack's contents in a neat assembly line order: the black, red, and yellow paint lined up in the correct sequence Plan 'C' required. He chuckled and repeated the adage his mother made him recite whenever he came out here: "Black on yellow can kill a fellow."

When he had finished painting, ninety minutes later, each former log was decked out in wide alternating bands of black and red, separated by narrower bands of yellow. As he admired his work, he heard rustling below.

"Harold," called a tiny voice. "You out here? It's me, Todd."

D. J. hunkered down in his stronghold. "It's not time for Plan 'C' yet, you little booger," he said softly. The tree fort was nearly undetectable from the ground. D. J. continued to lay low, waiting Todd to tire of his search.

Todd wandered haphazardly for a few more minutes, calling for "Harold" before giving up and heading toward the apartments.

D. J. stood and watched the distant figure. "Next time we'll have some fun, looking for" he glanced at the colored wood, "magic crawling sticks."

. . .

Donald James Galley stood in his tree fort, watching the distant apartments, ready to drop down if he saw Todd approaching. Next to him was yesterday's handiwork, the paint now dry. "Stupid kid's gonna come 'round lookin' for *Harold.* He was quite pleased for having given a fake name, on the almost certainty that Todd would mention him at home. "Unless," he mused, "he wants this to be a secret from his parents. In that case, even better."

He climbed down and quickly "hid" the colored logs so as to be easily detectable. "Just enough so he'll have to work a little," he said aloud. Then he climbed back up to watch.

Minutes later, he observed a young boy resembling Todd hitting a whiffle ball in his apartment's small backyard lot. A woman's head appeared at a nearby window. The boy waved at her. As soon as she disappeared, he dropped the bat and ran nonstop for the woods, as though legging out the world's longest single.

"You little sneak," said D. J. He hurried down before Todd could discover his secret whereabouts and positioned himself about twenty yards away.

"Harold, you're *here!*" Todd said brightly, finding D. J. by the bush he had rounded.

"That's right. This is my favorite place."

"Mine, too."

"Ya know *why* this is my favorite place?"

"Why?"

"'Cause it used to be a *magic* place."

Todd looked fascinated, but puzzled.

"There used to be magic colored trees here long time ago, but they're gone now."

"What happened to them? Did they die?"

"Somethin' like that. All that's left of them are a few pieces of their branches. They're hard to find. But I found one today." D. J. reached behind him and removed the remaining colored log from his back pocket, holding it near Todd's eyes.

The bright colors mesmerized him. He reached for it, but D. J. pulled it away, looking at Todd's shabby T-shirt and ripped jeans. "I'll give you a whole quarter for every magic stick you find me."

Todd's eyes widened. "Really? Where should I look?"

D. J. feigned deep thought. "Well, I been lookin' 'round here, but all's I could find was this one. Maybe if you looked over yonder there," he said, pointing in the opposite direction.

"Okay!"

For the next ten minutes, D. J. pretended to look in places he knew were barren, at the same time suggesting certain rocks, bushes, and clumps of grass to Todd, several of which concealed a colored wooden stick. D. J. laughed to himself. He could actually *see* some of them sticking out as he directed Todd to their location.

"Another magic stick!" Todd shouted, bending down and snatching his latest find from between two rocks.

"Boy, you sure have a knack for findin' 'um," D. J. said good-naturedly. "That's six, now." *This is perfect,* he thought. *He's grabbin' 'um before he can even tell what they are.*

"I'm tired, Harold. Can we rest?"

"I think that's enough for today."

"When do I get my quarters?"

"Right now," said D. J., reaching into his jeans pocket. He had been saving to buy a model car, but like the wooden logs, had decided to "invest" in a more important undertaking. He smiled patronizingly as he handed over the quarters. "Here you go. But yourself some decent clothes."

"My mommy and daddy do that," Todd said innocently. "But they don't have much money right now."

"Next time," D. J. stated casually, "maybe you can make five whole dollars."

"How?"

D. J. sat down on the pine needles. Todd copied him. "Ya see, sometimes the magic sticks can come to life. They turn into magic crawling sticks."

"Crawly sticks?"

"Yeah," said D. J., chuckling at the mispronunciation. "Crawly sticks. And you know what?"

"What?"

"If you catch one before it gets away, it will give you anything you want."

Todd's eyes turned to saucers, his mouth formed an oval. *"Anything?"*

"That's right. When I was little, I caught one, and it gave me lots of money and toys."

"Can I see it?"

D. J. dropped his head in mock sadness. "It crawled away one day when I left the door open. But there might be another one around here."

"Let's look. I'm not tired any more."

D. J. glanced at the sun. Todd did the same. "They only come out on cloudy days."

"Oh." Todd closed his hands and jiggled the six quarters.

"Remember, don't tell nobody, or you'll have to give the money back, and I won't help you look for a crawly stick," D. J. warned.

"I won't tell, Harold."

"You better get on home before your mama comes lookin' for you."

"Okay. Bye, Harold." He ran out of the woods as quickly as he had run in.

D. J. remained sitting, idly banging two of the sticks together. He snorted with contempt. *"Crawly* sticks!"

. . .

The day was perfect. At eight A. M. the cloud cover was so thick and dark it seemed like late afternoon. D. J. had risen early, left a note to Mom that he was taking a hike out on Highway 72, and gone out to the garage for a bucket, and the long metal strip Dad had bent at the bottom to form an 'L.'

He was going to the pond. He had never even gone close to it before, but today he *had* to. A lot depended on his bravery and success. Maybe even Dad's job at the mill. Today he would do what no one in South Sullivan, Georgia would even attempt. He was going to capture a Harlequin, the Southeastern coral snake.

He had always paid attention when the teacher talked about poisonous snakes. He knew they were shy and wouldn't strike unless stepped on or handled. And he knew their fangs were so small that nearly half those bitten were not poisoned because the skin was not broken.

He was confident that the plan would work if he could capture a Harlequin. His heart pounded. He had never felt so *scared,* or so *invigorated.*

He passed by the tree fort, yearning for the times he could just idle away the day there. Not today, though. There was dangerous, important work to be done. His musing had caused him to temporarily lose his vigilance. He didn't see the black, red, and yellow shape until he had stepped on it, that last instant seeming to play out in slow motion as he watched his foot come down.

He shrieked, trying to move every muscle at once, in every possible direction. The hard shape gave way, as he sprawled on the ground, the bucket and metal rod clanging against each other as he rolled, heart jackhammering. He leaped up to determine the snake's location.

The colored bands *rolled* down the slight incline, then stopped. It was one of the logs he had hidden. D.J. wanted to laugh at his foolishness, but couldn't. He put a hand over his pounding heart. "Damn it all," he said. He rounded up the bucket and rod and continued toward the pond.

He approached slowly, one step at a time, as though sneaking up on an enemy. Ten feet from the mushy, reedy shores a bullfrog sprang into the water, followed by other splashes around the pond. Circling, he watched the water's edge intently. "Gotta be careful," he reminded himself. Dark shapes revealed themselves in the shallow water, most of them in flight. Halfway around the pond he came upon several sheets of long-rotted plywood, possibly discarded by a builder of the houses on the other side of the pond.

He laid the bucket down and eased the bent section of the metal rod beneath the plywood. With all his might, he lurched up and away, lifting the plywood and flipping it end over end. Part of him wanted to attack instantly, but was overruled by the awe at seeing the largest coral snake he could imagine. In a second, *half* of it had taken off in the direction he had come. There were *two* of them.

D. J. grabbed the bucket and rammed the metal rod onto the remaining Harlequin, but it wriggled free and took off in the opposite direction. D. J. gave chase, careful not to fall into the water on onto his prey. Several times he caught up to the coral, pinning it. But each time, after initially rearing back and biting the metal, the snake was able to escape, aided by soft, uneven ground, a loose rock, or D. J.'s reluctance to press down hard enough to hold the snake's furious movements.

Finally, at the head of the pond, where the ground was harder and less sloped, he pinned him two inches behind the black head. The snake could not reach up or around to bite, and the boy's resolute pressure on the rod held it fast.

He dropped the bucket, and gathering all his resolve, stepped on the thirty-nine inch serpent at its midpoint, sliding the metal rod up until its head was pinned. For the next two minutes, he prayed for the nerve to grab the snake behind the head.

"Please, God, don't let nothin' happen." He held his breath and picked up the snake, holding it at arm's length. The mouth was open, the body whipsawed beneath his arm.

He squatted, grabbed the bucket, and eased the snake to ground level, pointing its head directly up to prevent it taking off immediately. When he had jockeyed the opening directly over the coiled reptile, he released his grip and slammed the bucket down. Keeping one foot on it, he reached for a nearby rock and placed it on top. He could hear thrashing and scraping sounds, but the bucket didn't budge.

D. J. waited for his breathing to return to normal, then looked admiringly at the fruits of his cunning and bravery. A slow, simmering smile appeared. He walked back toward the tree fort, carrying the metal rod. "Oh To-odd," he sang, "I've got a *surprise* for you."

. . .

D. J. held the five-dollar bill lengthwise. "Here it is. It's all yours if you find a magic crawly stick."

"Think we'll find some today, Harold?"

D. J. fought back a smile. "Well, maybe *one, anyways.*"

They walked towards the pond, D. J. pretending to look at the ground, raising his eyes to locate the bucket in the distance. Todd dutifully imitated him.

"Remember, Todd, crawly sticks *look* like snakes, but they ain't.

"How come they look like snakes, Harold?"

"Uh . . . so's not *anybody* will pick 'um up. Just kids like us."

"Oh."

They were fifteen feet from the bucket, the pond in full view. Todd halted. "Uh oh."

"What?"

"I ain't allowed to go near water, 'cause I---"

"Can't *swim. I know.* " D. J. realized he had to handle this carefully. "You don't have to get any closer than that bucket there, okay?"

"I guess."

As they approached the bucket, D. J. stopped and held his arms out, as though asking for quiet. "I think I hear one, Todd."

"Where?"

"Somewhere right around here." He pointed at the bucket. "Crawly sticks *like* to hide under buckets and stuff. Tell you what. I'll go on down by the water and look, and you look under there."

"Okay!" Todd started to rush forward, but D. J. caught him by the arm.

"Hold on there, Todd, old boy. Let me get down there in case he gets away from you."

"All right."

D. J. walked past the bucket, then turned and pointed at it, eyes wide, in a pantomime of discovery. In truth, he had no desire to watch. If by chance he was questioned, he could always say that he hadn't *seen* the snake. The trusty old bucket, of course would have to be tossed into the pond. Facing the water, he heard Todd's footsteps.

"Harold! A crawly stick! I'll get him!"

Any second now, D. J. thought.

"No you don't, crawly stick. Get back here!"

Yeah, get back there, crawly stick.

"I got you now, you little---"

The shriek that pierced the air gave D. J. a jolt. He was sure he had actually jumped. He turned to take in the scene he had orchestrated.

The bucket remained upside down, the rock still in place. *Bet he only lifted in an inch before that devil came flying out of there.* Todd was uphill about ten feet away, seated, wailing loudly. Twenty feet to the right the grass was a kaleidoscope of black, red, and yellow as the Harlequin made its escape toward the far end of the pond.

"Nice goin' big guy," D. J. whispered. He ambled up the hill, smiling at Todd. He bent and looked into the pale, frightened face, snapping his fingers in mock forgetfulness. "Oh yeah, Todd I forgot. Crawly sticks *bite* sometimes. *And,* they're *very* poisonous."

Todd struggled to get his voice under control. "I d-don't like y-you, Harold. You're *mean!"*

D. J. smiled a pitying smile. "Todd, old boy, I'd say you got more important things to worry about right now." Todd remained sitting, engaged in a new round of sniffling. "Well, Todd, gotta run. First, I better toss this old bucket in the pond."

He walked over to it, threw the rock aside, and grabbed it, in the same motion walking over the spot it had occupied. For the second time, his heart leaped as his foot came down on the black, red, and yellow color pattern.

The furious Harlequin struck, sliding up between the billow of D. J.'s jeans and his bare leg. He felt the stinging pierce in his leg, felt it again, and felt it a third time before his brain signaled to shake his leg vigorously. The coral was flung several feet away, making a mad dash around the pond.

No words came immediately. D. J. pulled up his pants and stared at his lower leg. Three neat sets of puncture wounds marked it. "Oh, *JESUS!* There were *TWO* of them!"

Todd had stopped crying, stood, and walked over to D. J. "Ha, ha, you got bit by a crawly stick, too." He peered at the wound, then seemed to lose interest in the entire episode. "I'm going home now."

Although numbness was already setting in, D. J.'s brain was still processing information. "But *you* got bit, *too!"*

Todd lifted his foot and pointed. "The other crawly stick bit my *sneaker."*

"You're not poisoned!" D. J. shouted. "Todd, listen to me. I need—"

"I'm not playing 'crawly sticks' any more, Harold" He turned and walked uphill towards the woods entrance.

D. J. attempted to rise, found his limbs unwilling. "Wait! Go get help! I'll *die!"*

Todd looked down at the older boy. "No! You lied!" He turned and ran out of the woods.

D. J. could feel his breathing becoming labored, his chest tight and burning, and the numbing sensation in his limbs growing.

His brain, in its last stages of usefulness, was reminding him that captured "crawly sticks" gave off a distress scent, often picked up by their mate.

"EIGHT-TRACK"
1995

It was one of those neighborhoods where the 'Have's' and 'Have-Nots' lived side by side. And true enough, the rich family, the Redmers, bordered on the property of Del Strobeck, the neighborhood Have Not.

We called him Eight-Track, after the obsolete tapes he collected, and spent as much time hanging out there as we did at the ball fields or each other's houses.

I know that a bunch of eleven and twelve-year-olds palling around with a guy in his late sixties seems kind of odd. But Eight-Track was more like an *advisor* to us. We'd go over there, six or seven of us, complaining about our parents, and nine times out of ten he'd take *their* side. But he'd *explain* it to us, at least. Most of the parents didn't care too much at first for us going over there. Eventually, they realized that he was okay. After that, they weren't suspicious, although I don't think any of them were really crazy about it.

Richard Kane, the eighteen-year-old half- brother of Mike Pfleuger, one of our gang, always gave us a hard time about it, though. "You guys oughta stay clear of that old coot!" he'd say. Richard had grown up bitter. His father was the fourth-to-last man killed in Vietnam. He took it out on the world in general, us in particular. We'd be sitting on top of the hill where Eight-Track's house was, and Richard would walk by, shaking his head and giving us dirty looks.

Marcus Wesley, a kid that talked as if he was from King Arthur's time, would say, "Ah, Richard the Fatherless passes."

Mike would whisper, "You mean Richard the *Asshole.*"

What did we do at Eight-Track's house? Mostly we listened to him tell of his life experiences. He had tons of fascinating stories, many involving some weird conspiracy to take over the country.

He claimed that one of his friends was there at President Kennedy's assassination. That got him going on his theory as to who was *really* behind the shooting. According to Eight-Track, it was a dairy corporation in Wisconsin and two infielders from the Mets. And don't even *ask* what the war in Vietnam had *really* been about.

"Tungsten mines!" he would exclaim. "We didn't want the Communists getting their hands on all that tungsten!"

All his tapes were narrations of his philosophies and stories. He tried a couple out on us, but they didn't hold our attention. Why listen to a tape of him when it was more fun when he talked live? We would interrupt with questions and objections to his weird theories.

For a retired truck mechanic with a bad back, a wife who had run off with a school custodian, and not much money, he seemed pretty happy. He still drove his sapphire blue 1976 Plymouth Volare, which he kept in great condition, despite his back. Everything with him, everything *about* him, seemed just right. But as he himself used to say, "Nothing in life remains static for very long."

. . .

We went over to his house one morning during the first week of summer vacation.

"Somethin' happened over there," he said grimly, pointing down his slope towards the Redmers. Their back yard, containing a luxurious built-in swimming pool, was visible even over the seven-foot stockade fence separating the two yards.

"What's goin' on, Eight-Track?" Lance Derwish asked.

"I don't know, but there's cops and ambulance guys there,"

We tried to get a better look, but that's when he kicked us out. No big deal. We ran around the block to the front of Redmer's property. Sure enough, there were two police cars, another marked "County Medical Examiner," an ambulance, and a couple dozen people standing around on lawns and the sidewalk.

"What happened?" we all asked, clamoring about.

The stern adults told us to simmer down, so we listened in on various conversations.

"Mrs. Redmer drowned in her pool last night."

"Probably had too much to drink, as usual."

"I heard she had lung cancer. Smoked like a fiend. Probably didn't have long, anyway."

We were shocked. Nothing like this had ever happened before. We didn't really *know* the Redmers. They owned several dry-cleaning stores, and mostly sat by their pool drinking all day. Finally, the ambulance guys wheeled a stretcher down the driveway. There was a long dark green bag on it.

We drifted over to Marcus's house for a while and talked about what it must feel like to drown, then headed over to Eight-Track's again. His old Plymouth was there, but he didn't answer the door. We yelled for him and everything. Norm Sutter even tried his back door, but it was locked. Marcus had that thoughtful look on his face.

"Perhaps Eight-Track is disturbed by the untimely passing of Lady Redmer."

The drowning was front-page news the next morning. Mr. Redmer told police that he and his wife had a few drinks by the pool before he went to bed around 12:30. She was going to take a short swim, then join him.

The next thing he knew, it was eight A. M. and he was alone in bed. When she didn't answer his calls, he went out to the pool and found her at the bottom of the deep end. He jumped in and hauled her out, but she was already dead.

The story mentioned that her blood-alcohol level was high, and was probably a contributing factor in her death. My mother was reading over my shoulder at the kitchen table.

"Fifty-nine years old," she said. "What a shame."

"Mom," I replied, "that's *old.*"

. . .

"Somethin's goin' on with Eight-Track," Mike said, as we sat around home plate in one of the lots we used. "Yesterday he wouldn't answer the door. Today he's not even home. His car's gone."

"Can't he go to the grocery store?" demanded Lance.

"He's been gone over seven hours!"

"Maybe he's *really* hungry, Mike."

Mike couldn't let *that* one pass. He chased Lance all over the outfield, with Lance laughing and managing to keep one step ahead.

The car that went by just then hadn't gone another twenty yards when the rest of us jumped up. "Eight-Track! Hey, you guys," we hollered into the outfield. "Eight-Track just drove by!"

Mike headed toward us. "Remind me to kill you later," he yelled at Lance. We sprinted towards Eight-Track's house, half a mile away. It looked like a road race in progress. We passed by Mike's house, where his half-brother Richard was sitting on the porch. He looked us over, scowling as usual, and picked out Mike bringing up the rear.

"Don't be late for dinner, jerk!"

Marcus nudged me. "Richard the Fatherless will make a fine mother someday."

We got to Eight-Track's house a couple minutes later, saw the blue Plymouth at the top of the steep driveway.

"Knock on the door, Marcus," I urged.

"Perhaps Eight-Track is deep in---"

"Oh, shut up. I'll do it myself." I knocked. After a couple of seconds we could hear him coming down the long, steep stairway that led to his second-floor den, where we usually hung out with him among his piles of tapes. We weren't sure what to expect. It was a pleasant surprise when he opened the door smiling.

"Come on in, boys. I've got ice cream sandwiches and soda for everybody."

We piled into his hallway, grinning ear to ear. Eight-Track was one of the guys again. Amid all the slurping and gurgling, Marcus asked, "Where were you, Eight-Track, pray tell?"

He leaned back, looking quite satisfied. "Well, I had to go pick up some groceries, for one."

"See, Mike, I told you." Lance said.

"And I had a little business decision to make. Needed some time to think it over."

"What kind of business?" I asked.

He looked at me and seemed to be stalling for an answer. Right then, Phil Chandler, who had gulped down a whole can of soda in one breath, let out a belch so long and loud it echoed and forced tears from his eyes.

The room erupted in laughter and insults. Phil was pelted with ice cream wrappers and empty soda cans. I started to repeat my question when Eight-Track jumped in with stories about guys he served with in Korea who were loud belchers.

Within seconds *everyone* was telling belching stories or trying to imitate Phil. Eight-Track often joined in our silliness, but it seemed that *this* time he did it to avoid my question.

For a couple of days things seemed normal. No more nosy questions from me, but I was still wondering why he didn't answer me.

Then, of course, things changed again. Like he said, nothing in life remains static for very long.

. . .

We were playing baseball in one of the vacant lots. About the time when everyone was tired, Tony Ondifer hit a foul ball in the woods behind home plate. No one except me moved a muscle to look for it. I never found the stupid ball, we all left, and the next day I was covered with poison oak.

I was confined to the yard, which normally would have been torture. But I couldn't do anything except scratch myself, anyway. To make things worse, that night was the annual Fourth of July fireworks at the park.

In a dull Ohio town of five-thousand, nearly everyone attended. A house-breaker could have had a field day on our street alone. Around eight, I could hear the explosions and cheers of the crowd. Feeling sorry for myself, I took a walk to Eight-Track's. He never went to stuff like that.

The itching had let up a bit, although my hands were still quite swollen. I was hoping Eight-Track and I could just shoot the breeze. And I would bet he had a theory about enemy agents planting poison oak.

About fifty yards from his house I saw someone coming out his side door. Although it was twilight, I could see the hands stuffed in the pockets, head down, that prowling walk. It was Mike's half-brother, Richard the

Fatherless, the guy who always hassled *us* for hanging out there. I didn't want him to know I'd seen him there, so I ducked behind a hedge opening until he was off the property. As we moved closer he looked up.

"Well, if it isn't little Eddie Cordelico," he said, with his usual nastiness. "Why ain't you down at the fireworks like a good boy?"

"I got poison oak. I itch all over." I scratched myself for effect.

He shook his head in disgust. "You guys. Every one of you is dumber than the one before, I swear." I looked at the ground. "Where you goin', Eddie? To see old man Strobeck?"

"I thought I might---"

He walked away, mumbling. It was so tempting, but I kept my mouth shut. Nobody wanted to rile Richard Kane. We all felt he was capable of killing somebody.

I headed up the driveway toward Eight-Track's. The only light on was in his kitchen. As I walked by his side door I caught sight of him inside, his back to me, the telephone receiver to his ear. Don't ask me why, maybe nosiness, or maybe because he avoided my questions that other day, but I stepped back against the side of his house and stood there, listening.

"That's right. Just a little piece of the pie for myself," he said. "No, don't worry about that. Just bag it and toss it over the fence. You know what they say. Good fences make good neighbors." He laughed.

I was pretty darn confused. Was someone going to throw *pie* over the fence to him?

"You just do that, now," he continued, "and I'm sure my memory will get fuzzy concerning . . .certain things. Fine. Five minutes, then."

He hung up and began to turn around. It was too late to pretend I just arrived. I dashed to the side and hid behind his baby pine tree. It was about as think as my arm, but had full branches, like a miniature Christmas tree.

A couple of minutes passed. Then he went out his back door, the one facing down the hill. I heard it shut, and could see his shadowy figure walking down the slope towards the fence separating his property from Mr. Redmer's. The lights were off by the pool, but I figured since his wife died, maybe he wasn't up to keeping them on.

I lost Eight-Track in the darkness, but I heard this crinkling sound, then footsteps as he materialized and went back inside. Wouldn't pie get wrecked being thrown over a fence? What was the big deal about it anyway? Sneaking back to the side of the doorway, I saw him sitting at his kitchen table, the bag open. But what he took out wasn't pie. It was *cash,* wads of it. I was scared, now. Dad once told me that when large amounts of money changed hands, something was rotten. I slid along the side of his house and ran home. Luckily, my parents were still at the fireworks. I needed to do some hard thinking.

. . .

It was tough pretending everything was normal, and not telling any of the guys what I'd seen and heard. The hardest part was hanging out at Eight-Track's and trying not to look guilty or suspicious.

About two weeks later I went over to Mike's house to see if he wanted to do anything. Just my luck, Richard answered the door. The instant I laid eyes on him it reminded me of the night of the fireworks. With all the turmoil inside over Eight-Track and the bag of money, I had almost forgotten the *other* mystery; Richard leaving Eight-Track's house.

"Nobody's home, runt," he said.

I was staring at him, possibly looking for some clue to all my confusion. Eight-Track was living some deep, strange secret, and so was Richard.

"You deaf or somethin'? I said he's not home. Beat it."

Maybe holding so much inside gave me the nerve to do what I did. "Richard?"

"What?"

"I saw you that night."

"Saw what, you little moron?"

"I saw you coming out of Eight-Track's the night of the fireworks."

He opened his mouth on impulse as if to deny it, but I could read something else in his eyes, a *trapped* look.

"So you saw me. Big deal. I do odd jobs for the old geezer. He doesn't know his ass from third base."

"Oh." I turned to leave, but he spun me around, his fingers digging into my shoulder.

"I get paid under the table from him, so you keep your fat mouth shut about me workin' there and you seein' me. Got it?"

"I got it."

Nice try, Richard, I was thinking on my walk home. Doing odd jobs, huh? The man had been a master truck mechanic, and could *still* make a living as a plumber, carpenter, or electrician if he wanted. He was about the handiest guy in Ohio.

So, Richard the Fatherless now had *two* secrets. He regularly went over to Eight-Track's, presumably when the rest of us were home. The big secret: *Why?*

. . .

For Marcus, Mike, Lance, Phil, Tony, Norm, and me, it was like seeing a nightmare acted out. And the worst part was, you knew the ending. On the morning of July

21st, three days after my conversation with Richard, the same ugly scene played itself out in front of Eight-Track's house. The police. The ambulance. The crowd. The stretcher with the dark green bag wheeled down a steep driveway. We didn't have to ask. We knew he was dead.

I looked around at the guys, all of us standing together, a couple of our parents among us. I saw the same thing on all their faces: shock, grief, the end of innocence, I suppose.

Across the street, by himself, stood Richard Kane, his fists clenched in front of him. The look in his eyes was one of pure rage. He ran toward his house.

I followed him keeping my distance. When he got home, he headed for their garage. I heard its side door slam. With my heart in my mouth, I opened it and stepped inside. He was sitting on an old storage box in the far corner.

"What the hell *you* want? Get outta here!"

"Richard, I've got to talk to you about Eight-Track."

"You gonna leave, or do I have to wipe up the floor with you?"

"No. I won't tell anyone about this, honest." He glared threateningly, but I just stood there. It wasn't all bravery, I don't think. I was sure he *wanted* to talk, he just had to overcome the tough-guy image.

"Shut the goddam door at least. You think I want the whole neighborhood to hear?"

I shut the door and sat next to him. I was right. There was a lot more to him than he let on. His anger over not knowing his real father was starting to overcome him. Then, by some odd twist of fate, he met Eight-Track. He had been going over there on the sly since he was fourteen. It wasn't the fun relationship that we had. It was more like going to see your guidance counselor, or one of those Big Brothers.

"He couldn't help me control anger," Richard said, "but he gave good enough advice to keep me out of serious trouble, even helped with schoolwork sometimes. He was the closest thing I ever had to a *real* father."

"What about your stepfather?" I asked.

"Pffffft! Him? All he ever cared about was Mike, *his* kid. I was the *other* kid, the one that came with the house when he married my mother."

"What are you gonna do now?"

He rose suddenly, shoved me off the box, and opened it. Digging down, he produced a small paper bag. *Oh, no,* I thought, *not another paper bag.* He removed a red, oblong plastic object from it. It was an eight-track tape. "I'll tell you what I'm gonna do. Just what he told me when he gave me this two weeks ago."

"What?"

"He said if anything …*strange* ever happened to him, to play this tape he made."

"What do you mean, 'strange'?"

"Dying, or disappearing without a trace! Jesus, how stupid *are* you?"

I shrugged. I had no idea how stupid I was.

"Tomorrow, when the paper tells what happened, if there's anything suspicious about it, I play the tape."

Did he say *suspicious?* "Richard, the night of the fireworks, I overheard him talking to someone on the phone, telling them to bag it and throw it over Redmer's fence. Then I peeked in his doorway. The bag he got thrown was filled with money."

He looked surprised, then his eyes narrowed. He reached back in the box and pulled out a square, metal device with a slot and buttons on it.

"What the heck is *that?"*

"It's the extra eight-track player he gave me." His eyes narrowed some more, and I could see the rage building again. "We're gonna play that tape *now."*

. . .

After "borrowing" Mike's stereo speakers, we listened to the tape. Eight-Track, looking out his second floor window one night, had *seen* Marv Redmer murder his wife. He got her stinking drunk, then teased her into taking a dip in the deep end of their pool, promising he would be right in.

In her condition, and with her lung problems, she was in trouble quickly. Redmer held out the pool's skimmer for her, then would move it just out of reach. Within minutes, the exertion left her exhausted, too exhausted to even yell, and she sank like a stone. Redmer shut the lights and went to bed.

There was no evidence of foul play, and nothing in his past to suggest a motive. He was just one greedy SOB who couldn't wait for her to die, which was probably only a year or two more. The dry cleaning stores were in her name, as she had inherited them. Only by her death could he own them. And he had found a buyer who could make him fabulously wealthy.

Eight-Track, apparently, was told all this when he contacted Redmer the first time, informing him of what he had seen that evening, and offering to forget about it in return for "a piece of the pie for himself."

"I don't condone what Redmer done," he said, "but I been poor my whole life. This way I can live comfortable, and Redmer can *pay* for his crime. He'll get his money, but I doubt if he'll ever enjoy it. *I* will, though."

The tape stopped.

"So *that's* why he hurried me out of there that night," Richard said bitterly. "So he could collect his payoff."

"I guess he wasn't *perfect.*" I offered, "but he *was* a pretty decent guy."

"And that bastard Redmer killed him," Richard said. "I *know* it!" He rose, and his fists were clenched like when I had seen him across the street earlier. He walked over by one of the windows, his face red and quivering. I looked down, embarrassed.

The sound of shattering glass snapped my head up. Richard was taking aim at another window pane. As I watched, feeling glued to the floor, he put his fist through all nine of them. He turned toward me, that expression still there. I opened the garage door and bolted.

I looked back. He was still in the garage, standing by the *other* window. All the way up to Liberty Street I could hear glass breaking.

. . .

"It's for you, Eddie," my mother said, after she had answered the phone around seven that evening. She looked puzzled. "It's that Richard character." She handed me the phone and left the room.

"Eddie, it's Richard Kane."

"How *are* you?" I asked nervously.

"How *am* I! My *hand* hurts, you shit-for-brains. I hadda have over thirty stitches in the emergency room!"

"Geez."

"You didn't say anything to anybody, did you?"

"Of course not."

"Good. You ain't half bad for a stupid runt, ya know?"

That was the first kind thing he had ever said to me. "Richard, what do we do about, you know, what's on the tape?"

"Wait for the newspaper. If he died of natural causes, we do nothing. But if somethin's fishy, then ..."

"Then *what?*"

"Then we have to decide. And we both have to do the same thing, or we'll look like liars and idiots."

I understood right away. With Eight-Track dead, there was no proof Redmer killed his wife. They would never believe a tape made by someone who was now dead. But if *Eight-Track's* death was murder, *then* the tape might help prove that Redmer *did* kill his wife, and murdered Eight-Track to protect himself. Or save money. Take your pick.

. . .

On page two of the paper the next morning, a headline read, *Police Investigate Death.* Eight-Track had died of injuries suffered in an apparent fall down the stairs that led from his upstairs den into his hallway. What caught my eye was the line, *Foul play is not suspected, but investigating officers have yet to rule it out.* Detective Sgt. William Tellerson was quoted, "It looks like a simple home accident, but there are inconsistencies." He refused to elaborate.

I was sure Richard would think Marv Redmer had *pushed* him down those stairs. Not twenty minutes later he was in front of my house in his mother's car, honking the horn.

Before Mom could object, I got in, noticing his bandaged right hand.

"We've got him, that murdering bastard." In all fairness he *did* ask me if we should go to the police, or right to Redmer himself, and "make him sweat."

"Are you nuts?" I screeched. "That's what Eight-Track was doing, and look what it got *him!*"

"Simmer down, runt. I was just makin' sure." The next thing I knew we were at the police station. From under the front seat he produced the tape and tape player,

then got Mike's "borrowed" speakers from the trunk.
"Well, I guess this is where I pay him back for everything
he did for me."

We went in, stated our business to a desk officer,
and were shown in to Detective Tellerman. I acted like a
scared kid about to wet his pants, but Richard did himself
proud. He spoke clearly and simply, and asked Tellerson to
play the tape. He did, right then and there. When it was
finished, he asked us to leave it with him and thanked us.

"That's *it?*" Richard nearly shouted. "Ain't you
gonna arrest the guy?"

"I'm not at liberty to discuss an investigation with
you boys. But this tape should be a *big* help in pursuing a
theory I've had. Leave your phone numbers with the
Sergeant."

. . .

Marv Redmer was arrested the next day and
charged with the murder of Delvin Strobeck. A small cut
on the side of Eight-Track's hand was inconsistent with
what he might have gotten in the fall. The police lab
examined a college ring Redmer wore, and came up with
traces of Eight-Track's blood and skin.

The tape was inadmissible as evidence, so Redmer
was never charged with killing his wife. But they had him
cold on the other one. At some point, his attorney advised
him to make a deal. Redmer pleaded guilty to voluntary
manslaughter, and eventually went to prison. The money
Eight-Track got from Redmer was never recovered.

Despite our brief alliance, Richard went back to his
old ways, brooding and glaring at everyone. If anything he
was worse after that. But I figured that had to do with
losing his friend and advisor, Eight-Track.

And us? After a few days we started hanging out
again, only not at Eight-Track's, of course. For a while I

was the hero, having helped solve a murder case. Almost every day the guys made me go through the whole story again, nearly word for word. They all liked the part where Richard was punching out the garage windows, except for Mike. He had to help his father replace them.

Yes, everything went back to the way it was before. But like Eight-Track used to say, nothing in life remains static for very long. We were all sprawled in the outfield one very hot day in August after a baseball game, picking out shapes among the clouds when footsteps sounded. We figured it was someone's little brother and ignored it.

"What're you idiots doin'?"

We all sat up, staring at the unlikely sight of Richard Kane, Richard the Fatherless, the neighborhood hoodlum. No one said a word.

"Whattaya all retards or somethin'?"

Finally Mike spoke up. "We were just---"

"You were just shootin' the breeze like you used to at old man Strobeck's."

We studied his face closely. For all we knew, he had decided to beat the crap out of the whole bunch of us. But Richard didn't look *angry,* he looked like he was doing something he *needed* to do, but to him it was like taking a large dose of bad-tasting medicine.

"That old man only told you guys stupid stuff," he declared.

No one dared to disagree.

"He saved the good stuff, the valuable stuff, for me," he continued. "I figure even a pathetic bunch of losers like you guys might learn somethin' from it."

It must have dawned on us that Richard had appointed himself as Eight-Track's successor. One or two of us may even have smiled, probably the same smile Eight-Track had seen on our faces countless times. Richard returned our smiles with a contemptuous sneer of disgust.

"You assholes know where to find me," he said, turning and prowling across the outfield grass, head down, hands jammed into his pockets.

"A CHRONICLE"
1994

I didn't *really* want to be here, but this community service stuff will look good on a college application next year. My "client," Mr. Leonard Pullig, age seventy-seven, had left a not for me on his front door: *Out walking Duchess, please wait.* I sat on the porch steps.

The City Youth Volunteers help the elderly with visits, light yardwork, and general cleaning. Names are taken from sign-up sheets compiled at the senior centers.

Mr. Pullig's was a new name, so the procedure was to visit three times and report back to Mrs. Zanders, the project coordinator. They wanted to make sure I wasn't being taken advantage of, like having to dig him a well by hand or something. He would be sent a sheet to fill out, too, to make sure I was polite and showed up on time.

After about five minutes I heard a low, grinding metallic drone. It was a sound I recognized instantly: skateboard wheels. I looked down Caitlin Avenue and saw an old man approaching, towing a skateboard with a wiener dog *riding* it. He approached me on the porch. Mr. Pullig, apparently, was back from "walking Duchess."

I was stunned at how perfectly the dog stood. My aunt had one of those dogs, dachshunds, I believe they're called, and I remember her telling me how uncooperative they could be. How did he *ever* get a dachshund to go along with a stupid pet trick like this?

I took a closer look. Duchess still hadn't moved a muscle and she was looking directly at me. Weren't these dogs notorious "yappers?" Only when Mr. Pullig undid a leather strap from a wooden on which the dog stood did I realize that Duchess was not a real dog. The man had been pulling a *toy* around!

Two more visits, I was thinking, and then file a "looney report" with Mrs. Zander.

I took a closer look at *him,* now. He looked normal, except for his eyes. They were huge, and bugged out of his head.

"I'm Leonard Pullig," he said, opening the door with his free hand, holding Duchess under his other arm.

"Ron Miles, from C. Y. V.," I said. As we went inside, I caught sight of a small metal plaque on the wooden stand. *Duchess, 1924-1937*, it said. This was even worse. Duchess *was* a real dog. A real *dead* dog.

He closed the front door behind us, and opened some French doors that swung in on a huge L-shaped living and dining room. Although the light was quite dim, one look had me debating whether to make a run for it, or just piss my pants right there.

There must have been at least twenty dogs, a couple of cats, and a baby mongoose in those two rooms. They were all on stands, which had plaques like Duchess's. They faced every which way, some at ground level, others on tables. And the eyes! They caught and reflected what little light there was. Politeness *had* made a run for it. "What the hell ...*is* this?"

To my surprise, the old man laughed, as though being a good sport. "It's a chronicle of my life. This is every pet I've ever owned." He nodded reflectively. "Here are all the things I've cared for, and cared about."

. . .

I stayed. I think part of it was curiosity. I'm not sure what the rest was. Mr. Pullig helped me into a chair, and immediately started explaining. He was raised in an isolated burg in southwest Kentucky, and became interested in taxidermy at age twelve, when Duchess was young. There hadn't been much to do except hunt, fish, and work hard. He wasn't big on any of those, but loved having pets. He thought that someday he could make taxidermy a career. In that environment, though, where people *ate* the things they hunted, there wasn't much call for it.

"I wasn't sure I'd be able to keep one of you Youth Volunteers after you'd seen this," he said, indicating the silent menagerie. He laughed again. "You'll get used to them."

. . .

Mr. Pullig turned out to be an all-right guy, aside from …*them.* Like many older men living alone, he let stuff go until there were piles of junk and clutter in every room of that two-story house.

He directed, and I cleaned. There were weeds, fallen branches, and scrub outside; trash, newspapers, and junk on the inside. I think he not only kept every *pet* he ever owned, but every *thing,* too. And I hadn't even set foot in the attic, basement, or garage. I didn't mind, though. It wasn't all work. I would come over after school and clean for an hour or so, then he would break out a two-liter bottle of soda, and we would talk. After three visits we gave each other a good report.

On many of the days, he was out "walking" one of them when I arrived, and I would sit on the steps and listen for that sound of skateboard wheels. I never asked why he did that. I didn't want him to think I was ridiculing him. I do remember asking him why he didn't have any *live* pets any more.

"I'm getting too old to care for an animal," he said, with some deliberation. "And," he added, "I'm not up to preserving them any more. It's very tedious and time-consuming."

It was quite a process, as I eventually learned. Special knives were used to remove the skin, which was treated with an arsenic-based soap. Measurements, drawings, and sometimes photos were taken of the specimen, and a life-like clay or balsa wood model was made, to which the skin was attached. Other sub-processes involved painting parts of the hide to duplicate natural color, and the inserting of artificial eyes. Benzene and carbon tetrachloride were used, also.

I was impressed, and figured he was happy with what he'd set out to do; preserve all his pets, and in a way, forego the passing of time. But something didn't seem right. He *sounded* and *acted* happy, but he never quite *looked* it.

. . .

Things progressed to the point where he gave me an extra key to let myself in if he wasn't home. One day I came in and noticed that the animals were all over the place, like he had been trying to clean around them. By the way, there were twenty-*eight* dogs, five cats, two guinea pigs, and a *ferret,* not a mongoose.

I took two steps and tripped over Sassy, the cocker spaniel. I thought it would be helpful to straighten up before he got back.

I began arranging the animals in my own way. Frisky, a black lab, and Pee-wee, a Doberman, had Onyx, a cat, cornered. I lined up all three dachshunds as one long wiener dog, with Smokey and Rusty two large dogs, looking down at them. And I put the two smallest dogs under the legs of Teko, a huge husky. When I finished, I thought it was a very creative piece of work.

Mr. Pullig came in minutes later, and his smile evaporated into a look of shock and anger. He looked around as though everything had been *destroyed.* "What have you done?" he shouted. "It's not a *chronicle* like that!"

He rushed in among the animals, trying to look everywhere at once. "These two never even *met*," he screeched, pointing at two Rottweilers I had placed nose to nose. "Nikita and Tippy wouldn't have gotten along," he bellowed, indicating two others. "I never would have owned them at the same time." On it went, for five minutes. By the time he finished reviewing my masterpiece, he was nearly in tears.

He looked at me, his hands trembling, his face a mixture of hurt and betrayal. I wanted to make things right, but I wasn't sure how.

"Want me to get started in the cellar?"

. . .

I'll give him credit. I had turned his world upside down and inside out, but he managed to calm down and quietly instructed me to begin bagging piles of stuff he'd sorted through in the cellar. "I'll be up *here*, trying to get the chronicle back the way it *should* be."

For the next two visits, I worked alone down there, feeling bad about what I'd done, and trying to figure out what was so wrong about it. He lived in an imaginary world, true enough. I could deal with that. But it was such a *fragile* world.

I made several trips out to the curb with garbage bags he'd labeled, "throw out." I came up one time to find him gone, hearing the drone of skateboard wheels in the distance.

I finished in the cellar on my next visit. He was waiting for me at the top of the stairs. Next to him was the skateboard, with Duchess strapped on and ready to ride.

"Would *you* like to take Duchess today, Ron?" he asked softly.

I knew this was his way of forgiving me, but it was also a test. He was laying himself open. I had the choice of ridiculing his very existence by refusing, or signing on as a partner in his time-frozen chronicle.

I did it. I walked Duchess. She was very well-behaved.

. . .

The attic was next. We were back to working together. In one of the piles I came across a framed certificate: *Member, Kentucky Mortician's Association, 1949-1950.*

"What's this, Mr. Pullig?" I asked.

"I couldn't make a living in taxidermy, so I became a mortician."

"What *is* a mortician?"

"It's what they called funeral directors back then."

"Oh."

"I didn't like it, though."

"Why not?"

"I hated the thought of burying my work. It didn't seem right. But in such an isolated area, someone had to do it."

I was eager to change the subject. "Did you have a family back in Kentucky?"

"Yes. I was married for many years. She's deceased. The only relatives left would be a couple of second cousins."

"You didn't have any children?"

He looked down. "No, I don't have any children." His brow furrowed, and he went over by the window and gazed off into the distance.

So much for changing the subject.

. . .

The garage was all that remained, but he kept putting it off. For the next week or so, my time was spent taking tours through his past. He would lead me over to a section of the chronicle and tell me stories about his pets.

One of the dachshunds, Gretchen, would *bite* him whenever the phone or doorbell rang. Eventually, he figured that she had very sensitive hearing, and the ringing sound drove her into a near frenzy. He fashioned a set of doggie earplugs, and that solved the problem.

Ace, a springer spaniel, loved the smell of money, literally. He would take Pullig's wallet if left unattended, *rob* him, and walk around the house with a wad of bills in his mouth.

One thing I noticed from reading the plaques was the overlap of the various pets. At any one time he would usually have three of them; one old, one in their prime, and one young. When the old one died, he immediately got another one. It was a revolving door type of thing. I happened to mention it to him one time.

"It's the natural cycle, Ron. First, you're young, then middle-aged, then old. Then you move aside for another young one to take your place." Then his huge eyes narrowed, and he started to tremble. "But the *young* one dying *first,* that's not right. I could *never* accept that."

He got up and staggered around, touching some of his favorites, before heading to the kitchen to get our customary bottle of soda. I left that day with the feeling that there really *was* something eating away at him.

The gap between cleaning seemed to have done him no good, so on my next visit I suggested we start on the garage. He reluctantly agreed.

The garage was a mess, too, but in a couple of sessions we had gotten trash, old tires, antiquated small appliances curbside, and were sweeping and straightening up. There was a large metal cabinet in one corner, and I wanted to clean behind it.

"No, Ron, don't move that."

"Why not?"

"There's knives and jars of preserving chemicals in there. Stuff might spill or break."

"Why don't we empty it first?"

"It's always locked. I don't have the key handy."

"Want me to get it?"

His hands fluttered nervously. "Let's just leave it be, Ron. We've done a good enough job out here."

"Are you sure? I'll do all—"

"*No,* Ron. It's fine the way it is. *Please.*"

"Whatever you say."

We went back inside for our soda. I thought he would be happy now that everything had been cleaned. "Well," I said cheerily, "we finally finished."

He nodded. "Finished."

"I guess from now on we can just visit. We'll have more time."

He nodded again. "Time."

As I got up to leave, he handed me the nearly-full bottle. "Here, you take this home with you." A puzzled look must have appeared on my face. "Don't worry. I've got plenty more. See you next time."

"Thanks, Mr. Pullig.

· · ·

With the heavy cleaning finished, I couldn't have been in a better mood when I showed up the next day and found the usual note on the door. I took out my key as I read it.

Ron, nothing to be afraid of.

Part of me went on red alert as I unlocked the front door and stepped inside. The French doors were slightly ajar. "Mr. Pullig, it's me, Ron." There was no answer, only the sound of a clock ticking in the dining room. I pushed open the doors.

The animals were gone.

I couldn't bring myself to take a step. From the doorway, I looked across the room divider into the dim dining room area. Highlighted against the darkness, I could see Mr. Pullig sitting in a chair at the far end of the room. He was staring at me, those huge eyes never blinking.

Half of me was wondering what was wrong with him, while the other half was wondering where the animals were. Just then, as my eyes became more accustomed to the dark, I saw a few of their heads over the top of the room divider. I stepped into the living room, and turned so I faced him.

All thirty-six of them were in the dining room. They sat in a huge semi-circle, their backs to me, facing Mr. Pullig, whose eyes still stared in the direction of the French doors.

I stepped into the dining room and stood behind the animal audience he had created. An overpowering chemical smell hit me, and I could make out a drinking glass and a sheet of paper on the window seat. It finally dawned on me that he had gathered them together and drank some of the chemicals. The same substances that had given them life, of sorts, had brought him death.

I carefully walked around the animals near the window seat. A key clattered down on the wooden surface as I picked up the paper.

There was an address and out-of-state phone number at the top. Below that, it said, *Thomas Pullig, Fulton, Kentucky. Second cousin. Please contact.* Then I read his final words.

I know now it was wrong to do this, to keep all of them. They weren't a chronicle. They were episodes to be remembered and then let go. All they ever did, really, was remind me how quick life passes.

The key is to the cabinet in the garage. I got nothin' to say about what's in there except that it ain't right, the young dying before the old. I couldn't bear to give him to the earth. He was only two years old. It was all my doin.' The wife never knew.

I had been about as dense as someone could be. How had I missed what now seemed so obvious? The way he looked when he said he didn't have kids. Of course he didn't. Not *now.* The way he flipped out about the young dying first. How he couldn't stand to bury his work. Even giving me the bottle of sods yesterday meant something. He'd never done that before.

And the locked cabinet in the garage. When I thought about it, it would have been easy enough for him to get away with. A funeral director, out in the middle of nowhere.

I felt so bad, I just sagged down on the floor. Then I took another look at what he'd set up with all of them. It was so dim, but as before, what light there was seemed drawn to their eyes.

I got up and walked in front of him, all the while watching them watching me. He had pushed the table and other chairs into the kitchen entryway, and I used my peripheral vision to locate one and drag it over next to him.

At that point I simply sat down and looked at them. I had no desire to unlock the cabinet in the garage. I just wanted to look at them.

The dimness, the clock ticking, the eyes reflecting; it was absolutely *mesmerizing.* Every animal was positioned so that it looked directly at us where we sat.

It was such an eerie, but *satisfying* feeling, like sitting at the right hand of some animal deity.

All those eyes, though! I'm telling you, it was … *indescribable.*

I knew I should be *doing* something instead of sitting there, but I realized that if I lived to be a hundred, I would *never* be part of something like this again.

It took every ounce of determination to force myself out of the chair and into the kitchen, nearly an hour later, to look for the telephone.

"TO THEMSELVES"
1995

Lamar Lauf bought fourteen acres of marsh and meadow, assuming that land in southeastern Washington would always be worth more than he would owe. He never used the land. He bought it in 1963 and let it sit there. Since then, the quiet burg of Lindenville had grown. Lamar's fourteen acres were now only eight-tenths of a mile from the high school.

Six boys, all juniors, who used the land as a hangout now hurried off its confines to two cars parked on a dirt access road. All were visibly shaken.

One, the only black youth among the six, shouted in a panic-stricken tone. "What the hell we gonna *do?*"

The tallest, Nick Eisner, a slim, angular youth with slicked-back brown hair, held up his hand against the growing panic. "You saw what happened. There's nothin' we *can* do."

"That's bullshit, Nick!" screeched a boy with dirty blond hair and red-rimmed blue eyes. "We can't do *nothing*. We gotta tell somebody."

"No, Warren, we *don't.*" said Bill Thayer, the stoutest of the six. "We'll all end up in some detention center."

"But I wasn't the one who—"

"It doesn't make any difference," Thayer said, more forcefully. "They'll slap conspiracy or complicity charges on us."

"Speak regular *English* for once!" shouted Warren Grivalsky.

"He's right, Warren," said Steve Basquin, who stood next to Eisner. Basquin wore his brown hair medium length and combed back. His drooping eyelids gave him the appearance of being half-asleep, but his prowess on the basketball court made him a valuable member of their six-man team. "We have to just shut up about this. There wasn't anything we could have done. And besides, it's too late now."

Nick Eisner surveyed the disturbed faces around him. "Gary?" he prompted, looking at a large blond boy, hair parted in the middle.

Gary Howst shook his head and looked down. "I don't *know* what we should do. I'm scared."

All were momentarily silent. Paul Joines, the black teen, spoke. "It won't be so bad if we do somethin' *now*. It'll look like we were sorry, at least."

"Hey, Paul, we *are* sorry," emphasized Nick. "We just can't *do* anything, and we got *way* too much to lose."

He surveyed the group again, seeing fear and indecisiveness. He would have to pull them out of the fire once again. "Everybody in," he commanded, assuming his aura of captaincy. Slowly, all six formed a circle, each extending an arm until all six right hands were piled awkwardly. "We gotta see this through the smart way," said Nick, "or we end up playing on some jailhouse team. I say we keep it to ourselves. Well?"

"To ourselves," several voices repeated.

Warren Grivalsky looked at the five faces scrutinizing his. "Yeah," he whispered. "To ourselves."

. . .

Detective Travis Newcombe sat in the principal's office at Lindenville High School, where he had graduated ten years earlier. As one of only ten black males at the time, he had been questioned in this office about the existence of an activist group, The Black Barons.

As a youth, Newcombe grew accustomed to being watched. Now, *he* was the one doing the watching. And he could spot a liar a mile away, mostly because he had told so many himself.

Across from him sat Dr. Edwin Hoak, age fifty-seven, successor to the man who had grilled him about the Black Barons. His slight build, thinning grayish hair, and brown glasses fit him almost stereotypically.

"Dr. Hoak, I'm here in response to a call from a Mrs. Bowlby. Her son Craig didn't come home yesterday. He was last seen here watching the after-school basketball."

"Yes, I know. She called both myself and the Superintendent. We are quite concerned."

"Do you have the rosters of the teams?"

"Yes," Hoak replied, handing over a typed sheet.

Newcombe glanced at the sheet, then covered his mouth, suppressing a laugh. "One of the teams has the same name as when I was here."

"Oh?"

"The Nads."

Hoak looked at him expectantly.

"The guys on the team would get their friends to sit in the stands and yell, 'Go, Nads.'"

Hoak recoiled slightly. "Well, *that* might explain why their games are so well-attended. Could I see that sheet again?" Together the two men read the roster sheet. "I'm not very knowledgeable concerning basketball, Detective. Perhaps you could help. You being *younger,* of course.

Newcombe smiled tightly.

Hoak read from the list. "Warriors, Rockets, The Good Shepherds. Those boys all attended the Catholic elementary school. Leo's Pizza, Krieger Hardware—"

"These teams have *sponsors,* now?"

"Oh, yes. The after-school basketball has become quite a community project."

"Wow. When I was here, they started it to avoid racial problems."

"Oh. Must have been tough back then, I take it."

Newcombe smiled again. "Still is."

"Well, let's continue. DP's. That's Drago's Pharmacy. Our friends the *Nads*, and Nick's Quad.

"What's that?"

"All the boys on that team are from the junior quad. Nick Eisner is the captain."

"Speaking of captains," Newcombe said, "Craig Bowlby's intent was to talk to team captains after the games. He told his mother that was the only way he could get on one of the teams."

"That's correct," replied Dr. Hoak. "As part of the Shared Leadership Initiative Program, the captain handles such requests."

"He stayed on Tuesday to talk to four of the captains, and again yesterday to talk to the other four. Which teams played yesterday?"

"Mr. Crane, our boys' gym teacher, would know. He was here, supervising."

Newcombe checked a small notepad. "I also want to speak to a boy named Kurt Pavelli. Mrs. Bowlby said he was Craig's best friend. His *only* friend."

"Yes, unfortunately, Craig is not very outgoing. Is there anything else I should be aware of, Detective?"

"I would want to speak with all eight captains and the boys from the teams that played yesterday."

Hoak looked annoyed. "That's a *lot* of students. Is this going to become a major distraction?"

Travis Newcombe couldn't choose between shock and anger. To him, Hoak was just another pompous, over-educated P. R. man. "Dr. Hoak, this may be nothing more than a depressed or angry kid staying out all night, but it could be *much* more serious."

On his way to the gym later, Newcombe spotted a poster showing the standings of the after-school three-on-three basketball league. He looked at them and laughed out loud. "Go, Nads," he said.

. . .

Captain Robert Nierenz carried a manila folder as he made the short walk from his office to that of his subordinate, Travis Newcombe. He buttoned his gray sport jacket over his slightly bulging stomach and knocked on Newcombe's door as he opened it.

"How'd it go at the high school, Travis?"

Newcombe shook his head. "We got a missing person. I talked to the principal, the team captains, and the boys who played yesterday."

"Anybody see him?"

"I'm sure they *all* saw him. Apparently, he's the kind of kid you just don't *notice.*"

Nierenz removed a photo of Craig Bowlby from the folder. "The kid's got red hair and *freckles,* for Christ's sakes. What's not to *notice?*"

"It's a social thing, Bob. Except for one friend, he's pretty much a loner."

"Well, what's his friend got to say?"

"He wasn't in school. I'll get him at home."

"What about the others?"

"Bob, a few of them looked like they wanted to *evaporate.*"

"Why shouldn't they?" Nierenz teased. "You the *Man,* now."

Newcombe frowned. "No, Bob, there's something else. Look at these statements from three different kids." He pointed to lines written on several pages of his notepad. "These three are all on the same team."

Nierenz read where Newcombe pointed. "The stories seem to match pretty well."

Newcombe exhaled loudly. "Bob, they match *exactly,* nearly word for word. Even their *phrasing* was the same. You know what that might mean?"

"A group lie?"

"Or," Newcombe suggested, "a group telling the same piece of the truth, and keepin' the rest of it to themselves."

"Okay, for now. I've got to get going on my own *big-time* case." He rolled his eyes.

"What's up, Bob?"

"A few complaints from people the past couple weeks about cars of teenagers heading out to the old Lauf property."

. . .

Travis Newcombe stood in the kitchen of the Pavelli residence as the woman waited for her son to come downstairs.

"He's so upset I let him stay home today. Craig's mother called here yesterday when he didn't come home, so we knew something was wrong."

Kurt Pavelli entered the kitchen, looked with surprise and concern at the black man standing by his mother.

"Kurtis, this is Detective Newcombe. He wants to ask you some questions about Craig. We can all sit here at the table, if that's okay."

They seated themselves, and Newcombe took out his notepad. He did a quick sizing up of the boy; a bit chubby, with short brown hair combed in a circular pattern, making his round face seem even rounder. Travis got the strange sensation that he was about to interrogate *Charlie Brown.*

"Kurt, I understand that you and Craig are close friends."

"Yes."

"What kind of things do you do together?"

"Mostly computer stuff. Shoot baskets at his house."

"You like basketball?"

"Not that much. But Craig does, so I go along, cause …we're best friends."

"Uh-huh. Is Craig good at basketball?"

The boy shrugged. "Better than me, but I'm not that good."

"And he stayed after on Tuesday and Thursday to try and get on one of the teams?"

"Yeah, he said he'd do *anything* to get on. He didn't even care which team."

Newcombe frowned. "What do you mean, 'do anything'? Doesn't the captain decide?"

The boy shook his head in frustration. "You don't understand. These captains …sometimes they make kids *do* things."

"Do things?"

"You know, like an initiation."

"Oh, I see. Something embarrassing, you mean?"

The boy's face reddened. He looked ready to explode. "No, not *embarrassing, dangerous!* Risky! Craig didn't run away. Something *bad* happened. I *know* it!"

"Kurtis," scolded his mother, "you shouldn't be saying—"

Kurt jumped up, pointing a pudgy index finger at the detective. "Go talk to those team captains. I bet at least one of *them* knows what happened." He bolted into the next room, bounding up the stairs to the second floor.

The woman looked aghast, then embarrassed. Travis nodded slowly, writing in his notepad, circling names.

"I'm so sorry Detective. I don't know where this came from. I guess he's been keeping things to himself."

"Believe me, Mrs. Pavelli," Newcombe said, "he's not the *only* one."

. . .

Travis Newcombe sat at his desk Monday morning, attempting to "assemble the pieces of the puzzle." Two team captains, Nick Eisner of Nick's Quad, and Ronnie Cordell of Leo's Pizza, left a bad impression. Cordell seemed indifferent, often a ploy of liars. Eisner was simply too *everything;* too polite, too smooth, too cooperative. That was something else he'd learned to watch for.

Several of Eisner's teammates seemed over-rehearsed, as though they had practiced not only *what* they would say, but *how* they would say it. He had already "flagged" their statements and brought it to Bob Nierenz's attention.

Now he had Kurt Pavelli's outburst to consider. The search parties organized by Chief Jenkins over the weekend had produced nothing. He was convinced that what they were looking for now was Craig Bowlby's body.

His thoughts turned to his own teen years; years he thought he was putting a lot over on his parents. He had been half right. His father didn't have a clue what he and his friends were into on weekends. But his mother did. She came to him one afternoon and delivered a lecture about choosing friends wisely and using good judgement.

"What's this all about?" he had asked.

"I know you've been smoking and drinking."

"How did you find out?" he asked, shocked, not even thinking to deny it.

"A mother just knows, sometimes, Travis."
A mother just knows, sometimes, he repeated to

. . .

Dirty beyond belief. Absolutely filthy. The words
seemed to want to fly off the notepad and slap him.
Newcombe sat in the parking lot of *Cumberland Farms,*
where he had stopped for a snack following his questioning
of the three non-working mothers whose sons played for
Nick's Quad.

He'd asked Virginia Eisner, Patricia Howst, and
Corrine Thayer for any "motherly intuitions" regarding
their sons' behavior recently. None seemed anxious to
cooperate. Who could blame them? You couldn't ask a
mother to sell out her own son.

There *was* one thing, though, mentioned in passing
by two of the women. A couple of weeks earlier, they had
each caught their sons attempting to wash the clothes
they'd worn that day.

"What's unusual about that?" he'd asked.

The two women had used the words he now stared
at on the notepad: *Dirty beyond belief. Absolutely filthy.*
And that was enough to make him ask how they got so
dirty.

"Nick said they played football in the mud," Mrs.
Eisner replied.

"They were hiking through some marshland, and
Gary fell in a swampy area," said Mrs. Howst.

"Thank you," said Travis Newcombe.

. . .

Nick Eisner stood before Charles Crane as boys
changed at nearby lockers. "Coach, I was wondering if we

could have an area to ourselves to talk strategy. We stink lately."

"I noticed," said the teacher. "Never thought you guys would lose to the Warriors."

"Yeah, well, that's what we want to talk about. We don't want the Nads to hear."

"Take that equipment room."

"Thanks, Coach."

Nick assembled his teammates and herded them into the far corner of the equipment room.

"We had *one* bad game," moaned Warren, "and we have to—"

"Shut up, you idiot!" hissed Nick. "I gave Crane a line. What do I care how we're *playin'*? This is about…the *other* thing."

Six tense, worried faces looked at each other.

"I don't know about you guys," he continued, "but my old lady's been on me like flies on shit." There were a couple of half-hearted chuckles.

"Same here," said Gary. "I been getting the third degree at home."

Nick nodded. "You know who's responsible for all this?" He scanned the five other faces.

"Newcombe!" grunted several voices.

"That's right. He's onto us for some reason."

"Wake up, Nick," said Steve. "He's been out to nearly all out houses. It's our *moms,* damn it!"

"*You* wake up, Steve. Talking to our mothers was just a follow-up on some hunch he already *had.*"

"I didn't want to do this," said Warren. "We should never have—"

Nick grabbed his arm, his patience wearing thin. "Wise up, Grivalsky. The rest of you, too. If we don't close ranks *right now* on this, the next set of uniforms we all wear will have *stripes* on them."

"Actually Nick," said Bill Thayer, "they wear those orange jump—"

"You shut the hell up!" screamed Nick. "We're in it up to our eyeballs and you're playing comedian! You're the brain here. Think of something!"

"Okay," said Thayer. "We gotta examine the situation." The others listened silently, showing him the respect accorded a top honor student who voluntarily read a dictionary and thesaurus daily.

"Somewhere along the line, we must have said something that wasn't consistent."

"Consistent?" asked Steve.

"Jesus," muttered Thayer. "Our stories didn't *match*. That Newcombe is gonna question us again. I'd bet anything on it. And the one thing we *have* to do is make sure our stories *match.*"

"What if they match *too* much?" asked Gary.

"They *say* we all talk alike anyway," Thayer retorted. "You gonna get in trouble for having the same vocabulary as your friends?"

"I guess not."

"The clothes, Billy. What about the clothes," reminded Nick.

"That's where I think we screwed up. Let's get straight on this. It was just a little harmless diversion, revelry among friends, you know?"

They all nodded. Steve Basquin mouthed the words silently.

"What if he presses us?" asked Joines.

"Just keep repeating the same thing," said Thayer. "You have to *outlast* him. If he asks you the same question forty-two times, give him the same answer forty-two times."

The door opened. "Let's go, guys," said Coach Crane. "People are waiting. You should see the crowd out there."

"Nads fans," murmured several voices.

"Everybody in," said Nick. The six hands formed a pile of seeming solidarity. Eisner narrowed his eyes. "Close ranks, guys."

. . .

Travis Newcombe sat at his desk. The pieces of the puzzle were coming together. Part of him was still laughing inside. Every time the Nads had the ball, the crowd started the familiar 'Go, Nads!' chant.

Nick's Quad had not looked anything like a first-place team. They missed easy shots, turned the ball over, and argued among themselves. Just before the end of the first half, he made eye contact with one of the players, a slightly-built blond boy. He could read the boy's lips as he mouthed the detective's last name.

The boy appeared to pass on the news to a teammate, who told another, and so forth. Nick's Quad, already playing poorly, went to pieces.

Nick Eisner went in for a layup and hit the bottom of the rim. "You stink, Nick!" yelled a sandy-haired blond girl next to him.

Newcombe decided to take a shot. "Kind of rough on the guy, aren't you?"

"I used to go out with him. He's a big blowhard. All he does is try to put one over on everybody. I couldn't *begin* to tell you the crap he pulled on me."

"I thought Nick was one of the school leaders," he said, baiting her.

"He gets involved and stuff, but—Go Nads!—he's just out for himself. *And* the other idiots on that team."

After the game he had gone down to floor level and stood behind Nick's Quad. They seemed to be avoiding *each other* as well as the Nads. "Tough game, guys," he said.

A couple of them looked around, saw him, and looked away. Nick Eisner, however, made eye contact. "I guess we just had a bad day, sir."

"Yeah," said Newcombe. "Gotta watch those bad days. "They'll get you every time."

He'd gotten a strange hunch since returning to his office. There was something about the team's *name* that didn't figure. Remembering that one other team name held a hidden agenda, he put the letters of Nick's Quad on scraps of paper. These guys weren't out to *promote* a school division, the Quad. They were in this for glory, to win, to impress girls. 'All he ever does is try to put one over on everybody,' the ex-girlfriend had said.

As unnecessary as it now seemed, Newcombe was trying for one more piece to the puzzle. He moved the letters around, getting one nonsense word after another.

Bob Nierenz breezed in through the open door, reaching back as an afterthought to knock. He came to an abrupt halt by Newcombe's desk, holding what looked like a report. He glanced down at the paper letters, which currently spelled "quasdinck."

"What the hell you doin,' Travis, playing 'anagrams?'"

"Nah. It was just a hunch that 'Nick's Quad' stood for something else."

"So you still think they're the ones?"

"Positive, now."

"Anyway, Trav," Nierenz continued, "I went out to see old man Lauf to tell him kids had been spotted driving out to his property. We get talkin' and he goes and gets this land survey he had done back in the sixties."

"Yeah, so?"

"So take a look at this paragraph. Doesn't that just blow your mind?"

Newcombe stared at the word jumping out at him from the page, a word simply impossible to ignore. He looked down at his latest creation, "quasdinck." "It *can't* be," he whispered, moving seven of the nine letters around. "It *is*. Mother of God, Bob, look at this."

"Hey," Nierenz said, grinning, "you spelled the same word. Talk about coincidence."

"Coincidence, my *ass*," Travis said, heading for the door.

. . .

Warren Grivalsky sat on a grassy bank, wiping away tears of grief and guilt. Forty yards away, obscured by marsh grass, floating leaves, and a thin layer of water, was the two-hundred square foot section of quicksand.

Gary had discovered it that past August, and told the others. Then Billy had looked it up, and found that because it was heavier than water, and water flowed *upwards* through it, there was no reason to sink if you didn't panic, and gave the quicksand time to flow around you and *support* you.

And it was Nick, good old Nick, who had come up with the idea that they should *all* take turns running into it and rolling to safety, the others nearby with long sticks in case someone panicked. And it was Nick's idea to take that nerd Craig there and have him do the same thing to get on the team. The kid had *begged* him to let him on.

Warren remembered the fear in his eyes, how quickly he had panicked, how quickly he went down. He could still picture the tree limbs extended, everyone screaming "Grab on, quick!" Then a moment of complete and utter silence, until one of them screamed. He couldn't remember who it had been, though.

Nick and the others would kill him if they knew he was here now, especially after Newcombe had waited for them after their game and asked more questions.

He hadn't asked about Craig, though. All he asked was how their clothes got so dirty that one time. And they had been ready for that one, thanks to Billy. "It was a little harmless diversion," he said. Their stories would match, and they would be safe, he told himself. But that didn't make the guilt go away.

Behind him, leaves crunched and twigs snapped. Warren looked around to find squirrels and chipmunks dashing about, gathering food for the winter.

Winter. He would be safe and warm. Craig Bowlby would spend the winter at the bottom of old man Lauf's quicksand, his life over, his family more distraught and desperate with each day. More twigs snapped and leaves crunched around him.

A hand came down on his shoulder. Warren jumped and turned around.

"Where's the quicksand, son?" asked Travis Newcombe.

"Down there," he pointed, half in shock, half relieved, still looking up at the stern face.

"What happened?"

Warren told him everything, then put his head between his knees. "How did you know?" came the muffled question.

"You were seen coming out here a few times. Nick's Quad is an anagram for 'quicksand,' and today when I asked you about your clothes, three of you said it was a 'little harmless diversion,' and three of you said it was 'revelry among friends.' You all lied at some point, and I can spot a liar a mile away."

"How much trouble are we in?" Warren asked meekly.

Newcombe shook his head. "More than you could ever imagine."

Warren's eyes teared. "Will they be able to get him out before …winter comes?"

Newcombe squinted in disgust. "What the hell kind of question is *that?*" Look son, you're in custody now. Until you have an attorney, I advise you not to say anything else. Keep it to yourself."

"WHEN YOU LIE DOWN WITH DOGS" 2013

I don't care what *anybody* says, one of the best feelings in the world is screwing someone over who has screwed *you* over. Especially when that person was someone you thought of as a friend.

Friendship with Charles " Chuck" Tratinni was always a bumpy ride. We were the same age, liked the same things, and spent many carefree hours together in the innocent world of the 1960's. It was a time when kids were *safe.* You could walk anywhere without fear, (and we *had* to walk everywhere, as our parents were not running a personal limo service) and if you had an argument with someone, or even a fight, you didn't have five government agencies involved in the "issue."

And God forbid, if our parents should lay a hand on us, it was assumed we had it coming. *They* didn't go to court, *we* went to our rooms. And somehow, in this non-child-centered environment, none of us turned into homicidal maniacs or serial killers.

But Chuck, he was something else. He was part comedian, part daredevil, and part con man. He lived across from me, two houses down on Pratt Hill, which abutted our back yard.

We did have some fun times, too, like the time we took my sled down Pratt Hill. It was a steep three-hundred yard incline, and on snow days from school, if you got there before the plows came, the ride down was like something out of an action movie. Once, with Chuck and I both riding my souped-up Flyer, we must have hit forty. Above the roar of the runners, Chuck yelled, "How fast can this thing go?" I screamed, "I have no idea!" Then someone backed out of their driveway and we swerved into the snowbank across the street from his house. It took five minutes to get the sled out and find my glasses.

Chuck and I, Duane Lovetere, came from similar middle class backgrounds. My father worked in a factory, and my mother kept house. I had an older brother John, whom I hardly ever saw. He was in high school, and played every sport and was in just about every club. Chuck's father was a lawyer, but was separated from his mom. Chuck saw him once in a while, but I never did. His mom waitressed. He had a little sister, Debbie, about five or so. She was always filthy, with a chocolate stain that resembled Antarctica seemingly embossed on her face.

Chuck's grandmother was often there babysitting for Debbie. I don't know how she put up with her. Debbie had to be the most annoying kid ever. She would always come up and ask me some ridiculous or disgusting question. "Dew-ane, can I pinch you? Dew-ane, wanna smell my fingers?"

Chuck had turned her into his little parrot. Once, his grandmother was trying to get her to go someplace, and she ran away, yelling, "Drag ass, grammie," over and over. With Chuck, you never knew when you were about to become the centerpiece in his next comedy inspiration. Once, we had finished having a catch and were sitting on my porch. I had a runny nose so I asked him if he had a "snot rag." He reached over and handed me my baseball glove. He was laughing hysterically over this bit of improvisation. He would remind me of it every so often, like it had been one of the greatest comedy routines ever. One time I made the mistake of telling him we had *Hamburger Helper* for supper. My nickname for the next two weeks: "Hamburger Helper."

His favorite routine: he would get me on the ground, sit on my chest, and take my wrists and make me hit myself. That in itself was nothing innovative, but with

Chuck, the narration that went with it was, to him, the funniest part of the routine. 'Duane, don't hit yourself like that. Duane, why are you hitting yourself?'

Yes, he was loud and domineering. But like I said, he was a fun friend, and those things I mentioned, it's not like they happened on a daily basis.

Chuck was very resourceful, and there were times out on our many explorations he would come up with ideas and innovative ways of doing or building things. I thought he would make a fine architectural engineer, and I made it a point to tell him. He had a big ego, and loved compliments. There was no mention of "snot rag" or "Hamburger Helper" *that* day.

Chuck liked living on the edge, or what passed for the edge at our age. Many of our adventures involved going to the end of dead-end street around the corner, traversing the farmer's field, and exploring the seemingly endless woods beyond. Sometimes the farmer's field contained a bull; yes a real bull, so we were risk-taking even before we reached our destination. Chuck's repertoire included climbing to the tops of trees and *jumping off,* jumping from the top of The Big Rock on Pershing Hill, raiding gardens belonging to the Casale, Hubbell, and Babonski families, and setting fires out in the woods and extinguishing them before they got out of control.

And how did I perform in this line-up? I could climb trees with the best of them, but wasn't fond of jumping out of them. The Big Rock I had conquered early on. I was mainly the lookout on the garden raids; that seemed too much like stealing to suit me. But what boy our age didn't like fire? Only one time, down in Hubbell's woods, did the fire get out of control. Chuck ran to their house for help, telling them that *I* was playing with matches, even though he *told me not to.* The Hubbell's two teenaged sons came down and put out the fire. Nothing ever came of it, but it was a real eye-opener to me that he would rat me out for something we *both* did.

The event of choice was a game called "Heads-Up." Looking back now, could anything have been more stupid? We would each grab two rocks, stand near a good-sized tree, and fling the rocks *at* the tree. You never knew if the rocks were going to ricochet away, or come screaming back directly at our heads. One time my cousin Nicky happened to be with us. With three rocks in play at the same time, it was pretty hairy. Chuck was in his glory, Nicky seemed to like it, and I was petrified. That was the one time anyone got nailed in the head. It was me, of course.

But none of this has anything to do with the incident that is the heart of this stroll down memory lane. It was April vacation of our eighth grade year, and we had a three-day deluge. Chuck knew that the streams that criss-crossed all the patches of woods would be swollen and running more rapidly than ever, possibly even flooded. It was like the Song of the Siren to him. He called and insisted that on the first non-rainy day to come and get him. We would have the adventure of a lifetime. He even hinted that we might be able to build a raft and sail on these normally narrow, weak-running streams.

It was a Thursday, and the rain had stopped. Nicky called me and said that the frog pond by his house above Pratt Hill had overflowed and created a new stream. I would have liked to explore that, with all those frogs getting washed right out of their pond, not to mention the brooks near Willard Street, which ran behind and parallel to Pratt Hill, but I told Nicky it would have to wait. I really didn't want to know how Chuck would react to getting blown off, since I had never had the nerve to do it. I was sure a new nickname would be the least of the problems.

So I crossed Pratt Hill and went down to Chuck's house. Debbie was playing with plastic figures from one of those new cartoon shows. She was already covered head-to-toe with mud and took one of the figures and thrust it head-first into a big mud pile. "Eat dirt, Gumby!" she shrieked. Nice.

I got Chuck and off we went, running from Debbie, who had decided to chase us with a big glob of mud in each hand. I had nothing to lose, so I suggested that we head up to Clearview Road to see the frog pond that overflowed, but he vetoed that idea right off.

We went behind Hubbell's house into their woods, sloshing through puddles. When we came to the first stream, we were astounded. We had never seen the true power of running water. The sound was almost deafening. Water collided with rocks, picked up speed, and rushed to its preordained destination.

The first order of business was to cross the swollen streams without falling in. We were successful at first, but the law of averages caught up to us. Within twenty minutes, we had both slipped into the knee-deep water. It was cold and damp out, and for me, the excitement and exhilaration of this new experience had worn off. Chuck was mesmerized by the scene, the rushing water, the roar, getting wet up to his knees. We worked our way down the torrent, towards the bottom of Pershing Hill, barely visible through the trees.

Around a bend we saw the dog. We didn't recognize it. It was out in the middle of the stream, on a rock just big enough for him to stand without falling into the water, which at this point had drawn all the water from above. Looking like a miniature Rocky Mountain rapids, it made the previous section of the stream placid by comparison. The dog was obviously afraid to move, and wasn't about to jump.

Chuck and I both called to him. You could tell he *wanted* to come, but there was no way he was voluntarily going back into the water.

"Duane, we gotta go get him."

"What if *we* fall in?"

"What if that was Penny out there?"

Chuck knew how to play my emotions. Penny was a collie mix, my favorite dog in the world. She belonged to Tony Anders, a kid who lived at the top of Pratt Hill. She was almost like my dog. Whenever Tony wasn't around, she would come over to my house just to be with me. Chuck knew how much I cared for *all* dogs, heightened by the fact that my mom adamantly refused to let me have one.

"I wouldn't let Penny just stay there," I said.

"Well, to somebody, this is *their* Penny."

"All right, what do we do?" I figured with Chuck's resourcefulness, we would build some device that would rescue the dog with no danger to us.

"We gotta wade over to him and carry him to this side."

"That's *it?* We're just gonna go in and carry him back here?"

"We gotta do somethin' before he panics and tries to get over to us. I don't think this dog can swim well, or he already would have tried. C'mon, Duane."

On the count of three we both stepped into the water, now *past* knee-deep and *pushing* steadily at us. We got out to the dog, and he was doing this crazy two-step like he was gonna jump into our arms, but he couldn't bring himself to do even *that,* so Chuck grabbed him. I immediately joined in, but we were not in sync and ended up working against each other. We both fell sideways while holding him. He started thrashing, but we got him under control and staggered back to our side of the stream. It wasn't as dangerous as it seemed, but we felt like heroes as we put him down.

"We did it Duane, we saved him!" Chuck exclaimed.

"Whose dog is it?" I asked. There was no collar on him.

We knew all the people in our neighborhood and the surrounding areas, but we had never seen this beagle mix, with the usual black, white, and light brown markings. Before we had even gotten back home we had decided to call him Butch, after a heroic dog in a story we had read in school.

We couldn't just turn him loose in the neighborhood. We agreed that if we didn't find the owner, he would be *both* our dog. Of course, he could not stay at my house, so Chuck "graciously" agreed to keep him in the empty fenced-in shed behind their house.

And that's how it went for a while. We asked around the neighborhood, in school, all over, but no one seemed to know anything about him.

Chuck was in his glory, coming over to my house with Butch, still giving lip-service to our agreement that we were joint owners, but I could see what was happening as the weeks went by. To Butch, Chuck was the *master,* and I was *the master's friend.* Butch was half mine, but I had nothing to show for it.

Then, at the beginning of summer vacation, Chuck came over my house one morning. To this day, I'm sure he waited until my parents weren't home. He seemed a bit subdued, but resolute, the way you look when you are about to give someone bad news, but there is no other option.

"You know, Duane, I gave Butch a place to stay, and I feed him, and we took him to the vet's."

I didn't like the sound of this, and part of me was kicking myself for never giving Chuck or his mother anything in the way of money or food for him. But part of it was my mom. She was so dead-set against me having a dog that whenever I mentioned him she just waved it off and said he really *wasn't* part my dog. So to avoid having my enthusiasm crushed I stopped talking about it. Meanwhile, Chuck had this tab running in his head, and I hadn't paid anything on it. I was sure, thinking about it later, that he was fine with how things had gone the past two months, and now he was going to collect on his "investment."

I said nothing, waiting for Chuck to deliver whatever bad news I was sure he had for me.

"You know, Duane, my father said possession is nine-tenths of the law, and he should know. He's a lawyer."

Again, I was dumbstruck. Chuck had pulled stuff on me before, but nothing like this.

"So what I'm saying, Duane, is that Butch is really *my* dog." He paused. "But you can visit him *anytime* you want, even if I'm not around."

Tears welled in my eyes. I searched for something meaningful to say. All that came out was a choked, "How come you get to have him? We *both* rescued him."

Chuck turned conciliatory, a ploy he used only when needed. "C'mon, Duane. Sure, you did your part in saving him, but *I* give him food and shelter, and anything else he needs." He paused, and assumed that "tough luck, buddy" tone again. "Like I said, possession is nine-tenths of the law."

Losing control, I quickly went inside. Chuck had the good sense to let things be at that point. At the kitchen window, watching him walk home, I found my voice, too late. "Possession is nine-tenths of the law, huh? You little shit. Wait till you see what the *other* tenth is!" Of course at that moment I had no idea what the other tenth was.

. . .

I'm not a schemer, but I remember that *something* in my head told me not to say anything more about this. Why? Because that same something was telling me that this wasn't over, and things would come out my way. And *that* was hard for me to believe, since I had never gotten the better of Chuck in anything other than the occasional board game.

So for the next week or so, I acted as though nothing had gone down between us. I went over Chuck's house, he came over mine, we explored with my cousin Nicky up at the frog pond off Clearview Drive, all kinds of regular stuff. Once, coming back from the pond, instead of walking down Pratt Hill, Chuck turned down Willard Street and cut across the Edwards's property to the back of his house. We were coming up on Butch's red fenced-in shed, and Butch was wagging his tail as we approached.

"Hey Chuck, I thought that was just a tool shed. Why is it fenced in?"

He rolled his eyes. "Remember Debbie's Easter rabbit from last year? That's where we kept it. Poor bastard never had a chance."

"Why did we come this way?"

"I was supposed to clean the garage out and I forgot. There's no windows in our house that can see us here. It's a blind spot. Now I can sneak in the garage and neaten it up from all the stuff we had to put in there so Butch would have room."

Again, I had to be reminded of the *sacrifices* he and his family had made for Butch. If Chuck had noticed that I had dropped the ownership conflict, he didn't let on. He wasn't much on complimenting others.

. . .

I'm convinced now that everything happens for a reason. Chuck was away one weekend in July, his father having taken him on some father-son thing. I started hanging out with my cousin Nicky and Tony Anders. We spent most of our time up at the frog pond and woods off Clearview Drive. I was allowed to stay out after dark in the summer. It was the '60's, remember? I was walking home and I suddenly got it in my head to go visit Butch, tucked away in his shed. On a whim, I cut down Willard Street and across Edwards's yard, approaching Chuck's house from the back. I could hear Butch in the shed, *crying* softly.

I went inside and comforted him. I wondered why he didn't bark or howl at night if he was sad. I would have heard him from my house. And then it hit me. He wasn't *sad,* he was *scared.* Was he scared of the dark, or of being alone? Did he miss his original owners? And all of a sudden I remembered this line from a story we had read in school. It was about some mean guy that was the boss at a store, and he fires this mentally handicapped guy, so the guy can't afford his place any more and moves. The boss sees him walking alone at night with his suitcase and suddenly feels badly. And he says to himself, 'The night makes cowards of us all.'

Just then I felt so bad for Butch *I* was almost crying. I hated Chuck for stealing him from me, and for leaving him out here at night, like Debbie's stupid rabbit. I lay down next to Butch and comforted him. He fell fast asleep, and I walked home feeling like more of a hero than when I *helped* rescue him.

. . .

And guess what? I did the same thing the next night. I even continued doing it when Chuck came back from his father-son weekend. After all, he said I could visit Butch *any time I wanted, even if he wasn't around.* I didn't feel the need to mention it to him, if you know what I mean.

I was getting good at subterfuge. I acted normal around Chuck. I called my cousin Nicky and told him that if my parents ever asked, I was up at the frog pond with him after dark, looking for the peeper frogs that come out at night. Luckily, Chuck had never been the type for doing stuff after supper. I think he was so intense during the heart of the day, he was used up by five or six P.M.

Whatever. I continued to lie down with Butch every night, approaching his shed from Willard Street, remembering there was a blind spot from Chuck's house, and no one there could see me coming. It was such a calm, *gratifying* feeling, taking the fear away from this beagle mongrel I had come to love. And I knew that every night I did this, I was becoming less and less the *friend of his master*, and more his *protector*.

Lying down with Butch every night brought back an odd memory from the end of the previous school year. Kids were acting up, and Chuck had thrown in with some real fools, kids who went to school just to make trouble. Mrs. Burke was upset that these losers now had Chuck in their group. In front of the whole class, she said, "Charles Tratinni, I know you think that Louis and George are so *wonderful,* but please remember that when you lie down with dogs, you wake up with fleas. And if you don't know what that means, I'll tell you. If you associate with people of low character, you will assume *their* qualities."

Ouch.

Chuck was furious, having been dressed down in front of everyone. Walking home later, he was raging. "When you lie down with dogs, you wake up with fleas," he mimicked. "When you lie down with dogs, you STINK!" he said, with finality. I nodded supportively, but oh, man, I was piss-my-pants laughing inside.

Yes, that was a fond memory for me. And Chuck had no idea that *I* was the one who was laying down with dogs. Literally.

As the summer wore on, it was obvious that whenever Chuck and I were together with Butch, he seemed to seek me out much more, coming over to me to be petted. Did Chuck notice? Was he suspicious? Not a chance. Egoists never think that they are anywhere but on top. I know he took care of Butch, and *liked* him and everything, but I think that to him Butch was just one more trophy to show off. *First Place, Dog Rescue and Care Competition; Charles Tratinni.*

· · ·

On August 24th, Chuck came over my house mid-morning, as he often did. He seemed very subdued. It reminded me of the day he came over and told me Butch was *his* dog, and all that nine-tenths crap, but the quiet righteousness was missing.

"Duane, my parents have decided to get back together."

I couldn't care less.

"Dad says things are gonna be *his* way this time."

I couldn't care less.

"He's makin' me get rid of Butch, so if you want him, he's all yours."

I'm listening, Chuck, old buddy!

"Let me know," he said, and walked home.

I was *close* to *almost* feeling bad for him, but this was no time for useless sentiments. I had to convince Mom to let me have the one thing she had so steadfastly refused since I was old enough to talk. And for once, my begging, pleading, and debating paid off. It didn't hurt that Dad had a dog as a child. Even John went to bat for me. Miraculously, Mom relented, and agreed that we could take Butch in, starting tomorrow.

I pushed my good luck. "Mom, he needs to be with me at night, or he'll cry. He's very sensitive." Behind Mom's back, John was making shoveling motions.

"Not on the *bed!"* was Mom's last gasp of defense.

I had finally triumphed. And it lasted all of five days.

Our regular paperboy, Allan Everett, was sick, and got a kid he knew to take his route for a couple of days. He came around to our back porch to deliver the paper and saw Butch and me sitting on our lawn. He stopped short. "Caesar?" he called. Butch's ears went up and he walked over to the kid.

"What?" I said uneasily.

"That's Caesar," the kid said, half in astonishment, half accusatory.

"You know him?"

"Yeah. That's the Nuhn's dog. They lost him back in April. Their house had some flooding, and while they were moving stuff, he wandered off. Where did you find him?"

This felt like a police interrogation, but I was taught to tell the truth. "My friend and I found him stranded in a stream off Pershing Hill. We asked everybody we knew, but nobody claimed him. How come nobody said anything?" I had the most awful feeling in the pit of my stomach.

"They go to Catholic school. So do I."

"Where do they live?"

"Down on Harrison Drive. Not that far from where you found him."

A weak "Oh," was all I could manage. And my mother had heard the whole conversation from the open kitchen window.

. . .

I suppose in today's world we could have demanded reparations from the Nuhns, or even got a lawyer and sued for ownership, claiming they were negligent. Then they would have countersued us for not making a thorough enough effort to find his rightful owners.

I remind you again, it was the '60's. The right thing was done just because it was the right thing. My parents made me call the Nuhns that evening and tell them everything. The next morning I walked Butch down Pershing Hill to Harrison Drive, which ran across it at the bottom. I purposely avoided going through Hubbell's woods. I did not want to see the spot where Chuck and I had probably saved his life.

At the Nuhn's house, Butch was mobbed by the three young Nuhn children, and their two small cousins, the Pervettis, who lived next door. Mrs. Nuhn thanked me profusely, the little kids said their thanks, and Butch, aka Caesar, was back in his rightful home. Mrs. Nuhn made sure I knew that prior to wandering off, Caesar had been exclusively an indoor dog. My former dog seemed very happy, sniffing and jumping all over the five kids he had grown up with. As I struggled for self-control, Mrs. Nuhn presented me with a fresh-baked cherry pie as a reward.

There was no reason to hold back my tears once I got to Pershing Hill. I cried a little. Okay, I cried a lot. I walked a few feet into the woods, and smashed the pie against The Big Rock.

The new school year started a couple days later, and it had my head spinning. But I knew *Butch's* night fears would never find him again. I was sad, but at peace.

Chuck and I had all different classes, and barely saw each other. We both made new sets of friends based on who was in our homerooms and classes. High school basically ended our close friendship, but no big deal. It happens to almost everyone, I think.

Seven weeks later it was Halloween. The freshman in me looked down on it as kid stuff, but I put on an elaborate goblin mask and trick-or-treated through our neighborhood, somehow ending up on Harrison Drive, at the Nuhn's. The little ones had just gotten home, and they looked up from their loot at my mask, whispering to each other who they thought I was. And from the next room came their dog, Caesar, who barked at me once, then wagged his tail and licked my hand. Mrs. Nuhn and her kids couldn't help but notice.

"Oh, he knows you for sure," she said.

"Michael!" the kids all shouted.

I shook my head.

"Raymond?" asked the oldest one.

Again, I shook my head.

"Are you gonna tell us?" asked Mrs. Nuhn, good-naturedly.

I shook my head a third time, tears now welling up in my eyes. I plunked the candy bar in my pillowcase and got out of there.

. . .

Believe it or not, I never saw Caesar again. I lost track of the Nuhn kids. I thought by my junior year the oldest one might be in high school, but I don't remember seeing her or hearing any of their names, including the Pervetti cousins. Maybe their parents found a Catholic high school for them. I'm glad, in a way. If I had seen them in school, I know it would have been a temptation to ask about Caesar.

But it was for the best, like most everything. In my mind he always existed as Butch, the lost, frightened mongrel who had his fears eased each night by me. The magic of those few weeks could not be erased by a substitute paperboy, or a conversation overheard by my mother, or a kid who had been taught to do the right thing because that was what you were supposed to do.

Oh, yes. Chuck's father landed a job with a big law firm in Allenbury, a city twenty miles away. He moved after our junior year. But there was to be one more encounter with him. We were both on our respective football teams, and senior year we went to Allenbury for a Friday night game. I played sparingly, but Chuck was a standout defensive back for them. We won the game, and afterwards, players from both teams were shaking hands. I saw Chuck working his way towards me, and I remembered him as the guy who had pulled the ultimate screw-job on me in eighth grade. But I had had the last laugh, and I thought it was time he knew it.

"Nice game, Duane," he said, as he shook my hand.

And here it came. "Hey, Chuck, remember that dog we rescued back in eighth grade?"

"Yeah, sure."

Something about it just didn't feel right, though. "That was neat, huh?"

He laughed. "Yeah, especially when you had to give him back the same week. Sucker!" He moved off, shaking hands with other players.

Oh, well, it's the thought that counts, right?

. . .

My mother, who had given in and let me have my first and only dog lived in our house on Lilac Lane until her death at age 91. Once, I drove around the block and slowly eased my car up Pratt Hill, stopping halfway up to look at the house where Chuck Tratinni lived. It had changed hands several times, the garage rebuilt, the big tree gone, but behind the house the shed still stood, without the fencing. It wore a new coat of paint, but still red.

In that shed in the summer of 1962, I had learned something that I'm sure helped make me a better person. If I have to tell you what it was, I guess you wasted your time reading this.

And I don't care what *anybody* says, when you lie down with dogs, you gain their loyalty, and their love.

"CROW'S NEST"
2013

Old man Fulton grabbed the note I'd been reading and tossed it on the floor of his den. "I don't want anybody puttin' words in your mouth. What's your name again?"

"Ronnie Davidson Kirts, sir."

"Let's just call you Ron, okay?"

"Okay."

"Ron, you got somethin' to ask me, ask it in your own words."

I nodded. "Mr. Fulton, I would like permission to go on your land to explore."

"That's better. Any of your friends have my say-so?"

"Yes, sir. All of them."

"They tell you my rules?"

"Yes, sir. No lightin' fires, no guns, and no destroyin' nothin'."

"You know how much land I own back of this house?"

"No, sir, but they say it's a lot."

Kendall H. Fulton laughed softly. "How does eighteen square miles sound?"

"Wow."

"Chesapeake Bay itself once ran on my land, about three-hundred years ago. Then the land shifted, or some damn thing. Where you live, anyways?"

"About three-quarters a mile up the road."

Fulton leaned toward me. "You know *why* I let youngsters use my land that comes and asks me proper-like?"

"No, sir."

"'Cause my sons and daughter didn't want no part of it *or* me, that's why. They all moved up north. They're just waitin' for me to die, so they can inherit all this and sell it to some land developers. Well, Ron, they are in for a surprise someday."

I nodded respectfully, shifting my weight nervously. He gave me a half-smile.

"You get goin,' now. Enjoy the land. It's God's gift, you know. And be *careful.*"

"I will, sir."

. . .

So there I was, the last one of my friends to go to Old Man Fulton and ask for permission to go on his land. It was a rite of passage here in Haydenville, Maryland, a couple miles from the Chesapeake. Between your tenth and eleventh birthday, you went to the large log farmhouse on Brewer Road, by yourself, and asked him man to man to "use" his land. He never wanted specifics, like what exactly would you be *doing* there. I think he knew that kids would revel in just *being* in such a place.

There wasn't a lot known about him. He had made a fortune sometime earlier. Parents didn't say much about him, except they respected him, and if he wanted you to ask in person to use his land, that was good enough for them.

I asked my dad how old he was, and he guessed he was about seventy-seven or eight. When I reported that all his kids lived up north and didn't want anything to do with him, they seemed to already know. I asked about his wife, and was told she had died about forty-five years ago, in her thirties. I felt bad about that, and asked if he ever got lonely.

At that point, Dad took me by one arm, gently, and said, "Ronnie, not everyone *feels* the same about things, like dying or being alone." He paused. "It's nice that Mr. Fulton lets kids use his land, but I don't want you going over his house pestering him."

"I won't."

"Some people just like to be left alone."

I had just gotten permission to explore the largest piece of private property in the entire state. That was good enough for me.

· · ·

I had turned ten in January, but Dad made me wait until April vacation to go see Old Man Fulton. I called my best friend, Jamie Nieves that Friday night and we agreed to meet in front of my house for our first adventure.

Jamie had been there a couple of times, and he told me of this great pond full of frogs, turtles, and even blackish-green water snakes.

We went in over half a mile, and passed rocky crags perfect for playing army, ponds, streams, and *dozens* of trees that you could climb.

That was my favorite. I love to climb to the top of a tree and get a birds-eye view of the world. Everything looks so small from up there, and you feel so *important* and powerful. We went a bit further, and Jamie acted like he needed a rest.

"Let's sit down a while, okay, Ronnie?"

"We just *got* here!"

"My mother told me to rest every fifteen minutes so my asthma wouldn't act up."

I turned away and muttered, "Oh, my God." Jamie's mother babied him quite a bit. His family had moved here from Mexico two years earlier.

It was just as well, though. While I was sitting there I happened to look up. And that's when I saw it. *The* perfect tree for climbing. It was a maple, and at the top was the most incredible arrangement of branches that formed a platform where you could stand or *sit.* It reminded me of the crow's nests on old sailing ships.

"Finish resting, Jamie. I gotta go look at that tree over there."

I ran about a hundred feet further, hoping that there would be good "starter branches."

The lowest branches were just out of reach, but there was an old stump next to it. I climbed up, reached across, grabbed the lowest branch, and swung myself into the tree. Looking up, I could see easy pathways to the top. I dropped back down and ran back to Jamie.

"Jamie, you gotta see the tree over there! You can go all the way up and *sit!*"

His face dropped a little. "You go ahead. I'll explore down here."

"Don't you want to climb it?"

"My mother doesn't want me climbing trees."

I exhaled loudly to show my disapproval. "Okay, I'm goin' up."

Not two minutes later I was in the crow's nest. Sitting up there was not as comfortable as I first thought, but standing was even better than I imagined. There were six branches to stand on, so I could get a panoramic view. I looked down to spot Jamie. He was nowhere to be found. The whole scene looked strange. I knew there would be a different *perspective* of the ground below me, but it seemed as though *things* down there were different. I couldn't find the path we had come down, or the pond we had just passed. I yelled to Jamie several times. No answer. I figured he had taken off exploring, so I started scanning the area. I had some small binoculars, which I always carried in anticipation of climbing trees. I looked south.

I could not believe what I was seeing. A hundred yards away was a body of water. At first I thought it was the Chygan River, but that was *north* of us. It *couldn't* be Chesapeake Bay; that was nearly two miles from here. And then came the unbelievable. I actually slapped myself to make sure this was real. It was a two-masted sloop, a *wooden ship,* the type from two-hundred years ago. It had pulled abreast on a direct line from me to this strange body of water, and was heading west. I got the binoculars out. The ship looked somewhat bigger, but I couldn't clearly see any people on it. I knew they had masted ships in the Inner Harbor, but that was usually on special occasions, like Fourth of July. I tried to find a name on it, but couldn't make one out. I looked atop the rigging. There was a flag flying, a British Union Jack naval flag.

I looked down to find Jamie. Still nothing. I yelled for him again. No answer. I quickly climbed down, and as I hit the ground found him standing right next to the tree.

"Jamie, there's a wooden ship out on that river over yonder."

He seemed confused and disturbed.

"It looks like a British sloop. Hey, where were you? I looked all around and yelled for you a bunch of times."

"I was right here the whole time."

"Didn't you hear me yellin' your name?"

Jamie had this odd look on his face, a cross between fear and uncertainty. "I could barely make out words coming from where you were, but I couldn't actually hear you."

"Jesus, get your ears checked."

"One other thing, Ronnie."

"What?"

"I couldn't exactly *see* you, either."

"I was right at the top of this *tree!*"

"I know. I saw you climb up, but when you got to the top, it was like all you were was an ...*outline* of you."

"Are you pullin' my leg?"

He got a little defensive. "Did you really see a British sloop where there isn't even any *water,* or are you pullin' *my* leg?"

We tried to talk it out like they teach you in school. We accused each other of carrying a joke too far, and our first adventure into Fulton's woods ended prematurely. We tromped out of there and went our separate ways.

. . .

They made us keep these dumb journals in school of our *thoughts* and *feelings* and all that rubbish. Well, I was going to keep a journal of all my trips up to the crow's nest. Darn Jamie almost had me believing I was imagining the whole thing. That was the last I saw of him during vacation.

I knew what I had seen was real, and that evening I recounted the whole story to my mom and dad, and my brother Todd, who is seven. Dad actually showed an interest and told me that back in the 1700's there *were* British ships in the Chesapeake.

"Dad, it couldn't have been the Chesapeake. It's two miles from here."

He smiled. "Well, what was it, Ron, the *Atlantic Ocean?*" Mom was smiling now, too. Todd was looking back and forth, trying to figure out what was going on.

Well, *I* knew. They thought I was pretending. This had always been a no-win situation for me, so I dropped it. I even managed a laugh, as though I had been caught red-handed in my little game.

My father was a guidance counselor at the high school, and a very practical man. He dealt in reality, tried-and true methods of problem-solving, and all that other *normal* stuff. He wasn't against a little pretending, but he believed in what was *real* in the conventional sense. My mother was typically average, had attended two years of community college, and worked in a pet store here in Haydenville. She was loving and supportive, but this was out of her comfort zone.

We had a new 2006 computer, and I tried to look up stuff to help me define what was happening. I had seen enough sci-fi TV and movies to give me a starting point. I was sure I was dealing with a *portal,* a window into the past. My theory was that at the top of that tree, the crow's nest, I had a portal, but it was a border zone. Jamie claimed he could barely hear me calling him, and could only see me in outline.

Then I looked up British ships in the Chesapeake, and remembered that Old Man Fulton said the Chesapeake once ran through here before the land shifted. I even found a date when British ships had been around here. It was *1761.* Had I really seen 245 years into the past?

So I made the journal entry for that Saturday. Every day during vacation I went back and climbed into the crow's nest. Nothing. And when I looked down, everything was the way it was supposed to look.

Meanwhile, school started again. Jamie was timid, but he had a big mouth. On the playground I started getting teased by "The Big Three." These jerks were always giving themselves nicknames, like The Three Musketeers, The Three Heroes, and so forth. Their real names were Tommy Bell, who had a nose the size of Illinois, Sam Giraud, the worst-smelling person in the school, and Louis Tharpe, a black kid with the largest head I'd ever seen. Too bad there was nothing in it. I called them Captain Big Nose, Buzzard Breath, and Potato Head.

At recess Buzzard Breath starts asking me if I had any more "visions." Then Potato Head chimes in with, "Hey, what you been smoking, Kirts? I wanna see me some ships in the magic river, or maybe a pile of hundred-dollar bills." Captain Big Nose finished it up with, "Ronnie, let's go climb the magic tree later. I wanna catch some imaginary visions. You make any imaginary friends up there?"

"You guys," I said, trying to sound *disappointed* in them.

It worked. All three turned and walked toward the school. I'm not sure if the recess bell had anything to do with it. Potato Head looked back at me. "Hey Kirts, you better book a couple sessions with Mrs. Evers, boy."

She was the school psychologist.

That Sunday, fifteen days after seeing the British ship, I saw my second vision from the crow's nest. An unpleasant one.

There were a man and woman, walking through the woods. They were right about at the spot where Jamie took a rest a couple weeks back. I tried to get a good look to determine the time period. Both were in their twenties, wearing clothes that seemed current. The guy had long sideburns and a moustache, wearing jeans and a red shirt. The girl had medium-length blond hair and jeans, with a white top. They seemed to be conversing normally, holding hands.

Suddenly the guy started trying to *undress* her. She resisted, then tried to scream, but he threw her down and covered her mouth. When she tried to scream again, he punched her in the head a couple times. All I heard after that was some moaning and crying.

I knew what this was, and I didn't want to see any more. I climbed down and looked back at that spot. It was as empty as when I had walked by it ten minutes earlier. I had witnessed a man brutalizing a woman, and I wondered if she had gotten the police on him, or if he had gotten away with it. And I was so disturbed by it that I knew my parents would sense something was wrong.

So, like a jerk, I told them.

It didn't go well. My mother was nearly hysterical, until my father told her I was reporting something that I *claimed* happened in the past. He was extremely agitated. What he thought was an innocent game of pretend had taken an ugly turn. "Do you want the police to come so you can tell *them* what you saw?" he yelled.

"I have no idea when this happened, Dad. What if this guy turns out to be a serial rapist or something?"

By now, Todd was confused, and scared at the violent reactions of our parents. "What's a serium rapus?" he asked, ready to cry.

Dad had my arms in his hands, trying to establish control, I guess. "Ronnie, where is your mind that you imagine things as unsavory as *this?*" He paused, and I braced myself. "I'm calling your school tomorrow. Edna Evers is a friend of mine, and I think you are going to spend some time talking things out. If you won't tell me what's wrong, then you need to tell someone qualified to help children having problems."

What a cruel irony that a jerk like Potato Head had turned out to be right. But I still needed to defend myself. I could not act like some stupid kid who happened to get caught doing something intolerable. "Dad, I don't have *problems,* except that no one believes me." And then came my second big mistake. "Maybe if we ask the police if there was an unsol—"

"You stop this at once, young man! You come home telling me you imagined the most insidious act a man can commit, and you want the *police* to know?"

Dictionary, please. *Insidious?*

. . .

Even though my teacher told me privately to go see Mrs. Evers during silent reading, by the second or third session anyone who made it their business to find out where I was going knew.

Mrs. Evers was okay and all, but she kept using phrases like "claimed to have seen" in our discussions. I tried to head her off by saying that if I *was* making this up I would have been doing it on a daily basis, but I don't think she was buying it.

Once, as I left her office to go back to class, I heard someone behind me. It was Captain Big Nose. He came alongside me.

"Hey, Kirts, you'll be just in time for creative writing. I got a great story I'm working on. 'I Was a Fifth-Grade Psycho.'"

. . .

I kept up my journal, and near the end of the school year, thirty-five days after seeing the young couple, came my third vision into the past.

About forty yards north of the tree were three tents set up in a clearing. There were six men nearby, talking, some holding rifles. They were dressed in the uniform of U. S. soldiers during the Civil War. Two were sitting on these side-by-side boulders, reading off pieces of paper. Letters from home, I guessed.

We had studied the Civil War, especially Maryland's role. Haydenville was east of Washington. Although Lincoln feared an attack on Washington from the west, he also knew an attack from the east was possible. I figured these guys were an outpost for early warning if the Rebs tried a sneak attack.

I watched them for awhile, and it was obvious that the two men sitting on the boulders were arguing. It became louder, and suddenly one threw his letter down and grabbed the other man by the front of his coat. It ripped. I could actually *hear* it as both men tumbled to the ground, scuffling. One of the other soldiers (probably their Sergeant) ordered them to stop. They did, and he made them shake hands and go inside different tents. I almost laughed out loud. (Go to your tent, young man, and think about what you've done.)

. . .

I was smart this time. With only a couple days of school left, I was not about to throw more fuel on the fire. I told no one about the third "sighting." When my parents questioned me about my sessions with Mrs. Evers, I let on that it helped, and she was showing me how to cope so I would not *feel the need* to fabricate or fantasize.

She also told me that having "visions" from above the ground is fairly common with creative people who need more control in their lives. I'm sure she also told that to my parents, so I didn't bother.

School ended on a positive note. I told my teacher, Miss Grinvalsky, that I was doing better with my "problems," and was looking forward to next year. She gave me a big hug and sent me on my way.

There was one casualty, though. A few days before the end of school I went over Jamie's house to see if he wanted to play catch. He said he didn't feel like it, then looked back at his parents, who looked away. The next day at school he told me they didn't want him playing with me any more. Adults, right? I'm tellin' you.

That may have been for the best. Now I had the whole summer to document this phenomenon. I was wondering if these sightings were random, or if there was a *cycle* to it. As it turned out, there *was*. Fifteen days after seeing the soldiers, I had another sighting. Twenty-two days later, another. Thirty-five days after that, a third. They were mildly interesting, but it was the fact that there was a predictable cycle that was fascinating.

In early July, I was witness to a bunch of boys playing football. From the football's old-fashioned shape and leather helmets with no facemasks, I knew it was the 1950's. I wondered if any of those kids were still around, now in their late sixties. No, I didn't go around asking. I learned my lesson. At the end of July I saw a guy pacing off distances, and pounding into the ground wooden stakes with colored pieces of cloth tied to their tops. I didn't think this area had ever been farmed. He could have been just marking land he'd bought. It seemed like the late 1800's or early 1900's. Just before school started I was witness to some kind of hippie celebration, probably from the late '60's or early '70's. I looked up some of the music blaring from their *tape players. The Beach Boys, Mamas and Papas, Steely Dan, Fleetwood Mac.* Groovy. And these would be the same people criticizing today's popular music. Go figure. And what the hell is a *Strawberry Alarm Clock?*

Were illegal substances used? Yes. I was secretly hoping to recognize an adult I now knew, like one of my teachers. Just as well I didn't. What if one of them had been Mom or Dad? Especially since some of the couples started taking a keen interest in each other, if you get my drift. It was still disgusting, but at least it was consentual.

. . .

There *is* such a thing as a clean slate. I started sixth grade with mostly different classmates than the ones that watched me schlep down to Mrs. Evers office the previous May and June. Mrs. Evers herself had been assigned to another school. And the state of Oklahoma was home to a new resident, Samuel Giraud, aka Buzzard Breath. It looked promising, if certain people had short memories.

A few started bad-mouthing me to kids that hadn't been in Miss Grinvalsky's class, but it was the beginning of a new school year, and nobody wanted to give anybody grief over hearsay from when we were dumb fifth-graders. As long as I didn't botch it up with tales from the crow's nest, I didn't even have to go see Mrs. Evers's replacement, Mr. Arthur.

I applied myself in school, kept my mouth shut at home, and stayed out of Fulton's woods. *Except* for every fifteenth, twenty-second, and thirty-fifth day.

Jamie was friendlier now, and a few cute girls started flirting with me. I returned the favor. Captain Big Nose and Potato Head were into girls, too, and decided they couldn't be bothered with me. Not a problem.

. . .

During the next six months or so, the sightings were unexciting compared to what they had been. I saw kids walking through the woods, beavers building a dam where there isn't a drop of water now, and some weird folk dance or religious ritual by a woman and about ten teenaged girls dressed in old European style. I tried looking it up, but all I got were dead ends.

And the guy who attacked that girl appeared again, with a different girl. He didn't do anything *insidious* this time. He and the girl brought a picnic lunch, picked flowers, talked for a while, then left. (Could this have been at an earlier time?)

It seemed as though this phenomenon had settled into what it was going to be: a time portal I could visit up to fifteen times a year. But it was something that I couldn't risk speaking of, especially when people claiming to have "seen things;" ghosts, the future, or even the past were marked as lunatics. I felt that my future was a bright one. I wouldn't risk jeopardizing it because I was fortunate (?) enough to have discovered a window to the past.

On April 14th, 2007, about a year after I first found the crow's nest, I climbed it for what, unknown to me, would be the last time. Thirty-five days since my last look into the past, I expected to see *something*. What I saw was a man about thirty-five yards northwest, dressed in a white tee shirt and jeans, furiously digging a large rectangular

hole. Beside him lay an oblong bundle about five feet long.
I was not a whiz at math, but I could add two and two.

When he had finished and pushed the wrapped
bundle into the hole, he frantically filled it in and placed
rocks, leaves, and whatever was handy on top to disguise it.

Nearly sick to my stomach, I descended the crow's
nest and ran to the spot. I looked mournfully at it,
wondering who was buried there, and who had done this. I
marked the now-indiscernible gravesite with three rocks.

. . .

Don't think I ran to the police, told my story, and
they came out, unearthed the body, ran tests, compared it to
missing person cases, and made an arrest.

First of all who was this, and when did it happen?
It was a missing person, obviously, not someone known to
be murdered. It took several days of computer searches,
and even then I couldn't be positive. My best guess was
that it was Rachel Ann McKay, aged 15, reported missing
by her parents on August 5th, 1967. According to what I
read, her parents had been having trouble with her,
skipping school, riding in cars with boys they didn't know,
smoking; all the ways kids went wrong back then. All
attempts to locate her turned up empty.

But the shocker was a follow-up article a week
later. Her parents, Harold and Lucinda, were pictured at
the top of the article. Harold looked exactly like the man I
had seen burying the bundle on Fulton's land. I looked him
up in the phone book and on the computer. Nothing. Same
thing for his wife. I knew I had to keep quiet. I would get
nothing but trouble at home or in school. The police would
want to know how I knew a body was buried on Fulton's
land from an incident that happened almost thirty years
before I was born. I finally decided on someone who might
be able to help. But then my father had a heart attack.

. . .

With my father's recuperation, my mother taking on more hours, poor Todd's emotional problems over this, I was basically the man of the house for quite a while. Even when my dad returned to school, there were lots of things I had to shoulder, all of them very time-consuming. Playing detective didn't even make the list.

Over two years passed before I could act on my plan to catch the killer of Rachel Ann McKay, her father, Harold. It was the summer of 2009, and I paid a visit to Mr. Kendall Fulton.

He looked older, but still seemed pretty sharp. He remembered me.

"Your name is Ron, right?"

"Yes, sir. I gotta talk to you about something that happened on your land in 1967."

"Well, Ron, unless my math fails me, you weren't born, and I was living in England, making my fortune."

"Mr. Fulton, I saw a dead body buried on your land, and I saw the guy that buried it."

His face scrunched up. "Wait a minute. You said 1967. What's goin' on here?"

For the next twenty minutes, I tried to explain everything, starting with the British ship, subsequent sightings, my credibility problems at home and school, right up to the burial of who I believed to be Rachel Ann McKay, and who I believed was responsible. I figured he would never put up with a story like that, but he listened intently, his face hardly changing expression. When I finished, he looked at the ceiling, then back at me for about half a minute.

"So what you're claiming is that there's a tree on my property that's a kind of window on the past, and you've been seeing things from it at certain intervals."

"You don't believe me, do you, sir?"

He gave me a hard, stern look, then shrugged. "Course I don't believe you, Ron. Who would? But I could use a little exercise. You ride?"

"Ride what, sir?"

"Horses. Let's grab a couple shovels and take a ride out there. If we go out my back pasture, we might save a little time. And we won't be seen out on the road here."

"Shovels, sir?"

"Well, Ron, you need shovels to dig. And it sounds like you been doin' your share of shovelin' already. Just in case you're right, though."

"How we gonna explain this to the cops if we find her?"

He winked at me as he threw on a western hat and riding gloves. "You leave that to me, Ron, old boy."

· · ·

So out his back pasture we went, him on Betsy, and me on Ol' Bess. We hadn't ridden for two minutes when he said, "I'll tell you something,' Ron. When I got back to the states and retired in 1995, I bought all that land and made it my business to learn everything I could about Haydenville and its people" He paused. "Tell you why you couldn't find Harold McKay or his wife."

I was listening intently over the sound of horse's hooves.

"Harold had a mental breakdown, lives in a rest home over in Vanderra, 'bout five miles from here. Same age as me, vaguely remember him from my school days."

"What about his wife?"

"She left him years ago, right after their daughter *disappeared.* Went back to her family in New Hampshire.

Harold was an okay guy, if I remember right. Bit of a temper, maybe."

"That could have been the reason he killed his daughter."

He gave me that look again. "You don't know any such thing, Ron."

"I'm pretty sure."

After a few more minutes, we were approaching the spot. "That's the tree, Mr. Fulton." I pointed to it.

He half smiled. "I see. Nice tall one."

We got to the gravesite, still marked with the three rocks. Fulton looked all around, and focused on a spot in the opposite direction. "Those two big boulders there, that where the two Union soldiers got into the fight?"

I was amazed at his recollection of detail. "Yes, they're a little askew from that day and tilted, but that's them." We dismounted and untied the shovels.

He pointed at the gravesite. "That where we're digging?"

I nodded. I moved the three rocks and we started. When we were down just over two feet, our shovels hit something. Fulton stopped me from digging, and started scraping away the dirt in an even pattern. When he was finished, there was some type of covering, bound in places by twine. His scraping had revealed an oblong, rounded shape.

"Oh, my," he said softly. "Harold, what in God's name did you do?" Then he pulled me close. "Ron, your part in this is done, now. I don't want you comin' 'round here no more. Let's fill it in, now."

"Fill it *in? Why?*"

"Animals, Ron. Can't have them diggin' and gnawin' at her."

"So what are we—what are you gonna—"

"Listen to me," he said sternly. "You ride back with me, go home, and keep away from here. Come back and see me in a week. We understood on this, now?"

"Yes, sir."

"And most important of all, Ron, you keep shut about this. It can only bring you trouble."

That, I already knew.

. . .

I did as he said, and went back to see him a week later. We sat out on his large, covered porch.

There were no preliminaries. "Ron, I went out to see Harold McKay at the home. I asked him to tell me what happened that day. And he did."

"Just like that?"

"Ron, Harold's got enough of his marbles left to know that people don't say 'no' to me. There was a big argument with Rachel that day; he grabbed her arm, and she pulled away, hard-like. She went flyin' down their second floor stairs. Broke her neck. The wife was scared of him bein' put away, so they agreed to bury her on what is now my land, and no one would be the wiser. Reported her missing, and that was the end of it. Until you and your *special tree* came along."

I was dumbfounded, but had an inner feeling of validation. "Now what happens?"

"Nothin.'"

"What about the police?"

"No police, Ron. That man has suffered enough for what he done *by accident.* He lost his daughter, his wife, his mind, *everything.* No point in draggin' him out to stand before a judge and jury."

I was speechless.

"I fixed up the grave proper-like, and had Pastor Flannery ride out there with me to bless the ground, in return for a very generous annual contribution to his church.”

My mind was reeling, but I still thought of another possibility. “Mr. Fulton, what about the crow’s nest? Some other kid could climb up there and see her being buried. Or *us* digging her up!”

“No one will ever climb that tree again, Ron, if you get my meaning.”

I did.

. . .

No one goes in Old Man’s Fulton’s woods any more. Shortly after our conversation, the “No Trespassing” signs went up all over the edge of the huge parcel of land. People knew enough to tell their kids to stay away. No one wanted Kendall Fulton on their back. I was in high school now, and found I had plenty enough to keep me occupied.

About a month after I had visited Mr. Fulton, I happened to look out our front window, and saw him sitting on Betsy in our driveway. I rushed outside and looked up at him, dumbfounded.

“Got somethin’ for ya,’ Ron. Went pokin’ around those boulders where the two soldiers had their little dust-up. You’re a smart lad, Ron, but you gotta learn to do a little diggin’ now and then.” He paused and smiled at me. “Even the unbelievable can be proved …sometimes.” He winked, handed me a small envelope, and sauntered down Brewer Road toward his massive farmhouse.

I opened the envelope, and a tarnished gold button slid out. It was very old. On the front, in raised letters, it said “U.S. Army.”

"SCOUT'S HONOR"
2013

Halfway between Millersburg and Woodston, on Ohio Route 83, lies Lake Sanganore. Its northern shore is home to a girl scout camp, and on its southern shore, a boy scout camp. They were renamed after a scouting couple, Chester and Marge Trolier, who dedicated their adult lives to the scouting movement. Upon their retirement, a ceremony was held at each camp.

The couple attended the ceremony, noting that even though they were on their way to retirement in Sebring, Florida, their hearts would always remain in Ohio, and in scouting. They believed scouting was one of the most honorable endeavors, and were proud of their service to it.

The incident which occurred at the camps three years later is in no way a reflection on the Boy Scouts, Girl Scouts, or Chester and Marge Trolier.

Camp Chester; Monday, July 17th, 1961

At four P.M. the half-hour "quiet time" at camps Chester and Marge began. Scouts were confined to their cabins for quiet games, conversation, tidying up, or resting.

In the Fox Cabin, Eddie Mintor had a meeting with his five cabinmates. All six were "lifers," scouts who stayed at camp all eight weeks of its summer operation. Most lifers came from families who could afford eight weeks of camp, or scouts totally immersed in the culture. There was a third category. Scouts that were there because their parents didn't want them around.

At the Mintor household in Woodston, Eddie's parents were in a downward spiral of infidelity, financial reversal, overindulgence approaching alcoholism, and mid-life crisis. They had subconsciously realized that he was the only element of their lives that contained no intrigue or instant gratification. He was, in effect, odd man out.

Although Eddie was a 'C' student, he had figured out this human equation years before he would be asked to solve equations on paper. Being an exemplary scout no longer held his interest. Eddie, in fact, wanted revenge on his parents by having himself kicked out of camp. He knew any one of several outrageous deeds would do it. Or two outrageous deeds if they were giving out second chances this summer. And it seemed they were. There was a different vibe this year. Maybe it had to do with the new optimistic young man in the White House. Fifty-mile hikes, new beginnings, people going into outer space. Eddie knew he had to pull something *really* outrageous. And, being Eddie Mintor, he wanted plenty of company when he did.

Eddie and his cabinmates sat in a circle on the floor. He knew that two would be a cinch to join his grand escapade, with two others a strong possibility. Only Reynaldo "Ronny" Cuesta might be opposed. This could not be done unless they were all in. Too much chance of someone squealing, either on moral grounds, or to gain favor with the counselors.

They had been guests at the girl scout camp that Saturday. Each camp hosted the other for an all-day festival of competitive games, scavenger hunts, canoe races, and the like. The day was topped off with a campfire that night, including storytelling, skits, and a marshmallow roast. In August the boys would host the girls. But Eddie planned on not being around then. At the girls' camp he noticed something that would be the perfect setting for his grand finale. He just had to convince the other five.

As Eddie laid out his proposal to Dennis Daignault, Steve Rossoman, Gary Williams, Mark Ollander, and Ronny Cuesta, he was mindful not to let it slip that for him, this was a "suicide mission," a deed done with no attempt to escape detection. But he had it planned that when the deed was done, he would take all the blame. There was a skewed version of scout's honor involved. He would owe up to what he did, but never squeal on his fellow conspirators.

"Okay, guys, here it is. There's this old cabin at the far end of the girl's camp, near the entrance."

"How do you know? We never went anywhere near that end," said Mark Ollander.

"Well, *you* didn't. I asked Robin Hebner about it."

"Yeah, 'Round Robin,'" jeered Ollander.

"She's not fat any more, peckerhead. Open your eyes," snapped Eddie.

"Easy, Ed," said Ollander. "If you got the hots for her we'll be cool with it."

"I don't. She's just a good kid. Listen. When everybody's asleep after midnight we take three canoes, cross the lake, and burn down that cabin. Whaddaya say?"

"Are you *insane?*" said Gary. "What if there's—"

"There's no *girls* in it, numbnuts. They use it for storage and junk."

Steve Rossoman raised an index finger. "Eddie, what are we gonna use to *paddle* the canoes? The oars are locked up. So that nobody *steals canoes.* Especially in the middle of the freakin' *night.*"

Eddie smiled. "I know where the key is hidden."

"Where?" asked Dennis.

"Under the rock by the flagpole. I been watchin' Mr. Renning for a few days."

"Bad idea, Ed. Too noisy," said Mark. "Launching three canoes. Bound to wake people up. We got tenderfoots here would piss their pants and start screamin' if they heard anything. Probably think we were bears."

"He's right, Ed," said Gary. "We could just walk around the lake. Probably take less time, too."

"How the hell we gonna *see* walking around the lake in the *dark?"* asked Dennis.

"You assholes, that's why we should take *canoes!"* hissed Eddie.

"How about we tie a rope around our waists, and the lead guy uses a light with a filter on it."

Everyone in the circle was stunned at Ronny Cuesta's suggestion.

"All *right.* Big *Ron!"* said Eddie. "You're *in?"*

"Why not? I'm tired of being odd man out."

Eddie looked at the five other lifers. "Okay, it would have been more interesting *my* way, but Ron has a good idea. We'll walk."

All five nodded in agreement.

"Just one thing, though," said Eddie. "If any of us get caught or are feeling guilty, you can only tell on yourself. No ratting out anybody. Agreed?"

There were nods from the circle.

"I mean it guys. No squealing. Scout's honor?"

Five hands went up in the three-finger salute. "Scout's honor," they echoed.

Camp Marge; Monday, July 17th, 1961

Cheryl Wiltz looked into the backpack Dody Lachance had opened on the floor of the Gazelle Cabin. Their other cabinmate, Robin Hebner, sat idly on her cot.

"Robin, could you watch the door?" asked Cheryl.

Eager to please the popular Cheryl, Robin scooted off the cot and stood in the doorway. "What do you have?" she asked.

"Dody's sister snuck in wine and brandy yesterday during visiting hours. Left it under the bushes by the main gate. We can party hearty tonight!"

Cheryl had grown tired of scouting, but had stayed in. As time went on there were more opportunities for socializing with *boys*. She was tall, with long brown hair and piercing blue eyes. Dody Lachance also had bright blue eyes, but her rail-thin body, stick-like arms, and scraggly unkempt light brown hair had earned her the nickname "Scarecrow" among many of the boys. Also, she was unpredictable in words and actions. Many scouts, boys *and* girls, steered clear of her.

Robin Hebner, after years of being overweight and enduring the moniker "Round Robin," had dieted and exercised under a doctor's care for a year, and was ready to make her mark. She knew that Cheryl was her quickest path to social acceptance, and was ready to do anything to gain it. But she couldn't just *ask* in. She had to be invited.

"I know the perfect place we can go tonight," declared Cheryl.

"So do I," stated Dody.

Cheryl looked at Robin, mulling it over. "Robin, you can come with us if you want, but you can't tell anyone."

And there was Robin's opportunity. "Sure, I'll party with you guys. Where we gonna go?"

"The old storage shed by the entrance. I gotta remember to bring my cigarettes. Makes the booze taste better," Cheryl stated.

"You got *cigarettes*, too?" Robin asked.

"I *always* have cigarettes, Robin. A scout has to be prepared."

. . .

At 12:45 that evening, all six boys of the Fox Cabin, attached at the waist with a rope, snuck down to the lake's edge. Eddie was in the lead with a scout flashlight fitted with a filter. He could see just far enough to avoid rocks and the lake itself.

Behind him in intervals of three feet were Steve, Mark, Gary, Dennis, and Ronny, who wore Eddie's pack on his back. Eddie didn't want it to be in his way.

What's in there?" Ronny had asked.

"You'll see."

Eddie had laid down the law before they left. Absolutely no noise, and no talking.

Within twenty minutes they could make out the main gate of Camp Marge, aided by a three-quarters moon. They sidled up to the shed and listened. All was quiet.

"Tell Ronny to open the pack and take out the tinder," Eddie whispered to Steve. Word was passed back. Piles of dry leaves, twigs, and long strands of dead grass were spread at intervals under the shed, which was built atop cement blocks.

Eddie couldn't resist. "Anybody got a match?"

"My ass and your face," several voices whispered back.

Eddie squelched a laugh, taking out a pack of matches. The tinder was lit, and more quickly than they could have imagined, flames jumped to the dry wooden boards of the storage cabin. "Let's go," he commanded.

. . .

The flames were visible on the south shore, but only the six residents of the Fox Cabin saw them. Screams, and raised voices soon followed, but not enough to raise the alarm at Camp Chester, three-quarters of a mile away. It was the smell of smoke that finally roused some of the lighter sleepers. By that time, Eddie and his co-conspirators were in their bunks, whispering excitedly to each other.

Word was spread in the camp, and within five minutes, every scout at Camp Chester, along with adult staff and supervisors were awake in various stages of dress.

Walter Renning, head counselor, quickly gathered the boys around him and selected ten of his most experienced scouts for a fire brigade. Shovels, rakes, and axes were procured, large lanterns were lit, and Renning commanded his assistant, Charlie Basson, to keep order while they went to the rescue. As they started the double-time march around the lake, sirens could be heard coming up the road to Camp Marge.

Eddid Mintor and Steve Rossoman were among the ten scouts dashing along the western shore. Eddie couldn't help but think, *Boy, twice in one night. What were the odds?*

. . .

A horrified Eddie Mintor and Steve Rossoman returned to Camp Chester at 4:45 A.M. It seemed that much of the news they learned had somehow beaten them across the lake. They gathered their cabinmates and withdrew inside.

"Guys, we're in big trouble," said Steve.

"No shit, Sherlock," retorted Dennis. "Nice goin,' Eddie."

"How the hell would I know there were *girls* in the freakin' *storage shed* at one in the morning?"

"What were they even *doin'* there?" asked Ronny. "Jesus, the one time I—"

"They had booze, all three of them. Cheryl Wiltz, Dody Lachance, and Robin Hebner."

"Didn't they hear us? Didn't they smell smoke?" asked Mark.

"They were so drunk they passed out and couldn't even *move,"* said Steve. "They took them to the first aid tent before we got there, so we don't know how bad they got burned, but it must have been serious. They called ambulances."

Eddie would not make eye contact.

Mark Ollander's eyes were wide. "Oh, my God! They're gonna find the tinder piles and know the fire was set, damn it!"

Eddie's head snapped up. "They won't find *anything,* Ollander, you pussy. The whole cabin collapsed!"

"You idiot, Mintor. They'll *examine* everything. The entire *scene.* This isn't some stupid Halloween prank you pulled this time."

"Let's just see what happens, Mark, before you go pissing your pants over it," Eddie said. "Maybe they won't find anything." He paused and gave everyone the once-over. "We're all in this together. You all swore on scout's honor."

"Eddie's right," said Dennis. "We can't be at each other's throats, or somebody's gonna get wise."

The other boys paused to think about everything that had been said, and *done,* and accepted the shared responsibility.

"Let's just keep our ears open for the next couple of days, all right, guys?" Dennis said.

• • •

On Wednesday, July 19th, camp director Renning called an assembly of all scouts and staff and had them sit by the flagpole.

"Boys," he began, "you're all aware of what happened yesterday morning. Three girls suffered burns in a fire. They are all in the hospital but doing okay."

Everyone breathed an open sigh of relief.

"Incidentally, their camp director, Mrs. Palomba, thanks us for sending a crew to help."

There were satisfied smiles from the crowd.

"But the reason I called you all here is to inform you *why* this happened in the first place."

Six bodies tensed, everyone listened in anticipation.

"Those three girls, and I'm not even gonna mention their names, had been drinking alcohol in that shed. Should they have been doing that, boys?"

A smattering of 'no's' was heard.

"And to top it off, they had cigarettes. And when you have cigarettes, you have matches and lighters."

A few murmurs from the crowd.

"Those girls were lighting matches and using a lighter. They were so drunk that they fell asleep and accidentally started that fire themselves."

Looks of disbelief abounded among the crowd, while six boys *inwardly* breathed a sigh of relief.

"Boys, I want you all to promise me, here and now, that you will *never* do anything as reckless and dangerous as those girls did."

Heads nodded all around.

Renning raised his right arm, forming the three-finger salute. "On your scout's honor, boys?"

Dozens of hands raised and asserted, "Scout's honor!"

. . .

The ensuing days were filled with rumors, theories, and information. Boys who knew someone who knew someone who knew one of the three girls were suddenly holding court, their peers hanging on every word.

Cheryl and Robin had second and third degree burns; Cheryl on one arm and back, Robin on one leg and side. Dody had gotten the worst of it. One entire side of her body had burns from her foot all the way to her back, neck, and hair.

Walter Renning took away everyone's free time on July 20th, for a mandatory session on fire prevention, fire-fighting, and first aid for burn victims.

On July 21st, anyone with a transistor radio listened as Gus Grissom became the second American to go into outer space.

"*That* was exciting," said Gary, after the near-disastrous mission.

"Yeah," offered Eddie, "especially when his capsule sank and he almost drowned."

"You think anyone suspects that it wasn't the girls who started the fire?" asked Mark.

Eddie was growing weary of Mark's pessimism. "Hey assface, the Fire Marshall himself was there, and *he* thought it was them. So why don't you just shut it?"

"I got news for you, Mintor. The Fire Marshall's son was in a mororcycle accident the day before. Maybe he wasn't doing his best job. He might just go back there."

"Doesn't make any difference, Mark. We're in the clear. Let it be, will ya?"

"Okay, Eddie, I can let it be for now. But how about in six weeks, when we're all in high school, and *some of us* have to pass those three in the hallway, or sit next to them in class?"

Unknown to the boys, the three girls, in the throes of alcohol, *had* been fooling around with the lighter and matches while in the shed, setting fire to odds and ends of paper and cellophane wrappings. So when they were questioned, they answered 'yes' when the Fire Marshall asked if they were doing anything that may have caused a fire. And Mark Ollander's information about the Fire Marshall being distracted, heard as a rumor from a scout who was the Marshall's neighbor, was accurate.

Fire Marshall Daylon Fisher had a son who had been in a motorcycle accident the day before, and was in serious condition. Fisher was operating on auto-pilot, and while he did everything he was supposed to, it was not his most thorough investigation. In all fairness, *everything* indicated that three extremely drunk girls, playing with fire, had burned *themselves.*

The remainder of the summer passed without incident. The six boys became so used to covering up what they had done that it was no longer difficult to keep up appearances.

In August, Camp Chester hosted Camp Marge for a day and night of games, socializing, and fun. Hardly anyone mentioned the fire. There were occasional comments from girls who knew the three that they were recovering, and would be starting high school on schedule, in three weeks.

Camp ended the last week in August. Eddie and Dennis would be attending high school in Woodston, the other four boys and all three girls attending Millersburg High. Eddie was relieved not to have to see any of the girls, as Mark had reminded him. He was not worried much about someone squealing. Scouting now seemed passe' to Eddie, but he still had a respect for the concept of scout's honor. He knew the others did, too.

· · ·

Although Millersburg and Woodston were only twelve miles apart, and rivals in many sports, in the day-to-day lives of high school students, they might as well have been across the country from each other.

Eddie ran track, and twice that year, he encountered Mark Ollander and Steve Rossoman. At one track meet, they made it a point to take Eddie aside and give him the latest news on the girls.

"Robin and Cheryl are fine, Eddie. You would never know anything happened, except that Robin limps a little, and Cheryl wears long sleeves, even if it's ninety out," said Steve.

"What about the other one?" asked Eddie, somewhat blandly.

Mark Ollander still carried a bitterness towards Eddie, and the casual attitude of his last remark provoked him. "The *other one,* Eddie? You mean Dody Lachance?"

"Yeah, okay, Dody."

"Well, Eddie, she's disfigured, skips school half the time, gets terrible grades, and her only friends are a bunch of pot-smoking, pill-popping losers. She's on the road to nowhere even before freshman year is finished."

Eddie smirked, making Mark even madder. *"Road to nowhere?* Ollander, where do you get this stuff? That girl was a freak show on wheels even *before* the fire."

Ollander lunged at Eddie, but Steve stepped between them and pushed them apart before anyone noticed. "Forget it, Mark." He gave Eddie a critical look. "Just forget it. See ya' around, Eddie." The two walked slowly towards the long jump pit.

Eddie stood there, arms folded. "Road to nowhere," he muttered. "What a weenie."

1983

At the scout camps on Lake Sanginore, there is no one left who can tell about the fire on July 18th, 1961. Occasionally, a scout will come to camp with a second-hand version, passed down by a parent, uncle, or aunt.

Sometimes the passing of years is like a strong wind, uprooting some, while others remain tied to their past. The ensuing twenty-two years affected the nine former scouts no more or no less than anyone else.

For Ronny Cuesta, the July 18th fire was not the only secret he kept from the Boy Scouts of America. He moved to Miami at age 23, where he lives with his partner

James, working as a reservation associate at Miami International Airport.

Gary Williams relocated to nearby Cleveland soon after graduation, working in the design department of *Lake Erie Publishing*. Divorced with no children, he remarried and gained a 14-year-old stepson.

Steve Rossoman went into insurance, and after two promotions, was living in Cincinnati with his wife and three children.

Cheryl Wiltz became Cheryl Larviere and gave birth to twin girls, now aged 12. She moved to Virginia, but following her divorce moved to North Carolina, then South Carolina, where she is the office manager at a medical practice. Working her way south one state at a time, she is currently considering a similar position in Georgia.

And there were five who could not or would not be uprooted.

Mark Ollander proved the "Theory of Relativity," marrying the boss's daughter and becoming a sales rep in a large tire business in Millersburg. He is the father of a boy, age 13, and a girl, 11.

Dennis Daignault is a car salesman in Woodston, happily married with two children.

Robin Hebner is now Robin Noonan. She has a 14-year-old daughter and works as a teacher's aide at the elementary school she once attended in Millersburg.

For Dolores "Dody" Lachance, life after 1961 was an endless procession of drugs, alcohol, rehab, failed marriages, a child in custody of her father, and countless menial jobs, between long periods of unemployment.

"Fast Eddie" Minton remained in Woodston, working for a lawn service. He keeps busy cleaning debris in the spring, mowing lawns in summer, raking leaves in the fall, and plowing snow during the winter. Divorced, he gets Wednesdays and every other weekend with his son Jack, age 13, and his daughter Abigail, 10.

. . .

Eddie pulled his Chevy Malibu into the driveway of 76 Brown Avenue. He was there to pick up his son, who had spent the last two hours after school with his very first girlfriend, whom he met at an away football game here in Millersburg. All Eddie knew was that the girl's name was Tricia, a year older than Jack. A lady's man in his youth, Eddie was somewhat impressed that Jack had landed an older girl.

Abigail sat in the back seat, frustrated that she was not allowed to stay home alone. Like many adults with a fuller appreciation of their transgressions, Eddie made sure that Jack and Abigail did not have opportunities to make bad choices because of him. No ten-year-old child of his was going to stay home unsupervised for even an hour.

Within seconds, Jack had bounced out a side door and plunked himself in the front seat. He wore an exasperated expression. "Dad, Trisha's mother wants to talk to you. Could you make it fast? I got homework, and basketball tryouts start tomorrow."

"What happened, Jack?" Abigail chimed. "Trisha's mom catch you kissing her?"

"Shut up, dorkwad. And no, she didn't."

"You didn't kiss her, or she didn't catch you?"

"Abby, stop with the teasing," said Eddie. "And Jack, what did I say about 'dorkwad'?"

"Not to call Abby 'dorkwad.'" He turned in his seat and grinned at her. "Even if she *is* one."

"Dad!"

"That's it, you two," said Eddie, opening the car door. "Try not to kill each other."

Eddie ran up the sidewalk to the side entrance. He was about to knock when the door was opened by Trisha. She was a typical attractive girl her age, fairly tall, long brown hair, and wide expressive eyes.

"Mom!" she called.

"Be right there," answered a voice from the next room.

Eddie could hear a drawer closing, then footsteps. Trisha's mother, Robin Hebner Noonan, entered the kitchen with an almost imperceptible limp, wearing the smile that adults often have when greeting a classmate of years past.

"Hey, Eddie, long time no see," she said extending her hand.

Eddie's mouth and eyes were wide as he shook her hand. "Wow, I had no idea *you* were Tricia's mom. Jack didn't even tell me her last name."

"Typical boy!" said Trisha.

Robin motioned toward the stairway.

"I got homework. I'll let you two reminisce," Trisha said. She called back as she ascended the stairs, "Dad will be home soon."

They could hear her laughing as she reached the second floor.

"So, Robin, how long has it been?" Eddie asked, discomfort oozing from his voice.

"Long time Eddie. Since the camp get-together."

"Sounds about right," said Eddie, his discomfort building.

"I remember how nice you always were to me, even when I was 'Round Robin.'"

"Kid, right?"

"Eddie, I know it's a long time, but do you remember asking me about an old storage cabin near the camp entrance?"

Eddie looked up and grimaced, trying to make it look genuine.

"*I* do, Eddie. That was the last time we ever spoke before today."

"Wow," Eddie said, shifting nervously, "what a memory on you."

"Not so hard to remember when two nights later I was *in* that cabin with Cheryl and Dody, drunk off my ass. We were so stupid. Booze, cigarettes, matches, and a lighter. We might as well have taken a stick of dynamite in there with us."

"We all make mistakes, Robin," Eddie said, now feeling more secure. It seemed that Robin was recounting what the *girls* had done to cause the fire.

"All those years, regretting *what* happened, and *why.*" Her voice sounded as far away as 1961. "Cheryl and I came out of it okay, but poor Dody."

"Yeah," Eddie replied, trying to keep guilt out of his voice. "She's had it pretty tough."

"That fire killed her last chance to turn things around. Her future got burned up that night." Robin seemed sad but resolute.

Eddie felt this was building to something he did not wish to hear. Like many parents, he now used his children as an excuse.

"Look, Robin, I got my kids in the car, and—"

Before he could finish, Robin reached into her back pocket and thrust its contents in his face. Uneasy and uncomfortable before, Eddie was now startled and *scared.*

"What's this?"

"Read it, Eddie."

He was looking at a faded three-by-five index card. His brain and eyes could not synchronize for what seemed like an eternity. The card read:

1. Mark Ollander, August 13, 1966 (in person)

2. Ronny Cuesta, August 21, 1966 (in person)
3. Dennis Daignault, October 1, 1966 (in person)
4. Gary Williams, February 23, 1974 (phone)
5. Steve Rossoman, December 3, 1975 (phone)
6.

Eddie finally grasped the meaning of it. The others had all visited or called Robin and owed up to having been involved in the fire. He noted that Mark, Ronny, and Dennis had done so the year following graduation. They must have tracked down Gary and Steve to tell them what they had done. They had all come clean. He was sure none of them had mentioned his name. But Robin was no dummy. He was their one remaining cabinmate. He was the one who had asked her about the old storage cabin.

Eddie looked at the floor. It may have been the first time since age six that he felt true *shame.* "Robin, it wasn't—"

"Eddie," she interrupted, "nobody's in trouble. There's a number six on that card, I'm sure you noticed."

"Kind of hard not to."

"Eddie, I work in a school. Every day I see ways kids can go wrong, and how adults can keep them from going wrong."

Eddie looked at her in confusion. Was she going to forbid his son from seeing her daughter? Was she going to make him confess?

"You were always a good friend, even when I was just another fat joke to every other boy in school."

"Yeah, big deal now."

"It *was,* and still *is.* I got a proposal for you."

Eddie couldn't believe he had to fight back tears. He had never felt like such a despicable excuse for a human being, another first for him.

"You have a great opportunity here to teach your children. Here's the deal. Go home, sit your kids down, and tell them a *certain* story from your past. Change the names if you want. You can give them something that no one else can, something they will remember and thank you for till your dying day.”

"Robin, I don’t—“

"You do that, Eddie, and I’ll cross off the number six on this card.”

. . .

Eddie Mintor climbed into his car, serenaded by two outraged children.

"About time!” yelled Abigail.

"Jesus, Dad. What were you doing in there?”

"Just reminiscing. Mrs. Noonan and I knew each other from scout camp.”

Abigail pounced. "Ooooh. Was she your girlfriend?”

"Just friends. Eddie drew a deep breath. "When we get home, I want both of you to sit at the table. I have something very, very important to tell you.”

Jack’s face resembled one of someone in intense pain. "Dad, have a heart, *please.* It’s after five. Can’t this wait?”

"No, Jack. In fact, it’s long overdue.”

"Dad, swear to me this isn’t gonna be a waste of time.”

Eddie smiled faintly and raised his right arm, three fingers pointed up. "Scout’s honor.”

"DIVISION"
2013

North Capston Junction, Montana

There was no doubt that Emma Halburton loved her three children. But it was just as obvious she didn't *like* them very much.

Born Emma Chisett in Billings in 1873, she adored children and aspired to teach. She got her teaching degree, but early in her career she met a man six years younger who caught her fancy, and who fancied her. Try as she may, Emma could not get him to commit to marriage. At 26, she was about to give up when war with Spain broke out. The man, Walter Halburton, enlisted, and during his duty assignment in Louisiana contracted a variety of serious illnesses. The army discharged him. He returned to Montana, weakened and dispirited.

His parents, wealthy landowners, taught him the art of speculation. Walter learned well, and within two years, had enough money and confidence to ask Miss Chisett for her hand. For Emma, better late than never. She made it clear she wanted at least five children, preferably six, and that she was now 30, and time was a'wastin.

In 1905 she gave birth to Madeline, a son Gilbert in 1907, and another son Ross in 1911. But the child-bearing came to an abrupt halt. Soon after Ross's birth, Emma took Walter aside and announced that there would be no more children.

"What do you mean, Emma? I thought you wanted five or six."

"Walter, I am finished bringing young ones into the world. We'll have to make do with what we have."

"But—"

"And to make sure, we will no longer engage in any activities that might result in a fourth child. Is that clear?"

"Emma!"

"You are free to take a mistress if you desire."

"A *mistress?* I don't want a mistress. I just want to know why you don't want any more children. What's *wrong?* What did I *do?"*

"T'wasn't anything *you* did, Walter, it's *them."*

"Who? The children?"

"Yes."

"What's the matter with the children?"

Emma softened her demeanor, led her husband to the couch in their sitting room, and sat beside him. "Walter, as a mother, I cannot bring myself to actually say what is in my heart, but you must trust me on this."

. . .

Try as he might, Walter could not see the problem that had stopped his wife from enlarging their family. An only child, he had nothing to compare. Emma and her sister had been raised in a strict, compliant manner.

All her babies had been "difficult," slow to accept bottles, naps, changes in routines and the like. That was something she had resigned herself to. Emma sincerely believed that her children were not *nice.* They weren't *mean,* as such. They were petty, competitive *squabblers,* something not tolerated in her childhood. She foresaw them spending their entire lives watching each other, looking to gain some advantage, obsessively worried that one would gain an advantage over *them.*

To Walter, witnessing the exact behavior and tendencies, it was "just kids being kids." Emma looked at the same pettiness, undercutting, backstabbing, and found it the most disgraceful display imaginable. It was especially evident on birthdays and holidays. Emma could not forgive or forget the plaintive indignation that one of her children would voice if the Easter, Halloween, or Christmas candy had not come out exactly even, right down to the last jellybean or chocolate Santa.

. . .

And that is how the three children of Emma and Walter Halburton evolved. The years passed, Walter blissfully ignorant or indifferent, Emma increasingly disheartened and disgusted.

Walter's land speculation flourished, and soon the Halburtons were very well off. During this time Emma was often heard to comment to her many friends and acquaintances, "I have the three children. Would've had a couple more, but the ones I had weren't turning out so good." This oft-repeated comment became the first thing people associated with her.

Walter's many illnesses from his youth took their toll on his heart, and he died suddenly in January, 1949. In the years following his death, the new President, Dwight Eisenhower, instituted a highway-building program across the country, and Emma was fortunate enough to own land that the U.S. government and State of Montana desired. She sold the land, and was suddenly quite wealthy. There was always much speculation in North Capston as to her financial worth. The guesses ranged from a quarter to a half-million dollars.

By this time, Emma's three offspring had more or less made their mark on the Montana landscape.

Madeline had married a man named Tim Martin, who worked in a grain and feed establishment. Like her mother, Madeline had a fondness for young children, and began a combination babysitting-nursery school in her home in North Capston. She was told bluntly by many that the concept of leaving pre-school children with a nonrelative would never catch on. Madeline's nineteen-year-old daughter Mikela helped her with the business.

Gilbert had married a woman named Lee, four years his junior, who showed no interest in working outside the home. She raised their two sons, Brian and Dennis, while Gilbert clerked at *Junction Hardware*.

Ross resisted adulthood. He loved toys, games, hobbies, and all the trappings of childhood. It was no surprise when his first job was working at *Big Sky Hobbies*. He eventually took over the business when the proprietor retired, helped by a loan from his parents. His wife Chelsea worked by his side. They had three daughters; Marilyn, Betsy, and Brittany. No one could figure out the family dynamics in Ross and Chelsea's home, but all three daughters implied they couldn't wait to turn twenty-one and get as far away as possible. Which they eventually did.

. . .

Walter Halburton was in his grave over ten years on Easter Sunday, March 29th, 1959.

Emma hosted her three children and whichever grandchildren could be in attendance.

She always cooked a huge meal of ham, potatoes, green beans, corn, and squash. This was followed by desserts of pie, cake, and a rice cobbler. She never asked for or accepted any help from her daughter or daughters-in-law.

On Easter Sunday, 1959, just three of the grandchildren were still in North Capston Junction. All of Ross and Chelsea's daughters had fled Montana; Marilyn to Colorado, where she worked in a railroad terminal, Betsy to upper Idaho, a hostess in a newly-built resort on Lake Cour d' Alene. Both were still single. Brittany had moved the farthest, living in Dayton, Ohio, serving as an ER nurse in a hospital where her husband was a doctor.

Emma had been in a strange mood for the entire meal, on edge, jittery, sometimes morphing into a melancholy seldom witnessed by her family. At the conclusion of the meal she asked for quiet and said she had an announcement.

"Well, I want you all to know that old windbag, Dr. Cerniglia, gave me the death sentence yesterday."

There was a moment of uncomprehending silence. Gilbert was first to speak. "Mom, what do you mean?"

"Don't be an idiot, Gil," said Madeline.

"It's Gil*bert.*"

"May I *continue?*"

"Sorry, Mom," said Gilbert. "Go on."

"Madeline?"

"Sorry, Mother."

"As I was saying, Doc Cerniglia found something inside me, been growin' for quite a spell, I guess."

Everyone at the table waited, barely breathing.

"He says I got about three months." Emma raised a hand and cut off anything that might have been said. "I got no problem with it. I'm eighty-six, lived a good life. I'll soon be reunited with Walt, the only man I ever loved." She paused, surveying the nine faces at the table. "So you people just go about your business of livin,' and leave the rest to me." She gave everyone a purposeful stare. "My affairs are in order, have been for some time. Mr. Unger will contact you after I'm gone, and you can get on with the division."

There was another period of silence. Madeline spoke. "By 'division,' Mother, do you mean—"

"You know what I mean. My worldly goods and financial assets. I got this house and land. Ain't worth that much. Walter and I had no use for showy stuff. My old Pontiac out in the garage. That ain't worth much either, but it runs fine. Mostly, I got the money from all that land I sold. A nice amount for you to split." Emma paused, and her face took on a no-nonsense look. "Mainly, I left a will behind, and you three will follow it to the letter. And Mr. Unger is gonna enforce it."

"Momma, what do you mean by 'enforce it?'" asked Ross. "Isn't everything split evenly?"

Madeline and Gilbert shot him disgusted looks, but Ross had spoken what they were already thinking.

"Well," replied Emma, "I been watchin' you three compete, undercut, and backstab each other to the point where I didn't want no more children."

Madeline, Gilbert, and Ross looked at the floor.

"I have decided that you three are gonna *work* for this money, and if you think it'll be easy, you are in for a surprise. You'll be well-off when this is over, but by God, you're gonna learn something."

At that point Emma politely asked everyone to leave; she wasn't feeling her best, and wanted some time alone.

* * *

The Mr. Unger Emma referred to in her big announcement was Rant Unger. He was a licensed attorney, but seemed unsure of the technicalities of the legal system. He was by no means unintelligent, and exhibited what would years later be referred to as "street smarts." As a young man, he took a passionate interest in local politics, showing up at town meetings in the community of two-thousand with an axe to grind about some issue or occurrence. He would usually take off on an ardent oratory, which earned him the nickname "Rant." Only the older generation in North Capston Junction even knew that his given name was James.

Rant did not make a full living off his dubious skills as an attorney, and dabbled in other areas, such as real estate, commodities trading, and the like. He and Walter

Halburton had been longtime friends, and was the recipient of much business from Walter. Following Walter's death, Rant made sure he kept a close business relationship with Emma. And he had, indeed, drawn up her latest will the previous year and continued to serve as her financial advisor.

Emma had an unusual will, and her first question to Rant was if it was even legal. "Don't worry about all that, Emma. It's as legal as it needs to be. And it's not *il*legal."

. . .

Emma's demise progressed faster than Dr. Cerniglia's prediction, and by mid-May she had Rant hire a woman to help during the daytime. Her children visited on a regular basis, but did not actually *do* anything for her. A local handyman tended to everything that needed attention. Rant handled all financial details in Emma's final days.

None of her children had the nerve to ask her anything about her will. The only family news was that Gilbert's sons Brian and Dennis had quit their jobs to buy a local diner.

Emma died on May 30th. Her funeral had been previously arranged, paid for by one of two accounts she had set up with Attorney Unger, the other for household expenses.

. . .

The day after the funeral, Rant Unger set up a meeting with the three heirs in his office. They were abuzz with anticipation and dread, not knowing what to expect.

All three were given copies of Emma's will, but Rant insisted they could read it on their own; he would explain the gist of things in his own words. There were no objections.

A sly smile broke on his face. "Your mother has divided her house and property into six areas; the house proper, attic, basement, garage, shed, and the grounds themselves"

Rant chuckled softly at the looks of confusion. "Madeline, you are to divide these six areas into three groups of two."

"What?" asked Gilbert.

"Let him finish," said Madeline. "Then what?"

"Ross takes two of the areas, then Gilbert takes two, and Madeline, you take the remaining two."

"Take them and do *what?"*

"Your mother and I have placed bank vouchers throughout those areas. What you find, you can cash against your mother's financial worth at Montana State Savings and Loan." At this point, Unger could no longer control himself. He looked down, laughing and choking at the same time.

"A freaking *treasure hunt?"* bellowed Gilbert. "Let me read this damn thing for myself." He began to pore over the document in his hands, as Ross and Madeline did the same.

"Holy shit," murmured Ross, as he read onto page two. "She actually did this."

"How much is. . .*hidden?"* asked Madeline, as she turned onto page three.

"I'm not at liberty to say, Mrs. Martin."

"Unbelievable," whispered Ross.

"Let me continue with the stipulations," said Rant. "Your spouses and children may help you with the searches, which may occur only when all three of you are on the premises."

"We got that," Gilbert said tersely.

"Wait a minute!" shouted Ross. "What the hell is this 'named representative living on the grounds' crap?"

"Oh, yes, that." Rant knocked on the wall of the meeting room, and a door to an adjoining conference room opened. A tall, craggy-faced Native American of about forty entered the room, holding a black Stetson hat in his hands. "This is Four Moons. He is an associate of mine, and will be living on the grounds during your search to insure that no one is poking around when they should not be there."

"God," said Gilbert, "she not only hated us, she didn't trust us, either."

"Gilbert," countered Rant, "your mother loved you all, she just didn't *like* you." Again, laughter won out in Attorney Unger's demeanor. "There is one further condition, which I emphasize because if it is broken, all of Mrs. Halburton's financial assets will be given to various named charities."

"I don't see that anywhere in here," Gilbert protested.

"It's an addendum," Rant replied. "I have the only copy right now. You can all read it for yourselves, if you'd like."

"Never mind, we believe you," said Madeline. "I'd believe *anything* after *this.* "

"Anyway, the condition is that any *currency or coinage* found by any of you is to be divided evenly. Madeline, I suggest we all meet here tomorrow at one with the divisions you are to make."

At this point, none of the three heirs had anything sarcastic or witty to say, and they tromped out.

Rant looked at Four Moons. "This is gonna be the damndest thing this town has ever seen."

The Crow Indian looked at the floor in disgust. "Not allowed to spit in here, right?"

. . .

Madeline had been a schemer since childhood. She used it to gain the upper hand on her two brothers when she thought it necessary, which was always. She now used it to second-guess her mother. Madeline wanted the house, so she teamed it with the grounds proper. No one would want to be digging in the spacious yard when they could have the garage, attic, shed, and basement.

She paired the basement and garage, and the attic and shed. She felt her two lazy brothers would take those two "divisions," leaving the house to her, Tim, and Mikela.

At the meeting the next day, Madeline was all smiles as Ross took the basement and garage, with Gilbert taking the attic and shed. Rant made it clear that the vouchers were hidden so they would be in plain view when found; no one would have to *disassemble* anything. They agreed to begin that Saturday. Four Moons would pitch a tent on the property and had brought provisions. He attended the meeting, sneering at the three adult heirs of Emma Halburton. As the meeting broke up, however, he flashed a gap-toothed smile at them, joining his thumb and index finger, making an "okay" sign. "Be good fun for everyone, yes?"

. . .

Emma had not been a hoarder, but she liked to collect things; knick-knacks, yard decorations, and handy-dandy household devices. She had several of anything a household could possibly have. With tag sales and online shopping many years off, she had apparently been a big fan of catalogues.

Rant was like the emcee of a bizarre game show. He couldn't help the contestants with the questions, but he knew all the answers. He knew the total of all the vouchers, but did not know how evenly they were distributed. And he had a few more to "hide," on Emma's orders, once the divisions had been picked.

. . .

Rant was discreet enough not to let on to anyone about the arrangements for the division of Emma Halburton's money, but the three heirs and their children were not. Brian and Dennis had told certain diner customers, Tim Martin and Gilbert told their bosses, Ross and Chelsea told some of their clientele, and Gilbert's wife Lee told her book club.

So when the three showed up at 9 o'clock, along with Madeline's daughter and Gilbert's wife, a smattering of thirty or so people showed up with them, ringing the property on both sides. Some were actually *rooting* for one of the three to "strike it rich." All of them believed that the late Emma Halburton was worth in the neighborhood of half a million dollars. If they themselves couldn't attain instant wealth, they would cheer on their favorite.

Madeline and Mikela were ransacking the kitchen, Gilbert and Lee plodded along in the attic, while Ross worked methodically in the basement.

Ever the lover of toys and such, Ross found one childhood treasure after another. Once, he came up from the basement with a plastic wreath of laurel leaves, once part of a Halloween costume, which he wore around his head.

"I am the emperor!" he exclaimed to Madeline.

"Hail, Stupidus Maximus," was her reply.

Four Moons and Rant Unger sat in folding chairs in the yard, smoking. Occasionally, Rant would go "work the crowd." Although there was nothing for them to see, most stayed for three hours, until the searchers had enough for one day. No one found anything, and went home disheartened and disappointed. Four Moons and Rant enjoyed themselves immensely.

The next day, Sunday, June 7th, the eight o'clock masses were overflowing in every house of worship in North Capston Junction. Nine o'clock masses were nearly empty, as those who normally went to mass then had gone to mass at eight, and headed out to Riano Street to watch the second day of the Emma Halburton Find Your Inheritance Sweepstakes, starring Madeline Martin, and Gilbert and Ross Halburton and their spouses, with guest appearances by Dennis and Brian Halburton, and Mikela Martin, and hosted by Rant Unger and Four Moons.

The law of averages being what it was, most of the eighty-six bystanders reckoned that someone was bound to find something.

Billy Arven, known to bet on anything, had a pool going, with odds on who would be the first to make a strike, and who would have the most by day's end. There were many takers on just about every wager he offered, including which hour would be the lucky one. Rant, known to sleep all Sunday morning, was not in attendance, but Four Moons was manning his chair, smoking. He did not work the crowd, however. He was not a fan of white society, often telling anyone who would listen that his tribe, the Crow, once held more land in Montana than any of the ten major tribes and whites combined.

The festivities started with a bang, Madeline finding the first voucher at 9:32, in the sum of 14,180 dollars. Billy Arven paid losses and collected winnings. Gilbert and Ross had a conference in the yard shortly after. Gilbert summoned his wife, and she left in their car. Everyone wondered what the hell was going on. Billy was giving odds on her return time.

More "strikes" were made that morning, two more by Madeline and her team, and one each by Gilbert and Ross. No one knew the amounts, and Billy had to convince some of his clients that on one was owed anything until the numbers were in. Lee Halburton returned at 10:30, and more money exchanged hands. Rant arrived soon after, and was seen to have a brief conference with all three "teams." They all seemed to be very pleased by whatever Rant had told them.

Mr. Unger never actually got to sit down, as people from both the front and back yards were constantly calling him over, asking for updates. Billy Arven in particular was quite insistent, reminding Rant that a lot of money was at stake, and practically *demanded* to know who had found how much.

"Ya know, Billy, this really ain't none of your damn business," replied Rant.

"Oh, c'mon, Rant. It ain't like we're askin' for a *cut* of it. Just a few details is all." Members of the gallery seconded his demands, and before long, there was the beginning of a ruckus growing.

Four Moons walked over to where Rant and Billy stood, nearly nose to nose. He was a tall man, and looked down on Billy with even more distain than he usually showed towards whites. He had never lifted a finger against anyone, but stories circulated as to why he no longer lived among his tribe. All versions of the stories involved Four Moons' retaliation against a tribe member who had wronged him. He deftly moved into the space formerly occupied by Rant.

"You go, now, Betting Man."

Billy turned and said loudly, "Let's go. We can find out what happened at the diner. Those three can't never keep their mouths shut nohow."

Things simmered down and by 3:30 the Halburton oppspring were spent. They reported to Rant, who took out a small notebook, collected the vouchers, and made an entry. Madeline, Tim, and Mikela left as though floating on air, while the other participants stomped off the property like ten-year-olds who had just lost a playground game.

"Looks like Madeline wins the day," someone said.

"Somebody call Billy."

. . .

Gilbert phoned Ross that evening. The operator, Nellie Barth, was listening in on every word.

"Ross, this is Gilbert. Madeline screwed us."

"How, Gilbert? She picked *last.*"

"I don't know how, but she did. She's got fifty-three thousand already, and we got fifteen *between* us!"

"What do we do?"

"We take a little ride over to Riano Street. There's an empty house there we should look in on."

"Are you nuts? That'll void the whole deal. We'll get *nothing.*"

There was a moment of silence. Gilbert said, "Nellie, are you listenin' in on a private conversation, damn it?"

"No,"

"Never mind, Ross." Gilbert hung up.

"You still there, Nellie?" asked Ross.

"No."

Nellie disconnected Ross's line and made a quick call to Billy Arven, earning herself ten dollars for her trouble.

. . .

While Madeline struggled with the huge area rug in the living room, Ross was looking under all the seats in his mother's white 1953 Pontiac. Gilbert was in the shed, pinned under several sacks of fertilizer and buckets of driveway sealer.

"Jesus Christ, somebody help me!" he yelled. Four Moons entered the shed, with Ross right behind him. Four Moons turned and put out a huge hand,

"You stay outside, Toy Man."

"He might be hurt."

"I will help. Go back to your white man's foolishness, looking for pieces of paper your mother hid on you." He looked at Ross thoughtfully. "Why does she do this? Why not give you the money she can no longer use?"

"It's complicated. You wouldn't understand."

"She does not like you three."

"Okay, so you do understand."

Following Gilbert's extrication from the pile of sacks and sealant, the search continued. Rant showed up, notebook in hand, giving the onlookers a second hand version of Gilbert's accident. The story brought down the house.

By mid-afternoon, several more vouchers were found. Madiline now had in excess of one-hundred fifty-seven thousand dollars, with Gilbert at seventy-three thousand, and Ross at sixty-seven thousand. They turned in their vouchers to Rant, who made entries in his book, looked at the three and said, "There's more. Keep lookin.'"

Fatigue and elation shared equal space in their reactions. By supper time, all three were exhausted. Ross had found another bank voucher deep inside the glove box of the Pontiac, bringing him to eighty-three thousand. Madeline and Gilbert, now limping, had come up empty. With Rant no longer in an entertaining mood, and Billy Arven now standing *across* the street, the spectacle had lost its luster. The crowd began to drift away, content to learn about the results secondhand. Rant added up the new totals. For the first time, he looked sympathetically at Emma's three squabblers.

"Well, you three have worked your asses off. I guess it's time for a little hint." Three adults leaned forward like children about to learn their prize in a contest.

"There's a hundred sixty-three thousand left."

The thought of that much money waiting to fall into their laps should have excited them, but they tromped back to their areas like miners returning to the deep underground.

By Monday, June 15th, Gilbert and Ross had found seven more vouchers. Madeline, for the second straight day, found nothing. As her brothers gleefully handed them to Rant and watched their totals soar, Madeline sat on the front porch steps, weeping, while Mikela tried to comfort her.

Gilbert approached, along with Ross, Rant, and Four Moons. "What's the matter, sis, not enough money to suit you?"

"You shut the hell up! I been searching that dump for the last—" She stopped, noticing the smiles on all four men's faces.

Four Moons made the circle with his thumb and index finger, still smiling. "Good fun for everyone, yes? You have many monies, now. Search over. You all go home."

"*What?* It's over?" Madeline demanded.

"He's right, Maddie," said Gilbert. "Rant added up the totals. We *each* got one-hundred fifty-seven thousand, five-hundred seventy-five dollars and thirty-three cents. It's all accounted for."

No one spoke, letting the irony sink in.

"Okay, folks, that's it," said Rant. "Meet me in my office tomorrow at nine. Make sure you bring any cash or coinage you found in your little Easter egg hunt, or you know, all of your mother's money goes to charities." Rant headed towards his car; Four Moons was already striking his tent and gathering his belongings.

"How much you find?" Gilbert asked Ross.

"Nothin.' What about you?"

"Not a cent."

Both men looked at their sister.

"I didn't find anything, either, you two morons!"

"You're gonna blow it for us, aren't you, Maddie?"

"Go to hell, Gilbert. What about little brother, here? Always the innocent act."

The accusations and insults continued for another ten minutes, until Madeline pointed out that Rant would also know of any cash and coin hidden, and they had until tomorrow to come clean if they were holding back. At that point everyone finally left, still failing to appreciate the fact that their inheritance in the 1959 Montana economy would make them financially carefree for the rest of their lives.

. . .

At nine the next morning they all showed at Rant's office. It was unlocked, with a sign on the front door: *Please come in and wait. I will be there directly.* Rant was habitually late to early morning meetings, so the three spent the time questioning each other about money found on the property.

"It's in your pocketbook, right Maddie? You came to your senses, right Maddie?"

"You can kiss my . . ."

And on it went.

At Billings International Airport, twenty-five miles away, a black 1957 Chrysler pulled up. Attorney James "Rant" Unger and Four Moons got out and headed for the Departures building, where they had booked a complicated, confusing series of flights which would land them in Phoenix by 1:45 P.M. Rant carried one suitcase; Four Moons wore a large backpack. Rant slapped his Crow friend on the back, breaking into a wide grin.

Four Moons made his familiar "okay" sign with his thumb and forefinger, flashing a gap-toothed smile. "Be good fun for everyone, yes?"

"A TEAR IN THE FABRIC" 2013

Green Pines, Georgia, 1987

"If he's not here in two minutes, we leave without him," snapped Renny Lamoin, leaning over the handlebars of his silver Huffy Sigma bike. "Why is he even coming with us, Jeff?"

Jeff Hodges turned his black and light blue Huffy Rage around to face Renny. "He's smart. He knows the battle pretty well." Jeff removed his new Atlanta Braves cap and readjusted it, trying to break it in. "Go, Braves!"

"How many times you gonna take off that hat and put it back on?"

"You only get one chance to break in a hat. And this is the best Braves hat I've ever owned."

"Really," Lamoin countered, sounding unimpressed. He turned toward the third member of their "battlefield exploration team," Yashuhiro Hito, known as Hiro. "You guys play a lot of baseball in Japan?"

"Oh, yes," replied Hiro, son of a Japanese steel executive and half-Japanese, half-American woman. "Play much baseball in Japan. Golf, too."

"Never mind golf. Just make sure you root for the Braves."

"Go, Braves!" injected Jeff.

"I will cheer for them very much," said Hiro. His polite Japanese manner had won him many new friends in the north Georgia town. When their sixth grade social studies teacher, Miss Gleason, had gotten to the Civil War, Hiro was excited to learn that a small battle had taken place six miles from town, in a fruit orchard. Maddin's Grove was the only real fighting that had occurred in the area, and was treated with a reverence accorded Shiloh or Gettysburg.

Jeff, eager to impress in school, learned that the battle was fought on May 16th, 1864, and while it involved only a couple of regiments from each army, there was a well-preserved grove of trees near Ten Oaks, with monuments, plaques, and a battlefield cemetery. He got three friends together and planned to bike there on the anniversary of the battle.

A hundred yards down Kenney Avenue a boy approached, riding a black Schwinn High Sierra bicycle.

"Look," shouted Hiro, "there is Craig."

"About freakin' time," hissed Renny. "He better have a good reason for makin' us wait."

The three boys watched as Craig Knudson neared. Even though he had known Renny and Jeff all their lives, he was more the odd man out than the Japanese-born Hiro. Craig had a penchant for expressing himself in a manner the others thought "prissy," even though he was just like them in most ways.

"Where the heck were you?" demanded Renny. "It's past eight-thirty."

"My parents insisted I bring enough water for the trip."

"Cripe, it's twelve miles *total.*"

"And I wanted to make sure I had the proper clothes. I, for one, don't like being uncomfortable."

"You, for one," Renny spat. "You *are* one."

"C'mon, guys," said Jeff. "This is gonna be great. Go Braves! We'll probably have the battlefield to ourselves. The actual ceremony is tomorrow."

"It would be an honor, yes?" asked Hiro.

Renny exhaled loudly. "Yeah, a real honor. A bunch of trees with bullet holes in them."

"Renny," said Jeff, it's where our ancestors made a stand against the Yankee invasion."

Renny Lamoin rolled his eyes. "Let's get goin.'"

For most eleven-year-olds, the ride to Maddin's Grove, on the outskirts of Ten Oaks, would have been filled with talk of sports and plans for the upcoming summer, but with Jeff Hodges leading the expedition, his three cohorts were "treated" to a blow by blow of the entire battle, beginning with the 27th New York regiment stopping at an orchard to pick fruit. As some of the soldiers made their way across the two-hundred yard expanse, they were surprised to find members of the 43rd Georgia regiment doing the same.

Shots were fired, and the New Yorkers sent word back of contact with the enemy. Union Colonel Franklin Tovars, receiving the message, sent another entire regiment to the orchard, the 61st Vermont, along with artillery.

The southern troops had done likewise, and within half an hour the 43rd Georgians had been joined by the 53rd Georgia, with *their* artillery.

Casualties were light at first, with men taking cover behind the trees, but the Union artillery joined in, half the guns firing high explosive shells, the rest firing canister, receptacles filled with nails and other sharp objects, designed to cause massive wide-spread destruction. The Confederates countered with their artillery, and before long the grove was a kill zone. Men from both sides died as much from falling trees and branches as from canister and musket balls.

The battle raged from about 10:15 until well past two that afternoon. The Rebels retreated as the Union brought up an entire division. When the smoke cleared there were 287 dead. A Union general went into Ten Oaks and made arrangements for the dead of both sides to be given a proper burial.

Over the next two days townspeople from Ten Oaks and nearby Dalton buried the dead in an unused plot of land half a mile away, taking great pains in identifying nearly all of them, along with their unit designations. The Yankee graves were placed on one side of the field in a mass grave, unadorned. The CSA dead were buried in individual plots in the other half, their resting places decorated with flowers and messages of gratitude.

"You memorized all that?" asked Renny. "Why?"

"It's important. Right, Craig?"

Craig nodded. With Renny around, he knew he had to watch every word.

By 9:10 the boys had arrived at the spot on Route 17 where a copper plaque marked where southern troops had rushed down a steep embankment into the grove. Jeff stopped his bike beside it and read for everyone's benefit. "On May 16, 1864, members of the Georgia 43rd and 53rd regiments bravely did battle with elements of the invading army of the northern states in the grove below." Jeff removed his Braves cap, sitting on his bike in a pose of reverent tribute.

The other boys did the same, until Renny broke the silence. "Okay, let's get down there."

Jeff, Craig, and Renny laid their bikes on the side of the road, while Hiro carefully pushed down the kickstand of his red Calico Cross and set it next to the others.

"We can just walk through these trees and go down this hill," said Jeff. "The grove is at the bottom."

The four picked their way down the embankment, avoiding rocks, large roots, and pricker bushes at they made their descent. It was so steep they had to go down sideways.

"Jesus, imagine *marchin'* down this to get to the battle," said Renny.

They reached the bottom, and after a walk of some thirty yards, came to another monument, a cast-iron rebel soldier with a plaque at its base. Jeff did the honors again, removing his cap. "Battle of Maddin's Grove, May 16,

1864. In this orchard, Georgia's native sons bravely defended their state from northern aggressors."

"Wow," said Hiro softly.

"Let's go all the way down," said Renny.

For the next half-hour, the four meandered their way down the grove of trees. Much of the orchard had been replanted over the years in an attempt to show the approximate number of trees originally there. Many trees were blown apart, huge splinters of their original selves. Each of these was examined and touched by the four visitors.

Jeff noted Renny's gruff exterior fading, and was bold enough to go over to him and quietly say, "Change your mind about this place?"

"Yeah, kinda. But not all the other crap you and Craig get off on. And shut up, will ya?"

"Sure thing."

They made their way to the far end of the grove, and found another monument. As they stood around it, Jeff put his hat down on the plain two foot by two foot stone. "Union position, May 16, 1864," he read.

"Not any kind words for the Yankees, yes?" asked Hiro.

"Filthy bastards," grunted Renny.

All four laughed, and without a word, began their trek back. The spell cast by the battlefield remained, hands touching long-ruined trees, eyes gazing in all directions. Before long, the four were making the arduous climb up the embankment.

As they gathered their bikes and turned toward Green Pines, Jeff smacked his forehead with his palm. "My Braves hat! I left it on the far monument. Crap!"

"You should go retrieve it, shouldn't you, Jeff?" asked Craig.

"And while you're there, you should *get* it," snorted Renny.

Jeff was down the road about fifty feet from where they had descended the hill, in near-panic mode. All he could imagine was someone walking off with his beloved hat. He dropped his bike with a thud and ran headlong into the light woods. "*Wait* for me, guys!" he yelled, not looking where he was going. Turning, he was forced to duck and go between two oddly-shaped small trees growing across each other, forming an arch. He looked back and saw *nothing.* His heart jumped.

Rushing back, he stopped dead. There was no *road,* only a wide dirt trail. His friends and all four bikes were gone. Jeff's heart raced. He was in *full* panic mode, now. How could he have gotten lost and be unable to find the highway? The others simply could *not* have gotten that far down the road as to be out of sight in a few seconds. *What the HELL was going on?*

He yelled for them a few times. No answer. Then he figured it out. They had taken off, bikes and all down the embankment and were planning to scare him in the orchard. That was just like Renny. But then came the undeniable fact that Route 17 was *not there.* He was *scared* now, not panicked. He was too afraid to wander down into the orchard. What if *that* wasn't there either, replaced by a swamp with snakes and quicksand. He paced around in a ten foot circle, trying to muster logical thoughts, but was overmatched by the incongruity of the situation. For no apparent reason, he walked back under the small tree arch toward the dirt trail.

On his left, Renny, Craig, and Hiro sat quietly on their bikes.

"What the *hell,* Jeff," yelled Renny. "You weren't gone long enough to even get down the hill."

Jeff looked at his friends, their bikes, and Georgia Route 17, its two paved lanes lying where he had seen an old dirt trail minutes before. He stared at the road as if it were one of the wonders of the world.

Hiro rode over to him. "Jeff, are you ill?"

"No. Yes. I don't know."

Renny and Craig joined them. "You pullin' something,' Hodges?" asked Renny.

"No, guys, honest. Somethin's really *wrong.*"

"What the hell you talkin' about?"

"I was goin' to get my hat, but when I looked back, you guys and the bikes were gone, and the road was just a dirt trail. Honest."

Hiro, naïve and polite, seemed to take him at his word. Craig sat open-mouthed on his bike, and Renny, predictably, looked angry and disgusted.

"Ya know, Jeff, we went along with your "battlefield adventure," and it was great and all, but now you top it off with this bullshit," said Renny.

Like most eleven-year-olds, seeing was believing, and each made several trips into the nearby shrubbery and woods, looking back and finding their friends and Route 17 unaltered.

In frustration, Jeff demonstrated how he had walked under the odd-looking arch. He looked back to see wilderness and a dirt road, nothing else. Stopping to think instead of panicking, he walked *back* through the arch, and found his friends staring at him, their mouths wide open.

"You *disappeared,* Jeff," said Hiro. "Where did you go?"

"It's the *arch,"* blurted Craig. The arch changes *time!"*

Jeff looked at Renny, eyes wide, frozen on his bike. "Hey guys, I just got the greatest idea *ever.* Go, Braves!"

. . .

The embankment was much more overgrown, and it was tougher going down.

"So what is this, like a time warp in science fiction shows?" asked Renny, when all had reached the bottom.

"It must be," ventured Craig.

"We have no idea what year it is, right?"

"Right," answered Craig, grateful for even the smallest conversation without Renny's insults.

"Look," shouted Hiro, after they had walked a little farther. "There is no monument, now."

Jeff's eyes widened. "The battle hasn't taken place yet."

"Unless it *has,* and they haven't put up the monument yet. It was erected in 1868," offered Craig, gaining confidence in his ability to contribute.

"Okay, Knudson," came Renny's sharp reply. "Either way, it's before 1868, all right?"

"Renny," Jeff said suddenly, "all we have to do is walk through the orchard. If all the trees are okay, we know they didn't fight here yet."

"What are we actually *doing* here, Jeff?" asked Renny, as the four made their way down the grove.

"Well, we get to see what it looked like before the battle."

Renny frowned. "You didn't bring us down here to go get your stupid Braves hat, did you?"

Jeff slapped his forehead again. "We won't *find* the hat, guys. It doesn't *exist,* now. The *Braves* don't exist."

"Guys," croaked Craig, his eyes welling up. "What if we can't get back to our own time? What if the arch doesn't work? We'll be stuck here without …without *anything.* No one will believe we're from 1987! They'll put us in reform school or a mental institution!"

"Shut the hell up, Knudson, you whining little pissbag!"

"Craig's right, Renny. We're almost halfway down. Let's just get the hell out of here."

At that instant, from in front and behind, slightly off to one side, came the shouts of men, followed by rifle and musket fire. Lead balls screamed past, slammed into trees ten feet away. More shouts followed more gunfire, and the sounds of men running. The boys instinctively dropped, then looked in both directions. Toward the road, men in gray and butternut brown were attempting to form a firing line, while at the far end of the orchard, men in dark blue did the same.

Renny crawled to where Jeff lay and punched him in the ribs. "Well, asshole, *now* we know what year it is!"

. . .

For twenty minutes, they lay on the ground, with soldiers seventy yards away in each direction. Jeff yelled to the others to crawl to the Rebel lines.

"No, Jeff, they might think we're Yankee snipers," replied Craig. "They'll shoot us for sure."

"Jeff," called Hiro, "lots of smoke now. Maybe they don't see us."

The heavy May air caused the smoke to hang just above the firing lines, then drop, obscuring almost everything. Men advanced and retreated. When the boys looked for each other, they could never find all three of their companions. Somewhere, Jeff's voice could be heard yelling to stay low and keep crawling towards the road, while Craig yelled back to Jeff to stop yelling, as it would give away their positions. Renny yelled at both of them to shut up or he would kill them himself.

After ten more minutes, they heard the first concussive roar from behind, followed by others every few seconds. The Union had brought up their divisional artillery, and the trees of Maddin's Grove were the first casualties. Canister rounds, mixed in with high explosive shells, burst everywhere. Men advanced, fell back, shouted orders, and tried to form firing ranks, with the trees interfering. Within a few minutes, artillery shells were fired from in front of them as the Confederate artillery arrived and countered with their deadly mix of canister and high explosive.

For the first time, the sounds that dominated were human beings in agony as tree trunks, branches, shrapnel, and musket balls tore into human flesh. The ripping and cracking of trees and branches soon drowned out all else.

There was chaotic ebb and flow to the movement of both armies. Because of the low level and denseness of the smoke, no one could clearly see what they were shooting at. Four figures, crawling desperately towards the rebel lines, gradually drifted farther apart.

. . .

"You boys git!" yelled Sergeant Caleb Foss, about to lead a rebel scouting party around the eastern flank of Maddin's Grove. "You two daft or something? What you doin' here now? You boys scoot up that hill yonder."

"Is that where the road is?" said one of two boys on their stomachs, looking up at the rebel soldiers.

"They ain't no road nowhere's around here, boy. Git on up that hill. They's a trail. Git on it and run home!"

Foss and his ten soldiers continued their flanking movement, leaving the two boys to negotiate the hill, now filled with members of the 53rd Georgia, reinforcing one of the most chaotic skirmishes of the war.

As the two crawled up the hill, soldiers yelled at them to get to safety.

"We gotta go through the arch, remember?"

"Yeah. Where the hell is it?"

"It's gotta be down this way. You see the others?"

"No."

"Here it is!"

Renny Lamoin and Craig Knudson crawled under the arch, ran a few yards, and found themselves on Georgia Route 17. It was May 16th, 1987. Craig looked at the four bikes, then looked up and down the road and saw no one.

Renny stared at his clothes, then examined Craig's. "All the dirt and grass stains and gunpowder smell is gone, Craig. What the hell?"

"They existed on the day of the battle, Renny. One-hundred twenty-three years ago."

Renny sighed. "We might as well sit here and wait for Jeff and Hiro."

After ten minutes, they sensed a movement by the arch. Hiro Hito emerged, his clothes as neat and clean as theirs.

"Hiro, thank God. Is Jeff behind you?" asked Craig.

"He was, but then I don't see him coming up the hill."

"Great, just great," muttered Renny.

Fifteen minutes passed. A few cars and a red pickup went by. It was nearly noon.

"Can't we go back and look for him, Renny?" asked Craig.

"And get killed *doin'* it? Jeff said they fought until after two. It's too dangerous."

"And after that the Yankees overran this whole place," Craig gasped. "Jesus!"

"We'll leave his bike here. He'll know we headed back. When we get home we tell our parents we lost him somewhere on the battlefield. Which is the *truth.*"

"Do we—"

"No, Hiro. If we start with any of this time warp crap, they're gonna think we did something wrong and are trying to cover it up," Renny gave his two classmates a long, hard look. "We stick to the truth. We got separated from him on the battlefield, and we *didn't* see him again,

and we *don't know where he is.* If he's not back later today, we're gonna be telling this to the police, got it?"

"Renny," pleaded Craig, "if he's hurt or captured he may *never* get back."

"I *know.*" Renny paused. "None of us did anything wrong. Just remember that."

. . .

By six that evening, Green Pines Police had contacted police in Ten Oaks. Police and civilians from both towns and nearby Dalton combed Route 17, the Maddin's Grove battlefield, and all roads and residences nearby. A blue and black Huffy Rage, identified as belonging to Jeff Hodges, was turned in to the police by a scout troop earlier that afternoon. At the far end of the battlefield, an Atlanta Braves cap was found on the stone marker. Jeff's parents and friends confirmed that is was his.

State Police and the Georgia Bureau of Investigation were on the scene by seven-thirty. Anyone with the slightest history of criminal behavior was questioned.

A Ten Oaks resident, Gary Buttrick, called and informed police he was driving his pickup on Route 17 around noon and had seen three boys there. He came in to give a statement, and was asked repeatedly if he was sure there were three boys, and not four.

"No," he stated confidently. "I remember three boys sittin' on their bikes, and a fourth bike just a'layin there on the ground."

Renny, Craig, and Hiro were questioned individually in the presence of their parents. They even volunteered to take a polygraph exam. "Sorry, boys," said Green Pines Police Chief Bertrand Rosseau. "We do that, and those commies in the ACLU and any lawyer looking for publicity will be up our behinds.”

On the third day of the search, all the lead investigators from the police, State Police, and GBI held a strategy meeting, along with newly-assigned FBI agent Kalina O’Brien.

“It *seems* these boys are tellin’ the truth,” Chief Rosseau said, not looking at all convinced.

“There isn’t a single clue as to any sign of abduction or murder,” added GBI agent Thad Morton. “No signs of a struggle, no blood, nothing.”

Chief Rosseau scratched his head. “This boy didn’t just *disappear, he evaporated.”*

“May I?” asked agent O’Brien.

Heads nodded.

“I suggest you question the three boys together.”

“Why would we do that? Their stories hold as it is.”

“I feel that they have *told* the truth, but there’s something they are *not* telling. *That’s* your key to finding out what happened, I believe.”

All heads nodded again.

“Watch closely when you question them,” O’Brien said. “Notice who looks at who for a prompt, who seems to be staring down the others. And who might inadvertently say something different in an answer.”

“You may have something there,” said State Police investigator Ed Gaffney. “They don’t seem *guilty* of *doing anything wrong,* but there’s definitely *something* they’re not saying.”

Agent O’Brien’s tactic did not work. No one looked for prompts, no one stared anyone down, and no one blurted out any contradictory information. By week’s end the consensus was that Jeff Hodges had been abducted, unseen, by someone unknown. Additional searches of woods and bodies of water turned up nothing.

At Green Pines Elementary School, teachers told students not to question the boys about the incident. But of course, they did. The three voluntarily stayed in their classroom for lunch and recess. Mrs. Gleason noticed them in quiet conference on the last day of school.

All three approached her desk. "Mrs. Gleason," Renny said, "we have to tell you something about Jeff. We waited until the last day so we wouldn't have to face all the other kids."

Thinking she was about to hear a death-by-misadventure confession, Julia Gleason nodded solemnly. "Go ahead, boys."

. . .

August 2nd, 1987

"It's called a "tear in the fabric" among those of us who hold to this principle of time and space," began Dr. Normand Boland, Ph.D. of Paranormal Studies at the University of Pennsylvania.

Dr. Boland stood at the Confederate monument at Maddin's Grove with a gathering that included the three boys, Renny's mother, Hiro's father, Craig's parents, Julia Gleason, Police Chief Bertrand Rosseau, Three Oaks Police Chief Edward Dodd, and investigators from the Georgia State Police, the GBI, and FBI agent Kalina O'Brien.

The "confession" heard by Julia Gleason back on May 29th eventually led to sensational news stories throughout the state, picked up by wire services all over the country and overseas.

"Dr. Boland," asked agent O'Brien, "we all walked through that odd tree-arch at the top of the hill. None of *us* were transported to another year."

"We believe it's a cyclical phenomenon. We think there are *layers*, for lack of a better word, between the past and the present. At times these layers develop what may best be described as a *tear,* allowing someone from the present to step into the past." He paused. "The incredible energy force expended on the day of the battle was, and still is, active. These three boys and Jeff Hodges accidentally found that tear on the anniversary of the battle."

Thirteen confused faces stared at him.

"So if I was to walk between those trees next May 16th, *I* would be here on the day of the battle?" asked Chief Rosseau.

"Not necessarily. It could open *anytime,* or never again. The tear repairs itself randomly."

The crowd looked at each other in silence.

"I realize most people scoff at this." Boland continued. "Jeff's own parents would have nothing to do with this, and prefer to believe he was abducted. Those of us who believe in this phenomena are still a small minority."

"Dr. Boland," asked Chief Rosseau, with Chief Dodd by his side, "what do we *do?"*

Edward Dodd spoke. "We can't have people swallowed up by the past whenever this "tear" decides to open up again."

"Chief Dodd, I suggest you cut down those trees and pave over that area."

Dodd took Boland aside. "Will that really work?"

Boland led the two men farther away from the others. "*I* don't know. It's worth a try."

. . .

October, 1987

When the seventh grade class trip was announced as going to the Maddin's Grove battlefield, Renny and Craig were determined not to go. Hiro had since moved to Birmingham, Alabama, when his father's consulting positon necessitated a relocation.

As the date neared, however, their guidance counselor convinced the boys that a visit might give them "closure."

The tour of the battlefield began at a small visitor's center in Ten Oaks, where a guide led them to a paved path which entered the east end of the orchard.

As they walked toward the Confederate monument, Renny whispered to Craig, "this is where we met that Sergeant and his men." Craig nodded. Kids stared at them, trying to listen in.

The tour continued with an explanation of how both armies collided in the orchard, called in reinforcements, and fired volleys at each other in a smoke-filled chaos, until artillery made the grove a deathly nightmare.

As the class traversed the orchard, their classmates looking and touching some of the original ruined trees, Renny and Craig looked at the scene with both nostalgia and sorrow. The official narrative ended by the Union positional marker.

Renny once again took Craig aside. "If only he hadn't left that damn hat down here." Again, nearby students strained to hear their conversation.

The group retraced their steps to the Confederate monument, then back to the visitor's center, where they boarded their bus for the short ride to the battlefield cemetery. Their guide, who identified himself as Warren, a college student, took the group onto the grounds.

At the Union gravesite, he said, "One-hundred thirty soldiers from the north are buried beneath this monument. Most were identified. Their names are on this marker." Without another word, the group walked to the opposite end of the field. A dozen or more rows of individual graves were situated there.

"One-hundred fifty-seven of Georgia's soldiers are buried here," said Warren. "Please take some time and pay your respects to these brave men." He walked off a few yards, hoping that the visitors would appreciate the sacrifice.

Renny and Craig walked down the rows, realizing that they had *seen* many of these men just five months ago, and over a hundred years ago. They randomly read aloud names, thinking Jeff would have done the same.

"Davis McCutcheon, 53rd Georgia," said Renny.

"Caleb Foss, 43rd Georgia," countered Craig.

They continued this for several minutes, suddenly noticing that their classmates were farther away than they had been previously.

"What gives?" Renny asked Craig. "Look at where everybody else is."

"I overheard Mrs. Gleason tell the other teachers to have the kids give us a little space."

"Good, because those jerks don't—"

"Renny," hissed Craig. "Jesus H. Christ, Renny. Look!" Craig was pointing to a headstone which read, *Unknown Boy, Approx. age 12.*

Renny dropped his head and covered his eyes. He quickly pulled Craig along the rows farther away from the others, as he wiped his eyes. "Let's see if the tour guide knows anything." While their classmates continued paying their respects, Renny and Craig, both red-eyed, hurried over to him, a few yards away.

"Warren," asked Renny, his voice shaking, "we found the grave of a twelve-year-old boy down there. Do you know anything about it?"

Warren smiled and nodded in acknowledgment. "Yes, somebody finds him on every tour we do. If I remember the notes correctly, there was a young boy fishing on the far side of the grove when the battle broke out, and he was trying to get to safety. He was never identified. He was probably a runaway, just fishing to survive." He saw two conflicted faces looking back at him. "Tell you what. At the visitors center there's a blond guy with a goatee named Willie. He's had family here since the battle. If anyone would know, he would."

"Thanks, sir," said Craig. "We'll ask him."

The cemetery visit ended, and the class walked back to the bus for the ride back to the visitor's center for a quick lunch before returning to school.

"Okay, it wasn't him, so those tears back there don't count. Got it, asshole?" Renny broke into a rueful smile. He was no longer capable of being truly nasty to Craig.

"Got it. We're gonna find that Willie guy, right?"

"Of course, nerdface."

While everyone was eating their bagged lunches outside and buying soda and snacks at the little shop nearby, Renny and Craig found a blond, goateed man behind a counter inside the visitor's center where one could buy souvenirs. His nametag read, *William*.

Renny and Craig walked up to him with a purposeful stride.

"What's up, fellas?"

"Our guide said that 'Willie' could help us. Is that you?"

"Yes. What can I do for you?"

Renny took a deep breath. "We saw a boy's grave in the cemetery. Were there any *other* boys at the battle? Caught in it, you know?"

Willie's face lit with pleasure and curiosity. "Funny you should ask about that. Everybody knows about the fishing pole boy, but we have some soldier's diaries donated by families of men who fought, and several of them mention seeing *three or four* boys trying to get off the battlefield when the fighting started. One even said one boy was *Chinese.* "

"Japanese," whispered Craig.

"Pardon?"

"Nothing."

"Well, little-known fact, and this is the truth. There *was* at least one other boy caught in the fighting." Willie paused for effect, noting two boys looking at him with incredible anticipation. "And that boy was one of my great-grandfathers. He was almost off the field and got blown off his feet by an artillery shell, hit his head on a rock and got a bad concussion. Medics found him and got him into town before the Yankees overran the orchard."

"So *that's* why he didn't—"

Renny's elbow stopped Craig's next words.

"I'm sorry," said Willie. "You were saying?"

"Keep going," said Renny. "We won't *interrupt* any more," he said, giving Craig a forceful look.

"Anyway, my great-grandfather kept his own diary, and he also wrote about that day. He was here with three friends, he said, but he never named them, and nobody ever found them. Most likely that blow to the head got him all confused."

"Yeah, probably," said Renny. "What was his name?" He and Craig didn't dare breathe at this point.

"Well, another funny story. Turned out he was an orphan or something. Didn't have any family anyone knew of. Just seemed to come out of nowhere that morning. He called himself Jefferson Hodges, but went by the name Jeff."

Renny bit his lip and looked down. Craig blinked repeatedly.

"What happened to him?" Renny asked in a hoarse whisper.

"Somebody must have taken him in, I guess. He stayed in Ten Oaks, got married, had kids, worked in a dry goods store. Died in 1935, I believe. He's buried next to my grandfather on the other side of town." Willie paused, looking at the two subdued boys. "I gotta ask, guys, what's your interest in this?"

"It's for school," Craig offered. "We have to do a report on children in the war. We'd like to use your great-grandfather's story, if you don't mind."

"I'd be honored. Come back some weekend. They might let me off for half an hour. I could take you out to his grave. Would you like that?"

"Very much so," said Craig. Renny looked at the floor.

"Thanks, Willie," Renny said. "What's your full name? So we can give you credit in our *report.*" He rolled his eyes at Craig.

"Willie Hodges." He grinned "William *Jefferson* Hodges. My parents had him in mind when they named me."

As the boys turned to leave, Willie called out, "Say, here's something you might want to put in your report."

"What is it?" asked Renny.

"Well, he was sort of an oddball all his life, always talking about things no one ever heard of and the like. Everyone thought it was from the concussion, you know?"

"Sure."

"Well, when he was happy or excited, he would yell, 'Go, Braves,' and no one knew what it meant. Of course now we have the baseball Braves. I thought that was kind of strange, almost like he knew the future."

Renny smiled through teary eyes. "Typical Jeff," he said, and turned and walked away, Craig following.

William Jefferson Hodges watched them depart, as proud and confused as he had ever been.

· · ·

The bus carrying the junior high field trip left Ten Oaks, and headed up Georgia Route 17, passing a monument dedicated to soldiers of the Confederate States of America who fought bravely in nearby Maddin's Grove on May 16th, 1864. Fifty feet west of the monument the bus passed a small section of light woods and shrubbery, containing pavement where a vehicle could pull off; pavement that would bring the vehicle to a point where two trees, recently cut, had formed an arch.

"LOCKER 75"
2013

Kelton High School, Kelton, Pennsylvania, 1970

Thomas Frederick looked up from his desk to see Lyman Hubert standing in his classroom doorway, holding a small gift-wrapped package.

"Lyman, no seniors have any final exams today."

"I just wanted to stop by and give you this," he said, walking over to Frederick's desk, and handing him the box.

"That wasn't necessary, Lyman," Frederick said, looking truly touched.

"It was to me, Mr. Frederick. I know it was your first year teaching, but you went out of your way for me, and I appreciate it."

"Lyman, I don't know what to say, except thank you. Someday the whole country and maybe the world will know who you are. I just did what any teacher would do; keep you pointed in the right direction."

"You're too modest, Mr. Frederick."

Frederick opened the small gray box with a tiny red bow and removed a tie clip. It was an American flag on a gold shield with eagles in each corner.

"I noticed you go for that patriotic stuff."

"Indeed I do, Lyman. I will wear it proudly and think of you and the great contributions you will someday make in science, or physics, or mathematics, or let's see, what else are you a gifted genius at?"

"That's about it, sir."

Frederick looked pensive, almost sorrowful. "So you'll be off to USC in the fall?"

"Actually sir, I'm going to drive there in the car my parents gave me for graduation. I'm gonna leave around

August 10th and get there early to kind of get the lay of the land."

Frederick raised an eyebrow. "That's quite a trip alone for someone your age. How are you going to manage a route that long?"

"I already memorized it, sir."

Frederick slapped his forehead. "Of course you did. What was I thinking?"

Lyman Hubert laughed nervously. "Well, Mr. Frederick, in case I don't see you between now and August." He extended his hand. "Thanks again, Mr. Frederick. You'll never know how much your guidance and everything meant to me."

"Lyman, I feel honored to have crossed paths with a phenomenon like yourself, especially in my first year. What I've learned from you I will be able to pass on to thousands of young people for as long as I am teaching." Frederick stood and saluted.

Lyman Hubert began to laugh, then realized that it was a sincere gesture of praise. He awkwardly returned the salute, turned, and walked briskly from the room.

. . .

2013

Thomas Frederick settled in to his new classroom, down the hallway from the room he had occupied for forty-three years. His seating charts and lesson plans were set for the opening of the new school year, only an hour away.

Frederick was a practical, pragmatic man, but once in a while he would think back to his early years teaching, in particular his first year, remembering the most brilliant student he had ever encountered of the over five-thousand teens who had set foot in his classroom.

The years had been kind to Frederick. He had developed a classroom style that caused even the most boisterous students to take a period off from causing problems to listen to his offbeat delivery, one that included a few 'hell's' and damn's' sprinkled into the English lesson. He gave some students his own nicknames, and discovered that some were actually *trying* to earn one. It had somehow become a badge of recognition.

When frustrated with their ineptness, he would call them knuckleheads, dodos, nincompoops, or blockheads. Sometimes he would hear students departing his class boasting to the incoming ones: 'we got two 'blockheads' and a 'nincompoop' this period.

But the most gratifying, and most frustrating aspect of his teaching had been for many years now, the constant questions he was asked about the legendary Lyman Hubert, class of 1970, the boy who was supposed to change the world by dint of his innovative genius, but who had simply disappeared without a trace that summer after driving as far as Sedona, Arizona.

. . .

There was always a "grace period" for Frederick, a few days, sometimes as much as a week, at the start of the year when his students paid strict attention to the lesson. The 'do-nothings' sat idly by, waiting for the colorful nicknames and insults to pepper the lesson with just enough spice for them to consider "sitting it out" for fifty minutes.

But the winds of change had blown this past summer. Frederick had not only been moved from his long-time classroom, he no longer taught all seniors. Perhaps the new principal, Dr. Hynes, was trying to tell him it was time to retire. He had assigned him three classes of *freshmen,* and one of *sophomores.* Frederick truthfully had no use in his mind for kids that young. He thrived on teaching *seniors,* and he only had one section of them, at the very end of the day.

He knew that questions about Lyman Hubert would not be forthcoming from the underclasses. Oddly, it was only seniors who showed the least bit interest in the boy who had become an urban legend in Kelton.

Frederick pretended that answering endless questions about him and entertaining the many theories kids came up with was an interruptive annoyance for him, but he really *enjoyed* reliving that magical year, 1969-1970. But there was still the lingering emptiness that accompanied such discussions.

. . .

The first two days were the usual; laying out objectives to the classes, reading ahead in the assigned texts, getting a feel for the strengths and weaknesses of each class. Frederick found the freshmen more enjoyable and challenging than expected. They were pleasant individuals, but there was so much he felt they should already know, but didn't. His sophomores were a chore; they had a surprisingly short attention span, and seemed to have no idea as to what was expected.

He found a note in his mailbox on the fourth day to see the new principal during his free period. During period four, he went to the main office and was announced by the secretary. Hynes sat behind his desk, just finishing a phone call, and motioned him to take a seat.

He stood and extended his hand across the desk. "Mr. Frederick, I just wanted to touch base with all the veteran teachers as soon as possible. I already spent a couple of in-service sessions with the new staff."

Frederick nodded.

"I'm sure you are in a state of transition, having moved and with underclassmen in your teaching load. I was wondering how things were going."

"Fine, so far, Dr. Hynes." Frederick wasn't sure where this was heading. Maybe the man just wanted to meet all the staff. Or maybe he was putting the word out that there was a new sheriff in town.

"Mr. Frederick, I'll get right to the point. I know you are an excellent educator and have been at this school for over forty years. Students and staff hold you in the highest regard."

Here comes the bad news, thought Frederick.

"That being said," continued Hynes, "I want to put everyone here on notice. I believe that all staff here, from teachers on down, should be constantly challenged." Hynes paused, and leaned forward in his chair. "I don't like the comfort zone that many staff here believe they have attained for themselves. Someone in a comfort zone is not doing the best job they can, whether they realize it or not."

Oh, shit, thought Frederick. He was probably the epitome of what Hynes was referring to.

"I just want to give the teachers here the benefit of knowing that things are going to be very different in terms of teaching assignments, room assignments, and in some cases, administrative expectations." He smiled in an attempt to reassure Frederick. "I'll be having this discussion with all the veteran teachers, so I don't want you to think you are being singled out."

"I don't think that, Dr. Hynes."

"Good, that's about it for me, unless you have—oh, there was one thing I was curious about."

"Yes?"

"Every now and then I hear the name Lyman Hubert, supposedly a multi-talented genius who attended this school many years ago."

"That's right."

"Well every time *his* name comes up, *yours* does, too."

"Yes, I was a first-year teacher. He was a senior in one of my classes."

"So, what's the connection, other than that?"

"I took him under my wing, saw the unlimited potential he had, and tried to keep all the extraneous stuff out of his way so he could attain what I believed would be a future that would affect this country, maybe even the world."

Hynes seemed to be mulling over his last words. He did *not* seem overly impressed by Frederick's bold statement. "Mr. Frederick, I appreciate history as much as the next guy, but I would be remiss if I didn't remind you that that was well over forty years ago. Nothing about that young man is doing anyone here now any good, as I see it. Let me leave you with this thought: It's okay to remember the past, but please live in the present, especially for the students whose education has been entrusted to you."

A stunned Thomas Frederick managed to keep a smile on his face. "Yes, sir, I will."

Frederick walked back to his classroom, astounded. Even Lyman Hubert had gotten his ass kicked in that little "getting to know you/there *is* a new sheriff in town" speech. He knew that this was going to be his last year of teaching.

. . .

Thomas Frederick did his due diligence with his freshmen and sophomores, consulting with the department head, Mrs. Barrett, to make sure he was doing what he was supposed to, and on schedule.

But his last class of seniors, that was different. His main goal for these young people, other than the curriculum, was to make sure they knew about Lyman

Hubert, if they showed the proper interest. Part of him still felt that Lyman's accomplishments could inspire present-day students. (Take that, Dr. Hynes.)

Like most other seniors, they waited a few days, getting the feel for his style, pace, and classroom demeanor. By that time, they had gotten called knuckleheads, dodos, nincompoops, and blockheads.

A few had already earned their classroom nickname. Andy Weymouth and his girlfriend, Hilary Scott, the senior class's most popular couple, were "Captain America" and "Hilarious." Tamara Thompson was "Tomorrow," Randy Doolittle, a reluctant learner, was "Randy Do-Nothing," and the trio of Lenny Duggan, Fred Donza, and Peter Williams, the laziest and most potential source of trouble he called "The Slugs."

When several students complained that they couldn't get their work done because they sat among Duggan, Donza, and Williams, Frederick declared, "Of course you can't get your work done there, you're in "The Slugmuda Triangle!"

The class roared. Even Donza and Williams thought it was funny. Lenny Duggan glowered. No one in "The Slugmuda Triangle" wanted their seat changed at that point.

And when Vincent Donofri found a jackknife he had inadvertently left in his pocket, he immediately became known as "Vinnie the Blade."

Within a few short days, Frederick had created the "village" atmosphere he loved in what would be the last class of his long teaching career. He had made it clear that they needed to work solidly and efficiently for forty-five minutes. If there were any "extraneous topics" they wished to discuss in the last five minutes, well, it *was* an English class.

Every morning Frederick would look at the senior class seating chart. Fourteen boys and ten girls. All decent or good students, with the exception of the "Slugs," and Randy Doolittle, who was just plain lazy. Frederick bet himself that Andy Weymouth would be the first to ask about Lyman Hubert.

. . .

With five minutes left in class the next day, Frederick couldn't help but notice that Andy and Hilary, who sat across from each other in front, seemed to be prompting each other.

Finally, Hilary raised her hand and asked, "Mr. Frederick, what's the true story about Lyman Hubert's locker? We heard the school can't get it open, so they left it unassigned ever since he graduated."

"That's right, Hilarious. Locker 75. No one can open it since Lyman rigged it senior year." Frederick noticed Ollie Freytag doing some quick calculations.

"Mr. Frederick," he called out, "the numbers on the lock go from zero to thirty-nine. With three numbers on the lock that's a total of sixty-four thousand possibilities."

"There's a set screw inside the locker, dipshit," scoffed Lenny Duggan. "They rotate it during the summer. There's only *four* combinations for each locker." He folded his arms across his chest in a smug manner.

"Lenny's right, Ollie," replied Frederick.

"So does that mean we can go back to the middle school and open our eighth grade locker?" asked Danny Hilton.

"You would, loser," sniped Patricia Bossio.

Frederick raised a hand for order. "Here's the story on that locker. During the school year, kids were opening Lyman's locker and stealing his homework, either as a prank or hoping to get all the right answers."

"He was getting bullied, Mr. Frederick?" asked Rachel Pruitt.

Frederick exhaled in exasperation. "You know, every little prank is not *bullying*. We didn't even *call* it that. It was 'teasing,' or 'getting picked on.' The world generally kicked the crap out of people who did that stuff, or they simply outgrew it. God, I am so sick of this hand-wringing, gutless-wonder mentality."

Kids looked at each other, some smiling or holding back a laugh.

"Lyman, genius that he was, fixed the locker so that only he could open it. When the school couldn't get it open that summer to change the combination, they thought it was fitting that they just leave it like that, almost like a tribute to him. To this day *no one* is able to open that locker."

"I can open it easy with a crowbar, Mr. Frederick," boasted Lenny Duggan.

"Disregarding 'Slug Technology,'" said Frederick, "that locker cannot be opened, and Lenny, I would not stick anything in there. Lyman had an extensive knowledge of electrical circuits, if you know what I mean."

There were snickers from the class.

It was time to wrap things up, so Frederick pointed at the classroom clock. "*Fortunately,* we're out of time, kiddies. Make sure you have the assignment in the Hemingway book, and if things go well tomorrow, we can continue your quest for information on the legendary Lyman Hubert."

As the class departed, Andy and Hilary stood by his desk. "Mr. Frederick," said Hilary, "you taught my mother. The same year you had Lyman Hubert in class."

Thomas Frederick looked at her in surprise.

"I know. She was forty-three when she had me."

"Who was your mother?" he asked.

"Cindy McCullough. You used to call her—"

"Scottie," said Frederick. "Because she was Scottish. She was such a beautiful girl."

Mr. Frederick!"

"That's a good thing, Hilarious. "That means there's still hope for *you.*"

Andy roared with laughter, then took off for the door as Hilary chased him out of the room.

. . .

Thomas Frederick sometimes wondered about himself. Here he was, at the end of a long teaching career, married forty-one years, two grown children, two grandchildren, yet part of him resided in a time that meant nothing, except to the extent he *made* it relevant to high school seniors. Maybe Hynes had been right about living in the past. He *still* knew that the combination to locker 75 was 9-26-8. It had been about fifteen feet down the hallway from his original classroom. He had actually *measured* it one day after school a few days ago.

He had been hoping to do this unnoticed, but he looked up to find a custodian a few feet away, sweeping the hallway floor.

"I know this must look kind of odd," he said, somewhat abashed.

The custodian smiled and shrugged. "I just sweep the floors after school. I don't need to know anything else."

"You're new, aren't you?"

"Yeah, I been in the elementary schools for twelve years, but there was an opening here on the three-to-eleven shift."

"I noticed a couple new custodians and secretaries. Think it has anything to do with the new principal?"

The custodian, a bald man with glasses so thick they made his eyes seem huge, smiled and winked. "What do *you* think?"

At that point, Frederick felt more comfortable about telling him why he was actually in the hallway. "I was just curious how far away I was from this locker." He was about to go into a story about the boy who once opened this locker years ago, but the custodian seemed to be in a hurry, or was not interested. "Well, I'll let you get back to your work. I'm Thomas Frederick, by the way."

"Nice to meet you, Mr. Frederick. I'm Bert Chiswell." He smiled and glided the broom down the hallway.

. . .

"So why didn't the police get a search warrant?" asked Danny Hilton.

"Well, Danny, when Lyman got to the Peace, Liberty, and Freedom Commune in Sedona, he sent his parents a postcard. He wanted to spend a week or so until classes started. They were suspicious and called the Arizona State Police, who said there wasn't anything they could do, since he was there by choice," replied Frederick.

"Then what happened?" asked Cassie Decamera.

"Lyman never showed for orientation, and his parents got a call from the university."

"That when the shit hit the fan?" asked Lenny Duggan, all smiles.

I'll do the swearing for the entire class, Lenny. And yes, sort of. His parents contacted the Sedona police, and they told them the same thing. Next day, they got another postcard saying he was staying at the commune for a few months and would start school in January instead." Frederick shook his head in frustration. "Over the next couple months they continued to get postcards. With each one, it seemed he was more into this hippie freak show and less into college. He *gave* them his car for their "motor pool" and eventually to use for spare parts."

"You think they brainwashed him?" asked Cheryl Wescott.

"Nincompoop," muttered Frederick. "That boy had more brains in his ass than that entire group of bottom-feeders had in their heads. He wasn't brainwashed. I always felt that Lyman was under a lot of pressure to be what everyone expected him to be. I guess we never considered what stress it may have caused him. He knew what lay ahead for the next four to six years, and I think he may have just thrown in the towel. It's sad, really, kids."

Frederick looked at the class, quietly listening. "To accomplish great things requires great effort, and I think Lyman, so impressionable, felt he could to more good for those forty dipshits than he could for the world. My God, maybe they *did* brainwash him."

You could hear a pin drop in the classroom until "Vinnie the Blade" Donofri spoke up. "Wait a minute, Mr. Frederick. Lyman wasn't majority age, why couldn't the police investigate when his parents stopped hearing from him?"

"They did, Vinnie, but it was too late. He had left the commune and struck out on his own, on foot. The police showed up, searched the place, questioned everyone. They all said he left a week earlier, heading west. That was around December 12th."

"Couldn't they, like, put his picture out, like on a milk carton or something?" asked Randy Doolittle.

Frederick feigned surprise. "He *can* speak!" Laughs from the class. "They didn't have milk carton kids back in 1970, Randy. There was no evidence of foul play, just an eighteen-year-old kid going out on his own. With that in mind, the police were not about to waste any time or resources on it."

Pedro Vargas raised his hand. "So what do you think really happened to him, Mr. Frederick?"

Frederick looked down, a half-smile showing. He was about to speak when the bell rang. "Fortunately, our time is up. See you tomorrow." He didn't even bother nagging them about their next day's assignment.

. . .

Thomas Frederick found that he was enjoying this school year more than he thought, but in October he informed the Board of Education that he would be retiring, and that it had been a pleasure serving the youth of Kelton, Pennsylvania.

Two normally quiet girls, Frannie McVay and Ronnie Hunt, asked him why Lyman's parents didn't hire a private detective.

"His father sold auto parts, and his mother was a part-time waitress," he replied. "They didn't have money to send a private investigator across the country when he left Sedona and the postcards abruptly stopped."

"Are they still alive?" asked Dino Scanlon.

"No. Lyman was their only child. They were hopeful for years that he would just show up one day, but that never happened."

"That's so sad," remarked Raquel Vasquez.

"I guess if he *had* resurfaced at some point, the high expectations would have just started up all over again," said Frederick. "Maybe all that just spooked him."

"Hey, Mr. Frederick," called out Lenny Duggan, "maybe he was never found because he became a serial killer, and didn't *want* to be found."

Amid the groans of several students, Frederick replied, "You know, Lenny, I think you're partially right. I *don't* think he wanted to be found. I wouldn't be surprised if he got a new identity or something along that line."

"How old would he be now?" asked Terrie Marcellino.

"Sixty-two or so, I guess. He was seventeen that year he graduated, and I was fresh out of college."

"He could be dead," said Dino Scanlon.

Al Wilkie raised his hand. "Mr. Frederick, Richy, Paul, and I did a computer search for him. We got nothing."

"You aren't the first to look for him and come up empty. Anyway, for extra credit, anyone who comes up with a paragraph on what someone like Lyman *could* have accomplished, both in his youth, and now, can read it tomorrow. It's a good exercise in divergent thinking." Frederick did his famous half-smile, which usually preceded a group insult. "Of course you have to be able to *think* in order to engage in *divergent* thinking."

The bell rang. "And, fortunately, our time is up."

As the class left, Juan Hernandez stood at his desk. A quiet immigrant from Mexico, he had never spoken except when called upon. "Hey, Mr. Frederick, I think this boy Lyman was scared of what might *happen* if he did something great. Some people are like that, you know. I had a cousin back in Mexico, very smart. His family talked big about what he would be some day, like President of Mexico."

Frederick, encouraged by the divergent thinking Juan exhibited, asked, "What happened to him, Juan?"

"He works on my uncle's chicken farm."

Juan departed, and Thomas Frederick sat at his desk, lost in the assignment he had given his seniors, who he now regarded as his second-favorite class all-time, behind only period 3 from 1969-1970, when Lyman D. Hubert had teased him into thinking he was the one who would change the world, or at least his part of it.

Frederick's reverie was broken by sounds of a ruckus down the hallway. He went to his doorway. Down by the magical locker there was a noisy gathering of several students. Although *fifty-three* away, (he had measured *that,* too) Frederick could make out all three "Slugs," and three others from class. There were raised voices and profanity.

He hurried down there, using his official "teacher taking over" walk.

"What is this, a 'slugfest'?" he barked.

Ollie Freytag and Danny Hilton came over to him, while Rachel Pruitt stood across the hallway. "We figured Lyman somehow changed the combination. We were trying a few when *these* guys showed up," Ollie said, jerking his head at Duggan, Donza, and Williams.

"No way these nerdasses are gonna open this locker," spouted Duggan. "Me and the boys got dib on it."

"Duggan, when are you going to wise up?" asked Frederick. "*Nobody* opens this locker, and not just because it *won't* open. Because I *said* nobody opens it! The whole bunch of you clear out!"

Ollie, Danny, and Rachel walked toward his room, while a sulking Lenny Duggan and his fellow slugs headed towards the near stairwell, nearly bumping into custodian Bert Chiswell, who stopped and stared at them.

"Whatta *you* lookin' at, Pops?" snarled Duggan. He grabbed the shaft of Chiswell's broom, then released it in a shoving motion. "Goofy-eyed bastard. Let's get out of this shithole, guys." They exited down the stairwell, shouting profanities.

Frederick approached Chiswell. "I apologize for them. Someday they'll learn, or end up in a ditch somewhere."

"It's okay, Mr. Frederick. They don't mean anything."

"Really? You believe that?"

"What I meant was, people like that don't *mean* anything."

"Oh, they don't *count* for anything?"

Chiswell shrugged, and moved down the hallway, gliding his broom ahead of him.

Both Thomas Frederick *and* Lenny Duggan knew enough to "lay low" the next day. Nothing more was said about the locker incident. Frederick told Ollie Freytag privately not to antagonize the situation by trying any more combinations on locker 75. "Believe me, Ollie, you are *not* going to be able to open it. It's been tried by better men than you and me."

Freytag smiled, possibly due to being referred to as a 'man' in Frederick's comparison. "Okay, Mr. Frederick."

Frederick did not hand out compliments liberally, but he was impressed with the ideas his seniors had come up with on the extra credit assignment. They included irrigation systems, space travel concepts, disease cures, physics, mathematical breakthroughs, and other innovative concepts and inventions as yet undiscovered.

Cheryl Wescott added, "He already *has* one great invention, Mr. Frederick."

"What's that?"

"The thief-proof locker!"

The class, realizing that Cheryl had put one over on Frederick, roared their approval.

. . .

The weeks flew by. It was a pleasant school year for Frederick, despite the bitter-sweet taste of having his second-favorite class, and knowing that they would be his last.

Parents night came in early December, and with it, a warm reunion with Cindy McCullough Scott, class of 1970.

He walked into his classroom the next day to find the entire class clustered around Hilary Scott's desk. She had brought in her mother's classbook, and everyone wanted to see a photo of Lyman Hubert. Where his picture would have been was a generic male silhouette with the words, *Photo Not Available.*

"This sucks, Mr. Frederick," moaned Al Wilkie. "He's not in the book!"

"I could have told you that, Al. He was extremely camera-shy. I tried to get him to submit one, but he just wouldn't. Even the clubs he was in. He left the room when the picture was being taken."

"What did he look like?" a girl's voice asked.

"Whatsa matter, Terrie, need a new boyfriend?" called Pedro Vargas.

Terrie Marcillino glared at Pedro and pushed her glasses up with her middle finger.

"Very subtle, Terrie," remarked Frederick. "Lyman was about 5' 10" and a bit on the thin side. He had medium-length brown hair and glasses."

"Those black-rimmed nerd ones?" asked Patricia Bossio.

"No. He looked like any other boy back then. Say, why are we on this at the *beginning* of the period? You people have a lot of mid-term review to finish to even have the slightest chance of passing the exam."

"Is your mid-term that hard?" asked Ronnie Hunt.

"No, it's fairly easy. But don't forget, you're all nincompoops and blockheads."

. . .

In mid-February, Frederick came down with the flu, followed by a virus, missing two-and-a-half weeks of school. He begged his wife to let him go in. "It's going to be one incompetent sub after another," he told her. "I'll just give them the assignment and sit there."

"You can sit in the living room or rest in bed, Tom, replied his wife Diane. "And I told Mrs. Barrett you would be out at least two weeks and asked to have the same sub each day, so there would be continuity. I *know* you have a file of every lesson you teach for those seniors. I can put them in a document and e-mail them to the school."

"That's not gonna help my other classes."

"You said yourself they were beyond help."

"And they are. They're all blockheads."

"And nincompoops?"

"That, too."

Frederick returned to school on March 2nd. His freshmen and sophomores seemed pleased, informing him that the sub, a Mr. Irwin, was "mean." As each member of his senior class found him behind his desk, their reaction made Frederick feel like a conquering hero returned home. They ranged from Lenny Duggan's, "About time. That other guy was a dick," to Andy Weymouth kneeling on the floor and doing the 'I am not worthy' supplication.

The class threw themselves into the lesson with a gusto that made Frederick proud. "At this rate," he said, "some of you will *not* be nincompoops by June. Of course, you'll still be blockheads."

At the end of class, Raquel Vasquez raised her hand. She seemed hesitant. "Mr. Frederick, my father is an army recruiter, and he said that when Lyman decided not to go to college, he should have signed up for the draft. That would make him a draft dodger, wouldn't it?"

Raquel, a sensitive quiet girl, had a definite sense of right and wrong. Frederick wondered how long this had been bothering her.

"Let me ease your mind, Raquel," said Frederick, noticing the shocked looks among the students. "When Lyman failed to enroll at USC, he lost his IIS student deferment, and was eligible for the draft in 1970. In that draft lottery, he had number 325, based on his birthday of January 10th. In 1970, they got as far as 175, I believe. So he wouldn't have had to report, and therefore is not considered a draft dodger, okay?"

Raquel smiled a relieved smile, as did many of the others in class.

The normally quiet Juan Hernandez asked, "You said his birthday was January 10th. Do you celebrate it?"

Frederick looked down, a reflective half-smile showing. "No, Juan, I don't *celebrate* it. I merely *observe* it."

. . .

Time really does fly when you're having fun, thought Thomas Frederick. Late winter melted into spring as the Pennsylvania snows receded to expose pale greenery. There was talk of spring sports, the prom, and college acceptances.

Sixteen of his twenty-four seniors would attend either two or four-year colleges and universities. Richy Ulner and Paul Lange, both computer whizzes, headed the list, having been accepted to Penn State. Two were enrolling in training courses in dental and medical assistance, and two, Raquel Vasquez and Cheryl Wescott, had enlisted in the armed forces.

Not surprisingly, the "Slugs" and Randy Doolittle were job-hunting. By June, only Lenny Duggan had found a job, taken in by his uncle in an auto-body shop.

With the last day of school approaching, Frederick often sat in his classroom during his free period, looking at a gray box with a faded red bow on top. It once contained the gaudy, patriotic tie clip presented to him in 1970 by Lyman Hubert. Frederick had worn it with pride the following year, until the news about Lyman had turned from hopeful, to concerning, to alarming, to disappointment and despair. The tie clip was home, and had been for forty-four years now. Only the box remained in school, hidden away in his desk.

Finally, Wednesday, June 18th arrived. He averaged final grades, filled out a "Lost and Damaged Books" report, and presided over a talking festival in his freshman and sophomore classes, wishing them a fun and safe summer.

He decided to make a "grand entrance" for his final class, sitting the teacher's workroom until the late bell rang. He made the walk up one flight of stairs and down the hallway to his classroom, passing locker 75, a silent reminder of what once was.

As he neared the room, Lenny Duggan's head popped out and back in again, accompanied by whispered shouts of "Here he comes!" Frederick entered the room to find Andy Weymouth "peeling out" around the corner of his desk. There were anticipatory smiles and giggles. Frederick looked at his desk, which had two rectangular boxes on it, one large and one small.

"Oh, my, what's this?" he said, in his "being a good sport" voice.

"Open the small one first," called Lenny Duggan.

He did, and laughed at the sight of three ceramic snails, obviously representing the "Slugs." "Well, guys, I certainly will never forget you. But I *will* try." Big laughs from the class. The larger box was now in his hand, and everyone was bursting with anticipatory laughter. He opened it and removed a large tee shirt in the school colors. The blue shirt bore the inscription *#1 Blockhead* in red letters and beneath it, in parenthesis *(And Nincompoop.)*

"Well, folks, I can't promise I'll wear it with *pride,* but thank you all very much."

Frederick gave the class permission to sit anywhere and visit, but he wanted the final minute of class to make a few remarks.

He enjoyed watching the class dynamic for the next forty-five minutes, guys hanging out together, one-upping each other as to what they were going to do this summer. The girls' dynamic was the opposite; teary-eyed reminiscences, mainly.

With a minute left, he flicked the light switch. Everyone scrambled back to their proper seats. There was absolute silence.

"I would like to thank you for making my final year a memorable and enjoyable one, and I wish you all much happiness and success in the future. I sincerely hope that I was able to be a positive influence on your lives. You're a fine group of …blockheads." There were a few laughs. Hilary Scott was wiping away tears. Frederick pointed at the clock. *"Un*fortunately, our time is up."

The bell rang, and while a few of the shyer kids headed for the door, most of the class, including the "Slugs," came up and shook his hand, wishing him a happy retirement. Hilary Scott hugged him tightly, still vibrating with emotion. Andy Weymouth shook his hand and slapped his shoulder. He and Hilary exited last, looking back and waving.

Frederick found that he needed to take several deep breaths. He waited until the halls were empty of students. The only sounds were a few teachers talking. He had no intention of returning tomorrow to clean out his possessions. He had come in early the past two days and loaded everything into his car. He would now turn in his final end-of-year paperwork and sit in his room until he heard the announcement for "official teacher dismissal."

He walked to the office and turned in his paperwork. Back at his desk a few minutes later, he noticed a folded piece of paper there. He had left the desk empty. He unfolded the note, written on a half-sheet of white-lined paper. It said, *Have a great retirement, Mr. Frederick. Thanks for everything. I will never forget you.* There was no signature, just the initials *L. D. H.*

The most telling feature of the note was the handwriting itself. He would know that writing anywhere. It was in all cursive, the cursive handwriting of Lyman Hubert.

Frederick, despite his sixty-seven years, bolted from the classroom. Bert Chiswell was by the stairwell, sweeping the paper-strewn floor. "Mr. Chiswell, was someone up here while I was at the office?"

"Yeah, some guy said he had a message for you, so I told him your room number. Was that okay?"

"What did he look like?" Frederick asked, frantic, and on the verge of panic.

"I don't know. Tall guy, bushy hair and glasses. Late fifties, maybe older. Was it all right that I—"

Frederick rushed down the stairwell. He had been sub-consciously waiting for this moment for over forty years. What poetic justice that it should come on his last day as a teacher. "You're not disappearing *this* time, Lyman," he panted.

Back at locker 75, a hand set the dial at '0', turning it 43 numbers, the sum of the locker's previous combination of 9-26-8. With the dial now showing a '3', a left hand pressed hard on the upper left corner of the locker. A voice counted off eight seconds, the hand releasing that corner as a right hand pressed the lower left corner, counting off another six seconds.

Locker 75 popped open like a large, metallic jack-in-the box.

Bert Chiswell smiled. "Still works like a charm." He closed the locker, grabbed his pushbroom, and glided it along the littered, silent hallway.

"THE REPLACEMENT KID" 2013

Please tell me you don't fall for that crap when parents tell their kids they love them all the same. My parents used it on my older sister Edith when she complained that my brother and I got special treatment. They used it on my late brother Todd when he complained he couldn't do the same things as me. And they used it on *me* when I voiced my displeasure at having to include Todd when I hung out with friends, or not being allowed to punch Edith when she was mean while babysitting us.

I don't know if Edith ever believed the "love you all the same" line; it was always hard to figure her out. I bet Todd believed it. Once, I told him if he planted some quarters, a money tree would grow. So he did. I dug up the money and put some pine branches there. He caught on eventually, but Jesus. There were about a dozen other scams me and my two best friends, Louis and Joey pulled on him. Their stuff was more nasty, and often involved them telling Todd to say certain promiscuous things to my sister, whom they both had a crush on. I had *no* idea what they found attractive about her. Now that I'm older I would describe her as aloof, unfeeling, and self-involved. But back then, I didn't know shit, so I assumed that's the way it was between boys and older sisters.

We lived in Fulton, Kentucky, had a nice house on a quiet street. Behind our house was a large expanse of woods, which led to a clearing. Just before the clearing was a stream and pond. As you might imagine, those woods were our own private kingdom for me and my friends, and unfortunately, my younger brother Todd. We created our own adult-free world, playing army, catching every living creature you could think of to keep as a pet, building tree forts, and using the clearing for baseball and football games.

At the other side of the clearing was an old guy who lived by himself, Mr. Pullig. We knew who he was from seeing the name on the mailbox.

I referred to my 'late brother Todd' a bit earlier, so you want to know what happened. That's only part of what this is about. There was a lot more to this than even *I* realized.

Let me set the scene. In 1994 I was nine, Edith was eighteen, and Todd was seven. I suppose I should have been flattered that he wanted to do everything I did, but I was too young to grasp the concept of imitation being the sincerest form of flattery. To me, back then, imitation was another pain in my ass, caught between an alien older sister and a tag-along brother, my parents' favorite.

That's right, favorite. They can deny it all they want, but it was obvious.

Did I resent my parents because of this? Heck, no. They were kind, loving people, and were good parents. I just wish they had sat Edith and me down one day (or just me; I'm not sure if Edith even cared) and stated, 'Look we love you two, but Todd is our favorite, so find a way to work around that and everything will be great, okay?' That's all it would have taken for me.

But that never happened. We got the party line. *We love you all the same.* Not even one of the caveats, like *only in different ways.* Like I said, I did *not* hold it against them. They didn't know what a manipulative liar he was. Yeah, seven years old, and already a manipulative liar. I don't know where he got it, either. Was there some Saturday morning cartoon show where all these animated, multi-colored beings with stupid names lied and manipulated for half an hour? My parents weren't holding the little bastard accountable for anything except throwing his dirty socks in the hamper and remembering to wipe his ass when he used the toilet.

So there it is. I hated Todd for all the times he lied and got me in trouble. If he broke something, I got blamed. My grandfather's WWII photographs all disappeared. My father was *positive* I had taken them to school and lost them. A few days later, I found some of them *floating* in the pond. Any injury he got, accidental or self-inflicted, was blamed on me. There are about a dozen other categories.

So we get to the day in question, June25th, 1994, about a week into summer vacation. It started like all days off from school: me running into the woods, and Todd pursuing me. I fooled him this time. I crossed the stream, ducked into a thicket, and doubled back upstream. My plan was to run home, get Louis and Joey, and run down the street past Mr. Pullig's house to a vacant lot almost a mile away. I don't know what we were actually gonna *do* there, but it was worth it to have ditched Todd. Of course, who knows what lies he was planning to tell about me when he got home?

As I doubled back, I looked to my left to see where Todd was. I didn't think he could have gotten past the stream at that point, and I didn't see him on the path. Curiosity must have moved me to run toward the stream crossing. It had several rocks strategically located so we could cross without getting wet.

Todd was in the water. At first I thought he was getting a drink, but he was stretched out in the water itself. My first thought was, *Todd fell in and got soaked; he'll have no trouble blaming this one on me.* I ran to the water's edge and looked closer. A rock in the middle of the stream had blood on it, and Todd was face down, not moving. I was scared, now. He really got hurt this time, and it's all gonna land at my doorstep. My only alternative was to help him up, act like the concerned older brother,

and try to talk him out of whatever tale he was determined
to tell.

I walked right in the water to get him. I was sure it
would look good if I was also soaking wet. I called him
and grabbed his arm. He still didn't move. I remember
turning him over and yelling that it was me. Then I saw the
huge gash on his right forehead, and his coloring, and I
knew that I was now in the most trouble someone could
possibly be in.

My mind kind of went blank, and the next thing I
remember is meeting Louis and Joey on the path.

"Pete," Louis said, "your mom said you and Todd
ran down here. Did you ditch him?"

"Guys, Todd's in the stream. He drowned," I heard
myself saying.

Louis's face froze, but Joey snorted. "You freakin'
liar, Colby. C'mon, let's get down to the lot. We can get
in some batting practice."

I was crying as I shouted at them, "I'm not lying!
Todd's dead!"

Joey's smirk evaporated into the frozen face Louis
still wore.

. . .

The next three days are burned into my memory. I
can't begin to describe the anguish from my parents,
especially my mother. As always, it was hard to read my
sister. She seemed more subdued than usual. And yes, I
was sad. Sure, the kid was a lying pest, but I didn't want
him to *die*.

My friends were very kind to me. Louis and Joey
did everything I wanted to do for weeks after. I think they
were pretty traumatized. They actually went down to the
stream and saw Todd lying there.

I was not held responsible for what happened. The police determined that Todd had slipped on a rock, fallen, and bashed his head on a second rock, and slid, unconscious, into the water and drowned. My testimony pretty much corroborated their conclusion.

The wake and funeral were unreal to me. I had never seen anyone in a coffin before. Mom had to be sedated. They kept saying Todd was *gone,* but there he was right in front of us. The priest said he would *sleep* for all eternity. So why call it a *wake?*

. . .

My brother Derrick was born on September 2nd of the next year. I called him "The Replacement Kid." To myself. He looked *exactly* like Todd as a baby. I was hoping his features would change. Todd ceased to exist. All pictures of him were put away, and Edith and I were cautioned never to mention him to Derrick when he got older. Mom and Dad planned to sit him down at some point and explain about Todd and his untimely death. I didn't get it, but it didn't really affect me, so I just said 'okay,' and let it go at that.

. . .

Six years later, and I'm a sophomore in high school. Edith had gone to college and become a social worker at the middle school one town over. She's still single, with no steady boyfriend, if you can possibly imagine that. Just my luck. Derrick is six now, and admires the hell out of me. The problem? He *still* looks *exactly* like Todd, the dead brother he still knows nothing about. But he's a good kid, for the most part. I still think about that Saturday afternoon back in 1994 when I found Todd in the stream.

Oh, the nightmares. I had bad ones starting about two weeks after the drowning. My parents finally made me see someone about them. It was some psychologist here in town, about a month later. They all involved Todd, me, and the stream. In some of the dreams, I pushed him into the water, and even held his head under. In some of them it was reversed, and he was trying to drown *me.* Louis and Joey made a few guest appearances, watching from the other side of the stream, yelling at me to hurry so we could go play ball.

I got nowhere with this, so I made a fuss until my parents relented and I didn't have to go any more. My friends all knew I was getting mental therapy, but didn't give me any grief over it.

But my sister. Jesus. One time, at Thanksgiving two years later, she came home from college and said I would be in therapy for ten years from the guilt I had from how I treated Todd, and not being able to get forgiveness. There was no **closure.** God, how I hate that word now. I told her she was nuts. *He* was the one who made *my* life difficult. But her take on it was that he was sad and frustrated from not getting the companionship from me he craved. I suddenly realized that one-year-old Derrick was five feet away from us in his stroller.

"Edith!" I jabbed my finger in his direction. "Not in front of—"

"Don't be a moron, Peter. He can't understand us."

"Pee-Pee!" yelled Derrick.

That was his name for me, before he could say 'Peter.' Great, huh?

Here's the really spooky thing. One time Edith sat me down when I was about thirteen and asked me to recall in detail what I remembered from that afternoon. Stupid me, I thought we were going to have a heart-to-heart talk about my nightmares. But she launched into this theory that I was *suppressing* what *really happened* at the stream that day. When I finally caught on, I felt like punching her.

"What the *hell,* Edith! You think I *pushed* him? Is that it?"

Her face didn't change; that haughty pickle-puss expression. "Only *you* know what happened down there that day. Peter, some things are so ...*repulsive* for us to think about that our mind *creates* an alternative. Todd was dead; there was no changing that, but maybe your mind came up with a more palatable way for it to have happened."

I stood over her, my breath coming in gasps. "I'll give you 'palatable,' you stuck-up skank!"

She merely looked vindicated, and pointed up at me. "See, look at the rage you're capable of. Everyone has it, Peter. Maybe there was one thing too many you perceived him doing to you, and you—"

"You shut the hell up, Edith," I hissed. "Did you ever say any of this to Mom and Dad?"

"Of course not," she said, somewhat reassuringly. Then her face took on a nasty twist. "There's no *proof* of anything. In my field, practitioners have to have a sense of confidentiality."

"In your field," I scoffed. "I wish *you* were in a field, about a thousand miles from here!"

She stood. "All right, Peter. I can see it's too soon for you to come to grips with this. But look how it touched a sensitive area—"

"I'd like to *kick* you in a sensitive area, you heartless bitch." (Okay, I was only thirteen, so I probably didn't say *that,* exactly.)

Thanks to Edith's little psychology session, I started having all kinds of weird thoughts. *Did* I just happen to stumble upon Todd dead in the stream, or had I been the one who caused it? No matter how hard I tried, I couldn't remember it any differently than what I had believed these six years.

Early in my sophomore year, I visited our school psychologist, Mr. Pender, without even my parents knowing. Of course I didn't know that while he couldn't reveal *what* I had discussed, he was required to *categorize* it. So I was in the district's records in the "psychological trauma" file. Nice going, everybody. I guess a guy simply can't have recurring nightmares about possibly killing his younger brother without causing a fuss. And, of course, my parents were back in the mix, now. Luckily, Edith lived out of town, and sweet little Derrick, the creepy Todd look-alike, was oblivious to all this.

. . .

Around Thanksgiving that year I was walking by Mr. Pullig's house on my way to the vacant lot. We just had a bad windstorm, and he was in his yard struggling with some branches knocked down by the storm. For some reason, what occurred to me were all the times we had played some loud baseball and football games in the clearing next to his house; lots of bad language, and a few guys smoking. Sometimes at dusk a few of us had snuck beer down there and hung out. Mr. Pullig had never chased us or called the cops. All of a sudden I felt I should thank him for his tolerance, or indifference, whichever.

"Could you use some help, Mr. Pullig?" I asked, walking over to him.

"Thank you, young fella. Mighty nice of you." He was trying to figure out which one of the kids I used to be. "You Rich and Barbara Colby's son?"

"Yeah, I'm Pete."

His face turned grim and sympathetic. "So that was your brother what drowned over there them years back."

"Yeah." I considered a moment. "But my parents had another baby the next year. Derrick. He's six now."

"Losin' family is tough. Lost my last cousin around that time. Killed himself back in Ohio. Drank poison."

"Jeez. Why?"

"He was a strange one, Leonard. Had every pet he ever owned, all stuffed. He also had his two-year-old son what died out in the garage in a cabinet. Just couldn't bear to bury him. I guess it all got to him, eventually."

I was astounded. "How the hell did that happen?"

"He was a funeral director here years ago. His son up and died, and he decided to keep him, that's all."

"God, that's creepy, if you don't mind my saying."

"Nah. Death brings out the best and the worst in people. I guess you know that in your family, what with your parents losing two kids and all."

"No, just the one, Todd." I was beginning to think Mr. Pullig didn't have a clear recollection of the past. We picked up branches, but I could see his mind working.

"Yeah, I remember Todd. I used to see you guys coming across the stream from my side window lots of times."

Oh, God. I had to ask. "You, didn't, uh, see anything the day he drowned, did you?"

"Nope."

"You're sure?"

"I'm sure. I remember reading about it and thinking, 'that's one of the neighbor kids.' Anyway, I remember saying to myself, 'God is really puttin' them poor folks to the test, takin' a second young 'un away.' Must have been bad enough on your parents when the baby died." He paused. "Were you even born then?"

I dropped the branch I was holding. "Wait a minute. In my family there was my sister Edith, me, and there was Todd."

"Right. But there was another baby. Paul, Peter, something like that."

"I'm Peter."

He scratched his chin. "So it was Paul, then."

"Mr. Pullig, no disrespect intended. I never heard of Paul." And then it hit me. We never told Derrick about Todd. Were my parents and Edith not telling me about Paul? Or was this some mismatched recollection of a man in his eighties?

He looked at me sympathetically. "Look, young man, I'm sorry if I gave away somethin' your folks didn't want you knowin' about."

I thought a moment. "It's okay, Mr. Pullig. You didn't mean nothin' by it. I think I gotta get going home now."

. . .

I'm not stupid. I knew enough to go home and do some thinking, instead of throwing accusations around. It really did make perfect sense. My brother Paul had died, and shortly after, I guessed, my parents had had me, just like when Todd died, they had Derrick. *I* was the *original* "Replacement Kid." How's that for irony?

When was I supposed to be told about Paul? How did he die? How old was he, and how much later did they have me? So many unanswered questions.

I was quite proud of the way I handles this. I just let it *simmer.* Gradually, my outrage and anger ebbed a little each day. And no way was I telling any of *this* to Mr. Pender. Within a week, I hardly gave it a second thought. There was school to think about, and Christmas was coming. I was asking for a new computer, and judging from my mother's reactions, I had a pretty good chance of scoring one. I really didn't worry about Mr. Pullig telling my parents of our conversation. He had always been the invisible man. But deep inside, I wished he had seen me or Todd crossing the stream that day in 1994 so I could *know* for certain what I truly believed: I had *nothing* to do with Todd's death.

. . .

On December 20th, my parents went to a Christmas party, and I was babysitting good old Derrick. For some reason, I got in one of those "snooping for Christmas presents" moods. I got Derrick interested in some animated Christmas special, and told him I had to go to the bathroom and would be back in a few minutes. I made him a glass of chocolate milk to keep him satisfied, and went to the master bedroom.

When we were younger, the Christmas presents were hidden in my father's clothes closet. How did I know? Edith showed me, about two minutes after she told me there was no Santa Claus. (C'mon, guys, she's still single!) My theory was that Mom now hid them in her cedar hope chest, by the window looking out on our front yard and driveway. I could look for my new computer and know if my parents were pulling in.

I opened the hope chest and worked through scarves, hats, and other junk. No computer boxes. Out of curiosity, I kept going. Near the bottom I found framed photos of Todd, some with Edith and me. I remembered all those photos, which had been in there over six years now. A few more were face down, so I pulled them out, too. There were several framed baby photos of me, but I had *never* seen them before. I knew Mom labeled the backs, so I removed them from the frames, looked on the reverse side, and forgot to breathe.

They were of *Paul* Colby at three, six, and nine months. And he looked just like *me* at that age. Merry Christmas, Peter!

. . .

I actually *did* get a new computer. My parents had wised up and hidden it at my uncle Steven's house.

Edith was here Christmas day, making a big production about what it was like working in a public school. Derrick was beside himself, going from one new toy to the next. Dad's eyes were pinwheels from watching basketball all day. Mom was quietly arranging things, picking up, and organizing all the desserts and leftovers in the kitchen. And finally Edith was in her old room, going through things she had left behind.

The trap was set. I slipped in and closed the door.

She looked half surprised, half annoyed. "What do you want, Peter? I'm busy right now."

"I want to know all about my older brother Paul. When did he die, and how? How come I was never told?"

Her face immediately developed blotches on each cheek. "There's no older—"

"Don't bother," I shot back. "I found his baby pictures at the bottom of Mom's hope chest. When was I supposed to find out? At sixteen? Eighteen? Twenty-one? Jump in any time, Edith."

"I don't know when they were going to tell you, Peter," she said softly.

"I assume *you* knew about it."

"Of course I did. I was eight. You were born the next year, just like with Todd and Derrick."

I can't describe the satisfaction I had from having Edith cornered. "So," I said, "what's the story on Paul?"

"I don't think I should be the one telling you this."

"What happened, Edith? You drop him on his head or something?" I was just being sarcastic, or glib, or something along that line. I had no idea of what I had just unleashed.

"It wasn't my fault!" she screamed. "Mom was upstairs cleaning and I was watching him in the kitchen. He wasn't supposed to *be* in that crib! I didn't know the bottom was too high now for him. Nobody *told* me. He fell onto the kitchen floor on his head. I picked him up and put him back and covered him. I was too scared to say anything. Mom didn't come down for another half hour. It was too late by then. Are you *satisfied* now?"

I was not.

She burst from the room and went screaming into the kitchen. "He knows, Mom! He knows about Paul!"

The next sounds were my parents yelling; at her, at me, at each other, Derrick screaming in fright and confusion, my father tripping over one of Derrick's toys and landing *in* the Christmas tree. And the phone was ringing. God bless us everyone!

. . .

It was twenty minutes before all the yelling, screaming, and crying had subsided. Half of me felt this righteous vindication, the other half was telling myself that I had stirred up pointless suffering. Too late now.

I couldn't believe my parents let Derrick sit at the kitchen table with us for what followed. Maybe it was for the best.

What ensued was a family history. Edith, the emotionless caregiver to her brother Paul, making a normal mistake for an eight-year-old, resulting in his subsequent death from head trauma. No charges were filed, the authorities coming to the conclusion that there was no ill intent, and the family's suffering far outweighed anything the law could dispense. My parents decided that for Edith's sanity and well-being that Paul would cease to be mentioned in our family. So his baby pictures went to the bottom of the hope chest, and the following year I became "Replacement Kid #1."

Edith claimed she was haunted in her dreams by what had happened to Paul. I had to give her that one, in light of my own troubled nights. What little affinity she had for others was probably sucked dry by the experience. Knowing what I now knew, it didn't seem so *wrong* for my parents to have kept Paul's life and tragic death a secret form me. Live and learn, I guess.

Then, of course, came tragedy number two, except that I was in no way responsible for Todd's death. I guess Edith didn't want to be the only one suffering, and thus began her quest to get me to blame myself, which I almost ended up doing. I *still* held that against her, but now I had a better understanding of the motivations and feelings involved.

Enter Derrick, "Replacement Kid #2." Funny thing, genetics. I looked just like Paul, and Derrick looked just like Todd. I wonder now how uneasy I had made Edith feel, with my resemblance to Paul. Probably the same way Derrick sometimes makes me feel. What goes around, huh?

I guess we go on, this family which has suffered two catastrophic losses. My parents go back to raising their sons, Edith goes back to her career, and the *two* replacement kids go back to their lives as brothers.

I seldom go into the woods anymore. I have mostly outgrown the need for it. But if I *should* happen to venture there in the future, and my brother Derrick follows, I shall not run from him.

We Colby offspring will probably be married with our own kids someday. (Even Edith!) I guess we would do well to have our children know that we love them all the same.

"WHEN THE MUSIC'S OVER"
2013

I guess I have a knack for finding things. Even though I'm only seventeen, I'm a darn good rock guitarist. But here in Calhoun, Georgia, not many kids are interested in the 60's and 70's rock classics I love. So you might think it would be hard to find some guys that would want to form a band.

But, I have a knack for finding things. In a high school of only 995, I found four guys who were willing to give it a try. At one point this past summer, I was scouring parks, swimming holes, parties, and other teen hangouts looking for the four people I needed to get my musical dream off the ground.

The drummer was easy to find. Norm Grant had been under my nose for years. We grew up in the same neighborhood. He had taken up drums in the fourth grade, the same year I started guitar. He was a good drummer, and a loyal friend.

Denny Davis was our rhythm guitar. He had a good singing voice, and had been in other bands. He was someone I thought I would have to compromise with at times, but if I threw him a few guitar solos and a couple vocal leads, I figured he'd be on board. I recruited him at this girl's birthday party we both attended.

Cal Wosney signed on to be our keyboard player. Cal's quiet, just seems to drift through life. His mother taught him piano at an early age, and made him play the organ for the church choir. That's where I found him, in church.

Our bass player is Zebulon "Zeb" Sippen, from one of the few Jewish families in Gordon County. To Zeb's credit, he's kind of the rebel in his family. "I may be Jewish," he told me one time, "but I'm not a very good

Jew." I had to laugh. So how does a boy raised in a traditional Jewish household end up playing the electric bass? His answer: "I just picked the instrument that would get under my parents' skin the most."

So we formed our band this past summer. I had to fight tooth and nail for the name I wanted: *The Gordon County Renaissance Band.*

"Too long," said Denny. "Who the hell's gonna remember *that?"*

"What's it even *mean?"* asked Cal.

I explain that it represented the fact that we were a "reawakening" of the great music from the 60's and 70's. Norm and Zeb just shrugged, and that was that. We were officially *The Gordon County Renaissance Band.* But there was no place to rehearse. A couple of the guys had garages, but there was a lot of stuff in them, like *cars.*

Enter my grandfather, Willis Trufaunt. He was the super in an apartment building near our high school. It's a new building, put up so that "no-account transients can have a place to drink and shoot dope," according to my grandfather. He's been more like a father to me than my real father, who runs a furniture store, and works insane hours. My mother is a volunteer at the historical society and the library. She was out of her league when it came to all that boy stuff here in a small Georgia town of 15,000, halfway between Atlanta and Chattanooga.

Grandpa had taken me fishing, taught me to shoot, play baseball, the works. When Grandpa Willis asks me to help him, I feel I owe him. The last week of summer vacation he came over to our house. He asked about the band, but there was something on his mind.

"Thad," he said, "I need your help moving a guy into one of our vacant units."

"Another dope fiend?" I asked, laughing.

"No, this guy's got a long history, but I can't get into it."

"What is he, some parolee from Raiford?"

"No. It's very complicated. That's all I can tell you. He's got no one to help him move in, and there's not much he can do physically."

"He handicapped?"

Grandpa Willis thought a moment. "Yes, he's got a lot of handicaps. Me and 'Captain Time Travel' just finished putting in a ramp for him."

The mention of 'Captain Time Travel' made me smile. That would be Renny Lamoin, a guy in his thirties who works for my grandfather. He's considered a nut case around town. He claims that in 1987 when he was eleven, he and three friends stepped through some time warp (he called it a "tear in the fabric") and were caught in a Civil War battle called Maddin's Grove in Ten Oaks, Georgia. He says one of the kids with him was hurt in the battle and never made it back to the spot where you could pass back from 1864 to the present. He stated that his friend lived his remaining years in that time and died there in the 1930's.

Everybody laughs at the guy, but I don't know. I mean, the story went worldwide, and some big-shot professors of the paranormal were involved. But the missing kid's parents maintained that he was abducted unseen and probably murdered. It's easy to make fun of Renny, but it *could* have happened, right? At any rate, whenever I'm helping Grandpa Willis and Renny is around, he'll take me aside and warn me, 'Don't get him started, okay, Thad'?

Anyway, I got in the truck with Grandpa and we drove over there, where Renny was finishing up the carpentry and plumbing that needed to be done. Grandpa told me the new guy's name was Adam Conway and his stuff was in a storage unit on the grounds. There were several of them there, as residents came and went at an alarming rate.

"Most of them stick around until the law or bill collectors catch up to them," said Grandpa.

"What about him?"

"He's in his *own* category."

That sounded intriguing. "Is he—"

"Thad, I told you I can't say much about him. Just help me move him in and don't say anything other than 'hello.' Got it?"

"Okay."

"And if Renny is working near us, don't get him started, okay?"

"Okay." As we pulled up at apartment unit 14, I saw a guy standing by the entrance. He was probably in his late fifties or early sixties, with two of those metal canes that have a brace on them to go around your wrists. His hair was long and frizzy, down to his shoulders. He had a small pinched-looking face, almost childlike. And he was very tall, probably about 6'5" or 6'6".

"Is that the guy, Grandpa?"

"Yeah, that's Adam."

"Wow, tall. Was he a basketball player?"

"No."

We got out, and Grandpa went over to him. "My grandson Thad, here, is gonna help me and Renny get you situated."

"Thanks." He nodded to me. "How you doin, fella?"

"Fine, thanks." Up closer now, I took a good look at his face. He looked pretty beat-up, like life had done a number on him. All his facial features had a grizzled, worn look, and you could tell that just standing was uncomfortable for him, if not downright painful. Grandpa got an old lawn chair from the back of the pickup and opened it next to Adam, who nodded his appreciation and began the slow, painful act of sitting.

For the next hour or so, Grandpa, Renny, and I made trips from the storage unit to apartment 14. In the back corner there was a pile covered with a large blanket. When Grandpa and Renny were busy I peeked under there. There were three guitar cases. The guy didn't strike me as the musical type. Renny came back and I quickly covered them up.

"What about this stuff under the blanket, Renny?"

"Yeah, we gotta be real careful with that. He's got a couple valuable guitars there."

"Is he a musician or something?"

"I guess he was, but he doesn't play any more."

"So what *does* he do?"

"I don't know. From the looks of the guy, I'd say all he does is sit on his ass all day. But he seems nice." He shrugged and lifted the blanket. "Okay, you take that top one, and I'll take the other two. Remember to be careful."

You couldn't tell what kind of guitars they were from the cases, but being a guitarist, I made it a point to carry the top one carefully, while the other two kept banging against each other as Renny hauled them across the parking lot. The chair was empty now, and as we went up the ramp into the living room we found Adam sitting on his couch. His face lit up as we tromped into the room with the guitars.

"Where you want these?" asked Renny.

"Just put them right there," he said, pointing to an empty corner.

I laid the guitar case down flat, and Renny started to pile the other two on top.

"No, no!" Adam shouted. "Stand them up against the wall."

Renny did as he asked, while Adam shook his head. I guess they must have been real valuable, like Renny said.

"I play guitar, Mr. Conway. What have you got there?"

"Nothin' fancy, but they're my last ones. Used to have a nice collection at one time."

After a few minutes everything seemed settled, and Grandpa came in to go over rules and regulations with Adam. Renny and I went outside to wait. I was *not* going to 'get him started,' but Renny looked as though he was in a self-starting frame of mind.

"Now *that* guy has a few tales he's not telling."

"Yeah, I think so, but Grandpa—"

"Thad, your grandfather doesn't have a clue about what this guy is holding in."

"Well, he said—"

"Listen, I know about secrets, and being tortured by the truth. When I was eleven, four of us—"

Fortunately, Grandpa came out, and Renny, who had been told not to fill me with his wild tales, stopped abruptly. He said goodbye and walked to his car.

"You didn't get him started, did you, Thad?"

"No, he started on his own."

"Well, I got a little surprise for you. For helping me, I'm gonna let your band use one of the storage units to rehearse in if you want."

My face lit up. "That would be great! Thanks a lot, Grandpa." A thought came to me. "What about outlets?"

"I'll give you a power strip, and you'll be able to get your instruments and amps plugged in, but no mikes. And you'll have to keep the volume low. These people need their sleep in the daytime since few of them work and they're usually up all night drinking and shooting dope."

That got the usual laugh from me. "What about the new guy? Is he one of those, too?"

Grandpa's face got stern. "What did I tell you about him?"

"Not to ask questions."

"Then don't. Just let him be."

. . .

When I got home I called the guys with the good news. Everyone was thrilled, and I was acknowledged as the guy who got things done.

Within a couple of days we were rehearsing there after school, as the apartments were within walking distance. I don't know if all the comments my grandfather made about the residents there were true. There was no evidence of big booze and drug parties, and no sign of Adam Conway, but we could see his side window and his entrance, complete with the new ramp.

I made it a point to tell the guys about Adam, how he had just moved in, and how my grandfather wanted him left in peace. They all agreed and didn't mention it again. I guess it was just me, then. I couldn't get it out of my head how Renny had said that he knew the look of someone with a secret.

We started rehearsing, being careful not to turn the amps up too high. We had five rock classics down so far, but you can't do a show or even a set with so thin a playlist, so we debated and argued for a while on what we should do.

We plodded on like this for a couple weeks. A high school dance was coming up and Marta King, head of the entertainment committee, asked me in history class if our band would like to perform.

"The entire dance, or just a small set?"

"Either one," she said.

"I don't know if we're ready, Mart. Could I check with the guys and let you know?"

"Okay, but I gotta know by Friday."

So I polled the guys over the phone and the debate was on. Norm and Cal were okay with it, but Zeb and especially Denny were dead-set against it.

"If we play now we're gonna make fools of ourselves and nobody will call us again, *ever,* " Denny protested.

Zeb stated we needed more time to "get the kinks out" and polish our delivery.

It ended up being my call, and the next day I told Marta we were gonna pass, but to keep us in mind in the future. She said she would, but I don't know if she meant it.

So *The Gordon County Renaissance Band* went back to the drawing board. We added a few more songs, and dropped the word 'Band' from our name. No big deal. I guess it *was* too long a name.

. . .

By mid-October we were a lot better. Everyone agreed that we were ready to play an extended set at the Halloween dance, if we were asked. We weren't. At our next rehearsal the guys were down, but trying to look at the big picture. Zeb suggested we get Marta over here to listen to us before the Thanksgiving dance. We all thought that would seal the deal, and were just talking among ourselves when we happened to look up and see Adam Conway in the doorway.

"You'll never get any better standing there talking," he said. "I can hear you from my living room. You're not bad, but you still need work."

"You play in a band?" asked Denny.

"Back in the 70's."

"A famous band?" asked Zeb.

Adam looked down. "I played with a lot of good musicians in my time. I might be able to give you guys some tips."

"Like *what?* " asked Denny, with an edge to his tone.

"For one, your bass and drummer are not synched up, and your guitars are not finishing their strands properly. Your keyboard man is almost inaudible. You gotta give him a melody or harmony line that brings out his sound."

I thought Denny was gonna tell Adam to go screw or something, but he stood there silently, then said, "Sounds like you know what you're talking about."

Adam smiled. "Believe me, it's probably the *only* thing I still know."

"So who did you play with? Anybody famous?" asked Norm.

Again, Adam looked down and sighed. "Why don't we focus on getting you guys where you want to be."

Everybody looked at each other and nodded. For the next ten minutes Adam gave us subtle tips we never would have come upon on our own. Little things, like at the beginning of a song Zeb and Norm should actually make eye contact, and the same for me and Denny.

"Who should *I* look at?" asked Cal.

"Whoever has the intro." He paused and gave us a critical look. "Do you guys even know how to count?"

"Like beginners in the school band?" scoffed Denny.

"Yes. A tempo count-off. If you don't start the song together, you'll be screwed up the whole way."

Then he asked Denny and me to play some of our riffs, and told us we weren't *phrasing* them correctly. We kept trying to do what he told us, but Denny was starting to lose patience. I shot him a look, and he soldiered on. He directed Cal to hold some chords longer, and play his strains with a little more "zip," as he called it. Norm was instructed to "accentuate his fills," the technical term for playing a crisper drum line. Anybody could see that the guy really knew his stuff. And I could see that standing there that long was taking a toll on him.

He looked at his watch during the next lull. "Fellas, I gotta get back and take my pain medication and lie down." He smiled. "Just more penance for some bad choices. Keep at it, fellas, and thanks for listening to an old has-been." He shuffled out.

A short time later everyone had packed up and gotten rides home. I locked up the shed, since Norm and Cal were leaving the drums and keyboards there, along with our amps. And despite my grandfather's warnings, I walked over to apartment 14 and knocked on the door.

• • •

I just wanted to thank him for helping us, since no one else had said anything. He called for me to come in, and I entered to find him sitting on his couch with an acoustic guitar, a vintage Martin D-20, worth thousands now. He noticed my shocked expression.

"Sweet, huh? The only acoustic I kept. The other two are electric."

"What are *they?*"

"A Gibson and a Fender Stratocaster."

"Wow."

He started playing the Martin, just improvising riffs up and down the fretboard. I had never heard any guitar *sing* like that. I didn't know if I should *kneel* in his presence, or take my own guitar and smash it. He stopped abruptly and laughed a bit.

"I can still play a little."

"I'll say."

In the next few seconds there was an imperceptible shift in the vibe. "So what is it you want, Thad?"

"I just wanted to thank you for helping us."

"No, no. What is it you want from *music,* from your *band?*"

I had to think a second. "Have fun. Have a little status, maybe." I wasn't entirely sure.

He nodded and put the guitar down gently. "That's fine, but do you realize how many millions of people are successful and happy and have nothing to do with music?"

"Sure, I guess, but they probably have something else that they're good at."

"Right. You're young. You got a million choices ahead of you. Don't make music some kind of god you worship."

"Huh?"

"Thad, when the music's over, you're stuck with the person you were before you strapped on that guitar. And it doesn't matter if it's a Stratocaster or a second hand piece of crap from a pawn shop." He lowered his voice. "When the music's over, all you got left is you."

"I'm not sure—"

"Look at me, Thad. I was rolling in it at one time. And now I take pain pills to get through the day and live in this tiny shithole. No offense, your grandfather and Renny did a nice job. By the way, what's with him?"

"He claims to have time-travelled when he was young. Can't stop talking about it."

He jabbed his finger at me. "And that's what *he's* stuck with now, because he couldn't move on from it. You get it?"

"I think so. Enjoy music, but move on if it's time."

He smiled broadly, struggled to his feet and stuck out his hand. As I shook it, he said, "Thad, I think you're gonna be all right. And who knows, one day you might strap on that Fender over there and amaze the hell out of your friends."

My thoughts were tripping over each other. *That* would be nice."

"You got a name for your band?"

"Yeah, we're *The Gordon County Renaissance.*"

The *what?"*

. . .

I decided not to tell the guys what Adam had said about music, and how incredible he was on guitar. I didn't want my grandfather to accidentally overhear anything from them. He wasn't going to hear it from me.

Two things really stuck with me. The guy was so passionate about keeping music in perspective with one's "real" life, and he was so talented there was no way, in my mind, that he was just some club musician. He said himself that at one time he was "rolling in it." That must have meant he was making a ton of money. He was famous at one time, or at least his band was. Some *bands* are famous without people knowing who the individual *members* are. I was sure he was one of those.

I was on my computer for hours trying to find him. I found *twenty-five* Adam Conways just in the professions, not to mention "regular people." But wouldn't he have been one of the twenty-five professionals? It came down to one of two things: he was lying about being a successful, famous musician, or the name 'Adam Conway' was just a cover.

I added this to what I was already keeping quiet about. For the next week things went back to the usual routine; school, homework, and band rehearsal. All the guys were making an effort to incorporate the suggestions Adam, or whoever this guy was, had given us. We didn't see him for days.

He finally showed up that Friday, having carried a folding chair out to the storage unit, and asked if he could listen in. We were okay with that, and played a few of our standards for him. There was a noticeable difference in our sound and technique now, and Adam seemed pleased that we had taken his suggestions. We were getting into such a "zone" when we played that we didn't even notice when he left.

. . .

I read in some story someplace that no situation in life remains static very long. But when you're seventeen, you don't spend much time thinking that things will change drastically.

We were rehearsing the following Monday when Grandpa Willis's truck came to a screeching halt by our open storage unit door. Instead of my grandfather getting out, it was Renny, hustling over to us. I knew right away something was wrong.

"Thad," he said, breathing heavily, "your grandfather had a heart attack or something. I called 911 and they took him to the hospital. They called your parents. I can drive you there if you want."

"Okay." My mind was whirling. Norm took over and made everybody clear out, taking the key from me to lock up.

On the ride to the hospital I asked Renny what happened.

"We were at the post office, and when we got back to the truck, he started having a lot of pain and sat down on the curb. He could hardly breathe, so I called 911."

"What were you guys doing at the post office?"

"Adam wanted two of his guitars shipped someplace."

"What?"

"Yeah, he was sending them to his sister in Florida."

At that point my brain couldn't process any more, and my concern for Grandpa Willis took over.

Renny left me off at the hospital entrance. "I'll wait at home until I hear something from your parents, okay?"

"Thanks, Renny."

Once inside, I asked the receptionist where Grandpa was and took the elevator to the second floor. Grandpa was in ICU with my parents already in his room. I was worried, scared, and angry. He was only sixty-seven, and kept himself pretty fit, doing manual labor and not smoking. This didn't seem fair. Dad told me he had a fairly serious "cardiac event" and was in a sedated state, but fully conscious.

A social worker came in and asked to see my parents in her office, so my mother asked me to keep him company while they were gone. He was conscious, like I said before, but all his defenses were down. He was talking about how he wished he could have done more for me, and how he wished my dad could have spent more time with me, and how he was going to give him a "good talking to" about it.

I'm not *proud* of what I did next, but I'm *glad* I did it. "Grandpa, why were you shipping Adam's guitars to his sister?"

"He didn't want the girlfriend getting her hands on them."

"What girlfriend?"

"The one in the car with him when he had the accident. She got paralyzed, and sued the hell out of him. That was a long time ago."

"So who is he?"

"I don't know. Part of his settlement with the girl was he couldn't benefit from his former fame. Adam Conway's not his real name."

"I already suspected that."

"You're a smart boy, Thad." He struggled to sit up. "When you see Renny, thank him for me and tell him to get his ass going on those three units we have to fix up."

I held back a laugh. "I will, Grandpa."

"And don't get him started."

. . .

They were keeping Grandpa in the hospital for a few more days, and then he was going to a nursing home. For the next few weeks things were different. I wasn't as available for band practice. It was just as well. Everyone was in kind of a rut. Even when we did practice we never saw Adam anymore.

In my grandfather's absence Renny was getting run ragged by the tenants. I bet there were days when he wished he *was* back in 1864.

When I visited Grandpa I knew enough not to mention all the things he let slip about Adam when he was heavily sedated.

And I had plenty to think about with Adam Conway. So he *had* been somebody in the music world long ago, and he messed it up with a car accident that left his girlfriend both paralyzed and vengeful. I didn't have the faintest clue as to who he was, and didn't have the time to search, but it did keep me wondering sometimes.

Weeks passed. Grandpa came home from the nursing facility, but refused to come live with us. Social Services of Senior Citizens had people coming over his house for meals, cleaning, and to monitor his recovery. He was itching to get back to work, but we all knew that was not going to happen any time soon. Renny had to hire a guy to help him. I felt sorry for the new guy. He probably heard the time travel story every day.

The Dance Committee had overspent on their first two dances, so there was no Thanksgiving *or* Christmas dance. They had to do fundraisers just to get back in the black. I stayed friendly with Marta on the off-chance we would get tapped to play at one of the remaining dances.

During the winter we rehearsed, but not as often. We no longer had an objective in mind, we just liked playing the oldies, and thanks to some of Adam's suggestions, we were starting to sound pretty good. About once a week we would find him in our doorway, sitting on a folding chair, listening. He never said a word to us any more, and would disappear as innocuously as he appeared. None of us, least of all me, felt comfortable initiating conversation with him.

. . .

On Monday, March 4th, Grandpa made his triumphant return, under some restrictions from his doctor, and more than a few protests about those restrictions. He could only do light carpentry and plumbing. The rest was supervisory.

The following Monday Grandpa called and asked if we were rehearsing the following day. I told him 'yes;' we played there on Tuesdays and Fridays now.

"Good. There's a little surprise for you in the storage unit."

"What is it?"

"You'll see."

When we got there the next day to rehearse, we found police, an ambulance, and the M. E. outside Adam's apartment. Grandpa came over to me, standing there with the rest of the band, dumbfounded.

"Thad, I'm so sorry. He left a note on his door, probably last night after I left."

"What note?" I was still not getting it.

Renny came over, bursting with news. "He overdosed on pain pills and tequila. Had a note on his door with one word on it."

"What was it?" I asked, still stunned.

"Enough," Renny said. "That was it. 'Enough.' Left a phone number on his coffee table. It's his sister in Jacksonville. The police are contacting her."

I didn't want to look at this scene any more. We trooped over to the shed and unlocked it. We had no intention of playing. We were just gonna hang out a while, then go home. I remembered Grandpa saying there was a surprise for me in there, and right by my place in our set-up was a black guitar case. Inside was a classic 1973 Fender Stratocaster. Taped to it was a plastic card, a Florida driver's license from 1986.

The picture showed a 35-year-old Adam Conway, under his real name, George Ramsey.

. . .

Everything happened so fast. Within minutes of getting home, everyone in the band knew that George Ramsey was a guitarist in the band *Hell House*, a famous and successful Southern Rock group from the late 60's through the early 80's. They were second only to *The Allman Brothers Band* in that time period. Originally from Jacksonville, they based themselves in Atlanta after they were discovered.

Fame and fortune got the better of them, though. From the mid-seventies until they disbanded, they were dogged by a series of misfortunes that included car accidents, arrests, addictions, a shooting in a bar fight, and other personal demons. Four years after they disbanded, George Ramsey, high and drunk, had wrapped his Jaguar around a tree, paralyzing his girlfriend. I already knew the rest of *that* story.

But his sister wanted the world to know about the sad final chapter. She informed the press, and two days later, reporters from everywhere were here interviewing my grandfather, Renny, (Oh boy!) residents of the apartment building, and the members of *The Gordon County Renaissance*. It wasn't long before everyone in town and the music world knew that I was "the boy with George Ramsey's guitar."

For a few days, our band had more publicity than we could have ever imagined. We even got to perform a song on the local newscast, with me playing the Fender. George Ramsey, alias Adam Conway, had made us the hottest musical ticket in northwest Georgia. I still sometimes wonder if he knew this would happen. Had he decided to help us get that "big break?" Was he leaving a final musical legacy? Or was it just that people can't get enough of that all-too-common combination of fame and death?

Needless to say, Marta asked us to play the "Spring Fling" in mid-April. We accepted.

By then, the news had faded, but at the high school, *Hell House* now had a cult following, and I was famously "the boy with George Ramsey's guitar." The anticipation of our performance grew, and we rehearsed our asses off.

On Friday, April 19th, we set up in the school cafeteria. Norm, Denny, Cal, Zeb, and I were ready to take our first steps in the musical world. Strange. As Marta stood at my mike introducing us, all I could hear was George Ramsey's voice in his living room trying to put me on the right path in life.

"Okay, kids, let's welcome a local band I'm sure you're all familiar with by now," announced Marta.

The audience was already cheering as I took Marta's place at the mike. The guys were waiting for my count-off to start our first number.

"Hey, everybody," I began. "We're *The Gordon County Renaissance!*" It got louder. "And yes, I'm the boy with George Ramsey's guitar!" I yelled, holding it up. I waited for quiet, then lowered my voice. "But when the music's over ..."

"HILLWALKERS"
2013

THE HISTORY

Long before the Ohio Indians were relocated to a Kansas reservation in 1843, the Wyandot inhabited northern Ohio. In what is now Fairmont, they worshipped the Nine Great Spirits who inhabited a steep hill. The spirits protected and guided the tribe, and the sacred hill was a place of worship and contemplation.

Nearly a century later, as Fairmont became a factory and mill town and grew into a city, citizens began buying land on the steep, half-mile hill to build homes and raise families. The spirits saw that the inhabitants were honorable people, and decreed that the first nine boys there would have the honor and task of protecting the sacred hill.

*Between 1949 and 1960 eleven children were born to the new inhabitants, nine of them boys. As the last of the original Wyandot were dying off in Kansas, the Nine Great Spirits ensured that the big hill, which was now three separate hills in a middle class neighborhood, would be honored and protected for all time. The spirits called the nine boys **Che'estaheh da seten: Hillwalkers.***

THE GEOGRAPHY

Lilac Lane was a deceiving name. The half-mile rise now had no lilacs growing anywhere on it. About two-hundred yards up it took a sharp left. At this point the houses started. The lower half of the hill contained an exit ramp and overpass from Ohio Route 15. As the hill ascended, there were side streets growing from it. Lilac Lane continued upward, giving birth to two more steep hills. Harrison Drive, one of the side streets was branched by Pershing Hill, shorter but steeper than Lilac Lane, running parallel, about seventy yards away. Between Pershing hill and Lilac Lane were houses and pristine woods.

Seventy yards further up, Richards Street sprouted off, going left, and forty yards down it had its own hill growing from it, Pratt Hill, a three-hundred yard incline running parallel to Lilac Lane on its other side.

Lilac Lane itself was a dead end, but at its top a right turn became Calvano Street. *That,* too, was a dead end, but before it could become Amicko's woods, it intersected with the top of Pershing Hill.

The four roads known as Lilac Lane, Calvano Street, Pershing Hill, and Harrison Drive formed a unique quadrangle of mystery and enchantment for nine boys who had grown up in that neighborhood. There were other children, but they were newcomers to the hilly east end of Fairmont, which had grown to nearly thirty-eight thousand by the mid-1960's.

• • •

Tony and Lee Temmons of 100 Pratt Hill stood at the window of their living room, looking out at the top of Lilac Lane where it turned onto Calvano Street. Nine boys, including their sons Tommy, Lonnie, and Roy were engaged in a rousing game of street football. The others included Duane and Denny Lovetere of 331 Lilac Lane, Len and Charlie Daignault of 309 Lilac Lane, and John and Frank Martin of 284 Lilac Lane.

Tony shook his head and laughed. "Those guys," he said, "it's only the first week of school and they're playing football."

"I think Tommy got outvoted," observed Lee. "He would play baseball all year if he could."

"They could go up to Redmont field and play there," Tony offered.

"Sometimes I feel sorry for Len and Charlie's sisters. They have no one to play with."

"They can play with the boys," Tony said.

"Really? Do you think those girls want to be running up and down the street trying to catch a football?" Lee took another look out the window. "They're gone. I didn't even see them leave."

Where Calvano Street met the top of Pershing Hill, nine boys raced down the steep incline towards "The Big Rock," a ten-foot ledge which served as their meeting place. The plan was to work back towards the woods that bordered Pershing Hill and came out near the top of Lilac Lane. There were rocks to scale, trees to climb, and frogs to catch in any one of several streams.

Lonnie Temmons saw it first. The Big Rock and surrounding area had been littered and defaced. Bright blue chalk writing covered the rock, the ground was awash in candy wrappers, soda cans, and broken glass. "Guys, look. Somebody wrote swears all over."

"Jesus Christ!" yelled John Martin. "I just stepped on glass!"

"Take off your sneaker," advised Tommy. "If there's glass in your foot you can pull it out."

While John attended to the wound, Duane Lovetere and the others surveyed the mess. "Who the hell did this, guys?" he asked.

"I bet it was Robby Faine," said Charlie.

"What about the Zhuckov brothers?" asked Len.

"You got Kenny Babonski and Jim Pender," Denny Lovetere offered. "They both live on Pershing."

"Don't forget Donny Casale," added Lonnie.

"Christ, that's seven people," complained Duane.

Tommy Temmons, the most resourceful, spoke up. "Take a look at what they wrote. That might give us a clue."

Thus began an intense reading of the chalk messages, most of which were profanities, some of which the boys had never actually seen *written* before.

"What's this word mean?" asked Lonnie Temmons.

John and Frank Martin roared with laughter. "Don't tell him!" John shouted.

"C'mon, you guys," whined Lonnie. He turned to his older brother. "Tommy, what does 'cont' mean?"

Duane Lovetere nearly fell over. "Jesus, he can't even *read* it! That's a 'u,' Lonnie!"

"What does it mean?"

Fred Martin pulled Lonnie aside and whispered in his ear, mindful of the two youngest, Roy and Charlie, who seemed to show no interest in the profanities, busying themselves picking up glass and soda cans.

John Martin put his sock and sneaker back on. "It didn't break the skin. Still, I'm *pissed!"*

Duane Lovetere positioned himself atop the Big Rock, and raised his arms as though orating to an audience. "Someone must die for this," he said, with mock seriousness. There were a few laughs, but they were all thinking of what must be done to the guilty party.

1969, THREE YEARS LATER

The nine were still close friends, but few occasions found them together. They had formed subsets of the main group, mostly based on age and interests. Duane, the oldest, was twenty, between his junior and senior year of college, and Roy Temmons was coming up on his ninth birthday. It would appear odd that a boy that young would be included, but there seemed to be an unwritten code among them: to be a brother of one was to be included.

Tommy, at sixteen was closest to Duane in age, and Duane often sought him out on summer days to talk, play chess, cards, or have a catch. He went out his front door to find Lonnie Temmons, two years younger than Tommy, on his porch about to ring the doorbell. Lonnie was a year younger than Duane's brother Denny, and they often spent time building model cars.

"I was just coming up your house to see Tommy," Duane said, laughing.

"And I came down here to get Denny," Lonnie said, shrugging.

"Denny's not home. He went golfing with my dad."

"Tommy's not home, either. He's down at John's. They're trying to form a band."

"So what do we do now?" Duane said, sitting on the porch steps as Lonnie sat next to him.

"I don't know. *We* never actually do anything." Lonnie racked his brain. "So you got one more year of college, then you'll be a history teacher, huh?"

"Yeah, be funny as hell if I got hired at the high school and you were in my class."

"That'd be so cool, though." Lonnie tried to think of something that would perk Duane's interest, wanting to show that he had "evolved" from the boy who complained about everything and everybody. "They're gonna land on the Moon next month."

"I know. Been waiting for this since seventh grade."

"Hope they make it."

"They will."

Lonnie searched for another topic. "Remember when Donny and Robbie messed up the Big Rock? Man, we got them good."

"Yeah, but I thought we were gonna have trouble with Robbie's sister. She was such a 'cont.'"

"Very funny."

"Well, I guess you've come a long way since then."

"Remember when Len tied Charlie to a telephone pole that Easter Sunday?"

"And perhaps I spoke too soon."

Lonnie's face sobered. He badly wanted to be taken seriously by Duane. He now chose a *personal revelation.* "Did I ever tell you about this dream I keep having?"

Duane ditched the sarcastic rejoinder he was ready to deliver and stared. "What dream?"

"It's really weird. All of us guys are in it, and we all walk around the neighborhood, like guards."

Duane looked intently at the fourteen-year-old he had known all his life. "You have a dream where we all walk around the neighborhood to protect it?"

Lonnie was encouraged by Duane's sudden interest. "Yeah, and we're all wearing—"

"Black hooded sweatshirts and only our eyes show, and they're *red.*"

Lonnie tried to breathe, but his wide-open mouth would not cooperate. His shocked silence was confirmation to Duane.

"We walk the three hills," continued Duane. "Lilac, Pershing, and Pratt."

Lonnie nodded slowly.

. . .

Duane and Lonnie agreed to bring up the topic to their respective brothers, then check back. No point in jumping the gun on something this eerie.

Lonnie learned that Tommy had had the dreams, but never told anyone. Tommy was a middle-of-the-road person, never straying too far into any category. He was smart, but not a brain, sports-loving without being a jock, fun-loving without being a clown, and forthright without being a goody-goody. He was intelligent enough to know that recurring dreams of himself and his friends lurking in the darkness, vigilant protectors of their turf could have a definite meaning.

Nine-year-old Roy was aware of the dreams, but feared ridicule by his brothers and some sanction from his parents, possibly an earlier bedtime. He did not have a grasp of the detail and nuances of the dreams, but had passed all the tests his brothers gave him, listing details of the dream, and not merely "rubber-stamping" anything they mentioned.

Duane Lovetere gave the same test to his brother Denny, now fifteen. Denny had been experiencing the dreams also. In his case, like Tommy's, his waking life was far more pleasurable and important to him than any nighttime images that did not affect his daily life.

Before Apollo 11 began its journey to the Moon, Duane, Tommy, and Lonnie had gotten each of the Martin and Daignault brothers alone and asked them if they had a recurring dream of walking the hills at night in sinister black hoods.

The Martin brothers had shared the dream experience with each other, but had kept it secret, their image as rough-and-tumble neighborhood guys more important to them than the dream's essence.

The Daignault brothers were, as usual, at the lower end of the scale. As Tommy once said, they were "okay guys, just not that smart." They admitted to having the dream, but wondered if the others were "trying to trick them" by getting them to admit it. The dreams meant little to them, obviously too deep to process.

"Maybe they'd get it if there was a female spirit with her tits hanging out," remarked John.

"And even then," concluded Tommy.

. . .

On the morning of July 21st the nine met on Lilac Lane in front of the Lovetere residence. The topic was not the eerie recurring dream. The previous night they had watched two human beings walk on the Moon. Although they had all stayed up till nearly 2 A.M. they seemed supercharged with emotion.

"That was so unreal."

"I was watching it and I *still* couldn't believe it."

"They looked like ghosts walking around up there."

"Too bad the Russians didn't get to see it. Stupid commie government."

"I kept waiting for some monster to come into the picture and attack."

"You're an idiot, Len."

· · ·

The drug and thief lifestyle had finally caught on in Fairmont.

This sub-culture did have one major characteristic in common with the mainstream: it was supply and demand, and cash was king.

Phil and George Chaussey had grown up on Richards Street, only fifty yards away from the bottom of Pratt Hill. They were seventeen and sixteen, respectively; lazy, clever, and hard-core drug users. With the price of marijuana on the rise, their skills as housebreakers and burglars were constantly needed. The hills of the east end of Fairmont were a low crime area, and the pickings looked good.

Phil and George knew that on the evening of July 26th, many residents of the surrounding neighborhoods would be at Fairly Stadium for the annual Northern Ohio Drum Corps competition, followed by fireworks.

They set out around 8:30 P.M. wearing boy scout knapsacks and carrying large gym bags. Many houses showed lights and movement, accompanied by the sounds of televisions through open screened windows.

"How come all these people are home?" demanded Phil. "Where's their sense of community involvement?"

"Shut up and keep walking," said George. "There's gotta be something up further."

The Chausseys did their "recon" all the way up Pratt Hill. When they were nearly at the top, they finally got lucky. Two houses, one on each side, numbers 97 and 100, were obviously empty, no cars in the driveway and no lights on.

George poked Phil and motioned at number 97. Phil nodded and the two teens stepped into the driveway. Nine figures stood between them and the house, seemingly materializing out of nowhere. They stood shoulder to shoulder, dressed in identical dark pants with black hooded sweatshirts. With the hoods up, their faces were obscured. Two red circles glared from each face, or where a face *would* have been.

"Jesus!" hissed George. "Who the hell are *you* guys?"

The nine figures advanced one step. They pointed at the would-be thieves, then held out both hands in a "halt" gesture. All was silent, but both Phil and George were getting *definite* vibes.

At this moment, on the corner of Pratt Hill and Clearview Drive, twenty-one-year-old Bobby Nichols had started up his super-charged 1956 Chevy Bel-Air, a vehicle he had spent a year rebuilding and customizing. He had promised Andrea, his girlfriend, that he would meet her at Fairly Stadium at 8:30 to watch the festivities. He was late, as usual, but the 356cc engine in the Chevy could help him to not be *as* late. He threw the red and white Bel-Air into reverse, peeled out as he shifted into first, and roared down Pratt Hill.

Sixty yards away, Phil and George Chaussey's blood ran cold. Although no words had been spoken by the nine figures, the message was clear: ***Run for your lives.***

"Phil," George said in a low voice, "these guys aren't screwing with us. Just turn around and run."

"Gotcha."

Without another word, Phil and George Chaussey ran from the driveway and into the front bumper of Bobby Nichols's Chevy, which had already topped forty mph.

. . .

The Temmons family, returning home after an evening of music and fireworks, were not allowed to get to their Pratt Hill driveway. They realized there had been a serious accident, turned around, and went up Lilac Lane to their other driveway. Lee hustled the three boys inside while Tony went down his Pratt Hill driveway to investigate.

He observed three police cruisers and two ambulances scattered on both sides of the street closest to his and Joseph Bassone's house. He recognized one of the officers.

"Hey, Mike, what happened here?"

"Hi, Tony. Sorry you couldn't get in. Bad accident. Young guy driving down the hill hit two people in the road."

"They hurt bad?"

"They're dead. Two teenage brothers from Richards Street. We got a car going there now."

"Who were they?"

"Read tomorrow's paper, Tony. That's all I can say."

A flashlight beam sliced across and fixed on a tree branch in the Temmons' yard. A voice called, "There's the other one, Al. It's up in the tree here. *Both* kids had knapsacks and gym bags with them. And I don't think they were going camping or to the YMCA."

The officer walked over to where Officer Mike Isseppi and Tony Temmons stood. "These two were obviously out to rob houses while people weren't home, and they got run over. Makes you wonder, sometimes."

Across the street, Bobby Nichols stood with another officer, making his statement. He had been reassured that it appeared the accident was not his fault. Still, Bobby felt he was about to throw up. He had stood up Andrea, and months of work on the Bel-Air was ruined.

. . .

Unfortunately for Nichols, further investigation revealed that he was travelling at a high rate of speed, and charges were preferred. His claim of being distracted by a "row of red lights" in Bassone's driveway was discounted, as the only red lights found were two small driveway reflectors. He was charged with vehicular manslaughter. The case went back and forth for months, with deals and counteroffers. A final settlement resulted in a jail sentence of three to five years.

From July of 1969 on there were many reports by residents of the hill neighborhood of seeing a "large group of men, dressed in black hooded sweatshirts," walking at night. Many of the reports included seeing "red lights or beacons" emanating from the head area of the prowling group.

Police investigated these reports vigorously, as it had the ear markings of a gang on the loose in peaceful Fairmont. The police never had a single sighting, and eventually surmised that people were imagining it, or were influenced by Bobby Nichols's claim that he saw a row of red lights in Bassone's driveway that fateful July evening.

The Lovetere, Temmons, Martin, and Daignault brothers were well aware of these reports. None had ever seen the Hillwalkers, as some people now called them. All the boys believed there was *something* going on in that area at night, somehow connected to their dreams.

One evening in November of 1974, Tommy Temmons, now twenty-one and studying music in Boston, was on Thanksgiving break and was making the short walk home from John Martin's house after jamming with him and a couple of others. Tommy had gotten to the top of Lilac Lane, just feet from his own back yard, when he saw in front of him, not ten feet away, nine figures in black, red eyes glowing.

"Jesus. Who—"

The figures advanced two steps towards him, arms extended at waist level, an almost welcoming gesture.

"Who are you?"

Although no words were *spoken,* they communicated to the second-born male child of the three hills. ***We are the spirit embodiment of the nine who have been deemed worthy to protect the sacred land.***

"You guys are *real?*"

We do the bidding of the Nine Great Spirits of the Wyandote

Tommy was speechless. He looked around to see if anyone was about. There was no one. After all, it was nearly 11 P.M.

You and the other Chosen Ones must begin your task to keep the sacred land pure.

"But I—"

Gather the others of the Che'estaheh da seten and walk the hills to keep them from harm.

"What if—"

You will do this, second-born. Gather as many of the Che'estaheh da seten as you can, and when the spirits call to you, walk here at night and protect the land on the three hills.

"But what if nobody wants to do it?"

You WILL all do this. You have been chosen.

Tommy looked down to think about how he would explain this to the others. He looked up to find the path to his backyard unblocked. In the glow of the streetlight, his watch read 11:05 P. M. He knew that five miles away, in another part of Fairmont, Duane Lovetere would still be awake.

. . .

"It was kind of a 'do it or else' thing," Tommy Temmons said into the phone.

"Jesus, I don't hear from you in months, and you lay *this* on me," replied Duane.

"They were pretty scary, Duane. It's like we have to do what the spirits say."

"So, the Che'estaheh da seten *are* real." He paused. "All those people calling the cops since those guys got run over, that was them."

"Yeah."

"I had a feeling. I been teaching here five years now, and the school library has a lot of info on this whole area."

"What did you find?"

"Our neighborhood *was* sacred land for the Wyandot. But they got moved out in 1843 to Kansas. I guess the spirits didn't make the trip."

"Yeah, and they appointed *us* to be the protectors because we were the first males born here."

"So exactly what do we have to do?"

"Walk the three hills when they tell us."

"Did they give you any idea how *often?*"

"I don't think they have a *schedule,* Duane."

"Jesus, I got a wife, a house, a kid on the way. What the *hell.* You go to school in *Boston. Nobody* knows where Len and Charlie are since they moved. Everybody else has jobs or is still in school."

"Duane, they said we had been chosen. And something tells me it wasn't up for debate."

"Do you realize the first time we go around that neighborhood at night people will have the cops on us like flies on shit. We're gonna be *exactly* what everybody was spooked about the past five years."

"We could tell the people on the hills what we're doing and why."

"Jesus, Tommy, c'mon. Who the hell is gonna believe the nine boogeymen made us do a Wyandot Indian version of a neighborhood watch?"

"That's *it!*" Tommy shouted. "Just inform the cops and the people on the hill that some of us original kids formed a neighborhood watch, and if they see us, we're just looking out for everybody. Whattaya think?"

Duane exhaled loudly. "Tell your brothers, and I'll call my brother and the Martins."

"What about Len and Charlie?"

"I have no idea where they are. Forget about them. But I got a question for you, Tommy."

"Yeah?"

"What do I tell my pregnant wife?"

. . .

Duane Lovetere and Tommy Temmons *did* inform as many residents of the three hills as possible that they planned to patrol the neighborhood. No other details or reasons were given.

A call to the Safety Officer of the Police Department was met with uneasy approval, with warnings *not* to carry weapons or confront anyone. "Just be a presence," they were told.

Then, of course, the now seven sons of the hills had to wait for some "sign." Eight days later, when Tommy was again home from school, all seven claimed to have had some type of subliminal message from *somewhere* that it was time. At sunset they set out from the bottom of Lilac Lane.

"How long do we have to be out here?" asked Frank Martin.

"Jesus, I don't know. Did anyone get any "message" on that?" asked Duane.

"Until 1 A.M." said Tommy.

"Really?"

"*I* don't know. Sounds good, though. Until the Hour of the Dead is over."

"That has nothing to do with *this.*"

"What do you suggest?"

"Once around the neighborhood."

And that is what they did. Occasionally they observed people at their windows watching. They ended in front of Duane and Denny's parents' house, 331 Lilac Lane.

"Hey," called Tommy. "Look over there," he said, pointing through the defoliated woods towards Pershing Hill. A line of red lights faced them.

"Christ, let's get out of here," whispered Lonnie.

"No," said Tommy, "we're supposed to be here. They're the spirit embodiment of *us*. Let's go over there and show them we're not afraid."

"But we *are!*" complained Lonnie.

"Tommy's right," said Duane. "We better do this." He laughed. "Hey, maybe they'll give us more *specific* instructions."

The seven walked to the top of Lilac Lane, turned right down Calvano Street and headed towards the intersection of Calvano and Pershing. Less than halfway down, the nine figures suddenly appeared directly in front of them.

"Wow," whispered Denny, "ask them if they could teach *us* how to do that."

"Shut the hell up, Denny."

After seemingly endless seconds of silence, Tommy mustered up the nerve to speak. "We are here protecting the three hills as you ordered."

It is good that you are here. The hills are sacred, and no bad should come to them. There are many evil ones who live among you now. You will do this as long as you are able

After another pause, Tommy finally spoke. "When should we return?"

"Good," whispered Duane. Some specifics, finally."

When the left half of the Moon is in the sky, the sons of the hills will gather here and become Che'estaheh da seten. Hillwalkers.

In the next moment the seven stood alone in the early December cold. From the nearest house a porch light went on and a front door opened. A man stood in the doorway. "You guys okay?" he called out.

"Yes, thanks," replied Tommy. "We were—"

"I know who you are," the man said reassuringly. "I'm Robert Willis. My wife and daughter and I saw who else was out here." He paused. "If you ever need a witness or anything like that, you know where to find me."

"So who do you think we are?" asked Duane.

"You're like a neighborhood watch, right?"

Duane stiffened proudly. "We are Che'estaheh da seten. *Hillwalkers.*"

DECEMBER, 2013

A half moon hung over Ohio Route 15 as Wallace Fairchild, his wife Theresa, and their seven-year-old daughter Briana headed toward exit 43. The night was cold, and the snow flurries which had begun earlier had picked up in intensity. It seemed as though the Fairchilds would get to their new home at 331 Lilac Lane ahead of the bad driving conditions that had been predicted.

They had bought a small, cozy ranch in a quiet neighborhood. Two brothers had put the house on the market the previous summer after their mother had passed away. The buyers and sellers had never actually met; all details and communications having taken place between lawyers and real estate agents.

As they pulled off the exit ramp, Wallace nudged his wife. "Terry, watch for the signs posted on the hill."

"What signs?"

"You'll know when you see them. Guaranteed."

At the end of the exit ramp, Wallace took a left and began the half-mile drive to their new home, the last house on the left. Fifty yards ahead on the right was the first of several signs, belatedly posted in 2002 by an act of the Fairmont City Council:

THIS AREA PROTECTED
BY SPIRITS KNOWN AS
"HILLWALKERS"
DISREGARD THIS WARNING
AT YOUR OWN RISK

Theresa Fairchild did not know whether to laugh or be scared. "Is that for real, Walt?"

"Yes. I never noticed then when we looked at the house, but they've been there for years, I was told."

"Do we have anything to worry about here?" she asked, half-seriously.

"No, but maybe these kids up here do."

At the first sharp corner of Lilac Lane, a group of figures plodded along the side of the road, bundled up in coats, hats, and scarfs against the cold.

"Those don't look like kids, Walt. It's a bunch of older people," she said of the group, which consisted of seven men, ranging in age from fifty-three to sixty-four. "What in God's name are they doing here at this time of night in this weather?"

"Maybe they're an athletic club for seniors, and this is their workout."

"Your daddy's a funny guy, Briana."

Briana Fairchild turned around in the back seat to look at the curious group. "Mommy?"

"What is it, dear?"

"Why do all those men have red eyes?"

"BACKWOODS TALE #71"
2013

There are *many* strange tales from the backwoods of northern Maine. This is just one of them.

Starting with the Micmac tribe, the French, the English, and finally the English who called themselves Americans; anyone who lived up here for any length of time eventually came to realize that some things in nature are *un*natural.

1953

Through eighteen inches of snow the couple trod through the woods. The sixtyish pair, through forty years of marriage, actually *did* grow to resemble each other. They were short in stature, hunched over, and had the time-worn, grizzled look of people who have lived a life without luxury.

Claude and Rene Fallione, American born, of French-Canadian descent, took turns carrying their five-year-old grandson, Rudolph Pierre Fallione. Rene carried him in her arms, while Claude put the child's legs over his shoulders, resembling a circus elephant and rider as he swayed towards their destination this January morning. The temperature hovering at the ten-degree mark, all three were bundled in heavy jackets, snowshoes, gloves, and hats. Their destination was a stand of pine trees in a large open field.

The Micmac had told the French about this particular stand of pines, and word had been passed through generations to the present. Yes, the trees had been there that long. Some were only four feet tall, the tallest standing just over twelve feet. In the real world this would be impossible. But these were not ordinary trees. According to the Micmac, they had *always* been there, would *always* be there.

They were trees, yes, but they were much *more*. When asked by early French settlers what that meant, the Micmac would not elaborate. The "Ghost Pines," as the natives called them, had the power to *do things*. Again, the curious French inquired as to what *things* they could *do*. Again, the Micmac would not elaborate. Many French settlers concluded that they were given no answers because of the Micmac's limited knowledge of French. But others sensed that some things are better left unsaid, and some things in nature are *un*natural.

Claude and Rene stood fifteen feet from the stand of pines. The heavy snow the night before lay heaped on the branches, giving them an almost-human shape. Claude set the boy down.

"Rudy," said Claude, "deze here are da trees Grandma and me tells you about."

The boy looked in wonder at the trees, as though meeting a celebrity in the world of a five-year-old. "How did they get here?"

"Nobody knows dat, Rudy. Dey just here, dat's all."

"They look like Halloween ghosts," said Rudy.

"Da Micmac call dem da 'Ghost Pines,' Rudy," said his grandmother.

"How many are there?"

"You can't count dem, Rudy," replied Claude. "You never get da same number."

"I bet there's a million of them, Grandpa."

Claude put his hands on the boy's shoulders. "When you grows up an' you comes here yourself, da trees might not be where we is now."

The boy looked at his grandfather in awe. "Where will they be?"

"Dey only moves a little bit, but dey moves. Maybe you finds dem right over dere," he said, pointing a few feet away. "Maybe back dat ways a bit."

"Why do they move, Grandpa?"

"Nobody know, Rudy. Dey just do, dat's all."

"Can I touch one of them?"

"Maybe we try one time, okay?" he said, as Rudy jumped in anticipation.

Claude again raised the boy in his arms, putting him in the elephant rider position as he and Rene approached the stand of pines. As they neared, it felt as if the ten degrees of temperature was now *minus* ten.

"Dis ain't good," whispered Claude.

"Closer," called Rudy. "I want to touch one of the branches."

Claude approached the trees the way one would approach a wounded, frightened animal. Rudy reached out and *petted* the nearest branch. Its snow dropped, creating a chain reaction throughout the eight-foot pine. Claude braced himself. Rene backed up, missing her previous footprints and fell over backwards. The sound of her hitting the snow caused Claude to jerk around, and he lost both his balance and his passenger. Within seconds, all three were lying in the soft snow. Claude and Rene prepared to grab Rudy and run for their lives, but the silence was broken by squeals of laughter.

"All fall down," Rudy yelled, repeating the last line of a song they sang at school. "Grandpa, Grandma, the tree made us *all fall down.*"

"Dey have a little fun wid us, eh, Rudy," said Rene.

"Okay, you seen da 'Ghost Pines,' Rudy," said Claude, picking himself and the boy up. "Let's get goin' now before sumtin' else happen."

"The trees *like* me, Grandpa. They're my new friends."

I don't tink so, thought Claude, turning to head home.

1956

As his son Rudy led the way through the snow, John Fallione plodded his way through the stretch of woods leading to the pines his son had begged him to visit. John knew his late father Claude, along with his mother, had taken the boy here when he was five. With Rudy now at the "age of reason," he felt it was his duty to do the same. But on this visit there would be information for the boy to process. Rudy had not been here since that day in January of 1953, and still insisted that the trees were his friends.

As they cleared the woods and came upon the open field, John could see confusion and wonder on the boy's face.

"It's like Grandpa said. They're closer to the woods now and farther right. They moved. Did you know they move, Dad?"

"Yes, he told me the same thing," John answered, wondering how a five-year-old could be so precise in his recollection.

"He was right."

So was his doctor about his heart, thought John. "Rudy, did Grandpa tell you anything else about the trees?"

"On the way home he told me to always be …nice to them."

"You sure he didn't say 'respectful'?"

"That's it. Respectful."

"He give you a list of taboos?"

"What's that?"

"Things you should never do."

"Uh-huh. Never try to cut one down, don't break their branches, no fires near them, all that kind of stuff."

"Good."

Rudy had a serious look as he faced his father. "Grandpa said they have powers, they can do things."

John Fallione paused. "Rudy, everyone who lives around here knows about these trees. Some people believe, some don't."

"Some kids in school don't. They say it's just a Micmac superstition to scare people."

"Well, *we* know it's not just superstition."

"Didn't you come here when you were a boy?"

"When I was a boy, we were living in the Depression. We didn't have time. We all had to work to get money to live."

"Can I come here sometimes?"

"As long as you behave and do good in school."

"I will. I promise."

1958

And that was how I came to know the Ghost Pines. In the next two years I went there whenever I could. It was true. Every time I counted them I got a different number.

And I found out one thing that Grandpa and my dad never mentioned: they had a way of *communicating*. They didn't *talk*. I did not hear any "voices on the wind," but there was *something*. I don't exactly know how to describe it, but one time there seemed to be an uneasiness in the air. For some reason I can't identify, I had the urge to go in among them and look around.

I found some trash in there, probably left by these two mean kids, Joseph LaFrance and Tommy Ozolinth, who lived nearby in the opposite direction. At first I felt good about helping them keep their land pure, but then I thought about it more. Was I the trash collector for a stand of ancient pine trees? I walked further down the line to see if there was anything else left by Joseph and Tommy. I heard a rustling in the leaves at the bottom of one of the trees, and my heart jumped. Was it a snake waiting to strike? I picked up a stick and poked cautiously where the leaves had moved. Out came a blue jay, one wing askew, running in a semi-circle. It had been hurt somehow.

I had a deep love of nature, passed on to me by Grandpa Claude. I covered my hands with the sleeves of my sweatshirt and picked him up. I brought him home, and after a debate with my mother, was allowed to make a place for him in our basement. I had food and water for him. Dad wasn't much like Grandpa when it came to nature, but he approved.

The jay got a little stronger each day, and by the third day, I found him perched on Mom's basement clothesline. He looked at me as if to say, "What do *you* want?" I knew when Mom or Dad saw this he would have to be set free, so I proceeded to chase him around the basement. I finally caught him as my parents and little brother Jimmy watched, laughing hysterically. Dad opened the basement doors, and I carried him up as he pecked me. I threw him into the air, and he flew and perched on our nearest tree before taking off.

In my mind, the Ghost Pines had saved this bird, leading me to him. Maybe they knew I would nurse him back to health. Joseph or Tommy would have had a rock-throwing contest until they killed him. So even an insignificant bird was important to the sacred pines.

We didn't have computers or the internet in 1958, but we did have encyclopedias and libraries. That year I did all the research and reading I could on the Micmac and the early white settlers who once inhabited northwest Maine.

I began to formulate some theories on what these trees really were. I wrote a big report on it (five whole pages) and used it in school for one of our assignments. Most of the other boys were writing about men going into space someday, or even going to the Moon. Sounded pretty ridiculous to me. But I guess my theory of the Ghost Pines being the reincarnation (I looked that word up) of the souls of great Micmac warriors sounded just as ridiculous to the rest of the class. Most of the girls gave me these pitying, disinterested looks. A few of the boys seemed interested, but Joseph LaFrance and Tommy Ozolinth glared at me like I had said something unspeakable. I knew there was going to be trouble with them, I just had no idea *why*.

When Dad got home that day, I read him the report.

"Pretty good, Rudy. What makes you think the Ghost Pines are Micmac warriors?"

I was ready for that. "They never grow. You get so big, then you don't grow any more. These warriors would be different sizes in their lives, right? So now they are all different sizes, too."

Dad smiled. "So were they between four and twelve feet tall in their lives, Rudy?"

He had me on that one. "No, but ..."

"Just teasing, Rudy. Size is relative."

Whatever that meant. I completely forgot to tell him about the mean looks I got from Joseph and Tommy and that I thought they were going to lay for me.

By Thanksgiving I had somehow gotten a reputation in school as an oddball who talked to trees. I do *not* know how that happened. Wait, I do know. In school I constantly talked about the Ghost Pines and may have said that I had a very special relationship with them. I didn't actually say 'very special relationship,' but whatever passed for that, I probably said it. A few boys were still friendly to me, but I was shunned by everyone else, except for this one nice girl named Diana.

Joseph and Tommy were starting to push me around, and I knew I couldn't beat either of them in a fight. And any fight I might have with them would be with both of them at the same time. They lived on the other side of the big clearing where the Ghost Pines were, and they knew where to find me one Saturday afternoon. I was standing near the front of the pines, just communing with them, as I often did. Most of the time there was no communication from them, although a couple of times they seemed to "tell" me of sudden shifts in the weather, like big rainstorms or blizzards coming. In Maine you always have to keep one eye on the weather.

For some reason, on this rather pleasant Saturday in December, the pines were "warning" me about something. I stood with my back to them, looking up at the sky. It was crystal blue. I couldn't figure out why there would be anything to beware of.

"Well, well, if it isn't 'tree boy,'" came a voice from behind me.

I turned to find Joseph LaFrance and Tommy Ozolinth emerging from the pines. I took a quick look at the woods I had come through to see if I had any chance of outrunning them. But they were onto me.

"You run, Rudy, and you're gonna get it ten times worse," called Joseph.

"Yeah, you little fartfaced nature boy," added Tommy. "All your stupid crap about your tree friends. Let's see what they do for you now."

"What do you guys have against the pine trees?" I couldn't think of anything else to say.

"We don't believe in any of this Micmac superstition bullshit," spat Joseph. "My dad told me some of the early settlers here were slaughtered by the Micmac."

"But—"

"My relatives were some of the people that were wiped out, you pansy tree-hugger. And there you go saying these trees are the spirits of great warriors. I hate them, and I hate you for talking like they were something special. They were murderers of woman and children!"

I knew there had been some rogue war parties in colonial days. It was in our social studies book. Most of the Micmac were honorable, decent people. It was usually the whites who started the trouble. But I didn't think Joseph or Tommy was up for a history lesson, so I just stared at the ground.

"How come we were able to come through those pines and get the drop on you without them *protecting* you, huh, Rudy boy?" asked Tommy.

It would probably have made things worse to tell them the trees *had* warned me, so I shrugged and said nothing.

"Get over here!" ordered Joseph.

"What are you gonna do?" I asked, starting to tremble.

"I *said,* get over here."

I did what he said.

"Take your boots off," Joseph ordered.

"*What?* Take my—"

Before I knew it, they grabbed me and turned me upside down, my outstretched hands touching the ground. Tommy continued to hold me, while Joseph unbuckled my boots and pulled them off, throwing them aside. Tommy dropped me and I got up quickly.

"Pants," Joseph said, smiling.

No words made their way out of my wide-open mouth. Not the most patient person to begin with, Tommy threw me down over his outstretched leg. Joseph undid my belt and started pulling my pants off. I struggled, but Tommy kicked me in the head. It hurt like a bastard, and while I was whimpering and holding my head, Joseph got my pants off and walked back towards the pines. He was headed for the tallest one, a twelve-footer I called "The Chief."

"You like the Indian ways so much," Joseph said, we're gonna make a sacrifice to the Ghost Pines, Rudy. You can't climb these freakin' things, so if I get these on top of this big one, you won't be able to shake it down."

He paused and looked at me with pure hatred. "Now your trees will *look* as stupid as they *are.* Hey Tommy, what do you think of a *tree* wearing *pants?"*

"Ridiculous, Joe. Don't you agree, Rudy?"

I knew this was not up for debate. "Yes," I said calmly, "a tree wearing pants looks ridiculous."

I didn't think Joseph could throw them up there so that I couldn't get them down, but he oddly seemed to have a knack for it. Maybe he practiced throwing pants onto treetops after school, I don't know. On his third try, the open waist went right over the Chief's top. Joseph shook the tree as hard as he could. They didn't budge.

"There you go, Rudy, old boy," Joseph said. "And you better not tell on us. We didn't actually hurt you."

"Tommy kicked me in the head," I said, holding back tears.

"That was an accident," Tommy replied.

"Yeah, an accident," said Joseph. "I witnessed it."

"See you in school Monday," called Tommy.

They began to trudge off towards their homes, a quarter mile through the far woods.

They were still in sight when I walked over to the Chief. I shook him with all my strength, but the vibrations didn't come close to reaching the top branch. I didn't think it a wise move to throw anything to try and loosen the pants. I just stared mournfully at them, my stocking feet cold and soaked standing in the couple inches of snow.

And then, the slightest creaking sound. Then a soft, but distinct cracking. And then, lo and behold, the top foot or so of the Chief bending toward me, cracking more, and finally breaking. My pants slid down a foot or two, their soaking weight making them incompatible with the symmetry of the now eleven foot pine. They pin-balled from branch to branch, finally stopping five feet off the ground, where I pulled them down. I quickly put them on,

got my boots on, and looked for my two tormentors. They
were about eighty yards away, almost into the far woods.

"Hey!" I yelled at the top of my lungs. They
turned, and I pointed at my pants and did a little dance.
"Magic tree!" I then yelled. I could see their open mouths,
and them looking at each other. I couldn't resist, knowing
they were too far away to catch me. "They're gonna get
you, so watch out!" It felt gratifying to be on the delivering
end of a threat, especially where those two goons were
involved.

I heard my own voice inside my head, saying 'safe
for now.' A message from the pines? It seemed like *I* was
the one saying it. There was no echo quality to it, like on
TV or in the movies, but it seemed to come out of nowhere.

I didn't say anything at home about the incident, but
in my room after supper, I did some thinking. The way I
saw it, the trees had tried to warn me those guys were
coming. But the big thing was that one of them, the Chief
no less, had *sacrificed* some of his stature so I could get
back what belonged to me. I'm positive they sensed that
this was not a harmless prank. They *knew* these two were
inwardly evil. Maybe they *would* get even with them.
They weren't going to get in any trouble on my end.
Squealers don't have it very good in a small school in a
small town.

On Monday morning they were both noticeably
absent from class. Everyone was whispering about it, but
no one would tell me until Diana did at lunch. It was funny
as hell, if you think about it.

Turns out those two were so enraged after I did my
little dance, they went through the woods grabbing
anything they could get their hands on and throwing it.
They broke branches off trees and used them for clubs. As
they were cutting across some guy's yard, they smashed
one of his bird feeders. He came out and yelled, and they
swore at him as they ran away.

He called not only the police, but the *school principal.* It's a small town, like I said. When the smoke had cleared, Joseph LaFrance and Tommy Ozolinth had to do chores for the guy until he decided that the bird feeder was paid for. On the school end of things, they had to spend the entire week in the principal's office, doing all their work. Every time they spoke, it would add one day to their "sentence." If you're keeping score at home, LaFrance got three extra days, Ozolinth got one.

I guess that's what 'safe for now' meant. But all good things come to an end. By Thursday of the second week in December, they were back in class. As they walked by me on the playground, Joseph said, "Have we got a surprise for you, *Judy.*"

That's what they called me now. Judy. "What surprise?" I asked, mostly out of wanting to know what I might be up against.

"You'll see, Judy," said Tommy. "Saturday morning at ten at the pines."

. . .

Even though the possibility existed they were waiting to beat the hell out of me, I showed up anyway.

I came through the woods and saw them standing in front of the pines. They were motionless, arms behind them, looking like soldiers at parade rest. I got as close as I dared, and called out, "What's going on?"

"We're not gonna hurt you. Christmas time, good will towards men, ya know?" said Joseph.

I got closer. "So what's the big surprise, then?"

"Well," said Joseph, smiling at Tommy, "I promised my folks I would bring home a nice tree for Christmas. We thought you might want to watch." He and Tommy brought their arms out from behind them. Joseph had a full-sized axe, and Tommy had a small hatchet. "I thought this one on the end would be the perfect tree for the family. Any objections, Judy?"

What was I supposed to have done, take on two bigger kids armed with deadly weapons? I actually walked closer, more out of curiosity than bravery. I could "feel" a message from the pines. One word: 'cannot.' I knew right then that there was no way these two morons were taking down one of the Ghost Pines.

"No objections, fellas. Chop away."

They looked surprised that I was being a good sport about it. About that time came the three word message in my mind that reassured me even more.

They moved to the left end of the stand, where a nice-looking seven-footer stood. I smiled, and that seemed to spurn them into action.

"Let me get it started, Tommy," said Joseph, "then you can join in on alternate strokes. We'll take this sucker down in no time." Tommy walked inside the stand, on the other side of the targeted tree, while Joseph flexed his arms. All the while the three words reverberated in my head.

Joseph got into position and swung the axe. I wasn't worried. I knew what was about to happen. 'Run the sap' played in my head. *The trees were going to run their sap.* Joseph was in for a rude awakening. The blade sank in almost an inch, and *stuck there.*

"What the hell!" he yelled.

"Blade stuck?" asked Tommy.

"Holy Christ! The whole tree is flowing with sap!"

Tommy leaned against a nearby pine. "Hey, I got sap all over me. This one's doing it, too!"

They looked at the trees in front and behind them. Sap was running from all of them like oil from a gusher. It took both of them to get the axe out. They came back out front. I was now in fear for my well-being. These two were not known for thinking things through. Maybe in their frustration I would be their next target. It didn't help that the message I was now getting from the pines was the word 'sacrifice.'

"You say one word and you're gonna get hurt bad," snarled Joseph.

I found it fairly easy to say nothing.

We all saw it at once; two small four-footers off to the side. I would swear they were not there before, or *ever.*

"Who needs some clunky oversized tree, right Tommy? Let's take these two. One for each of us. Our own personal Christmas trees."

"Good idea," said Tommy. "There's not any sap running out of them, either."

The word 'sacrifice' played in my head.

Within ten minutes Joseph and Tommy had felled both miniature pines and were dragging them away. Joseph stopped after a few feet and turned to me. "You're off the hook, Judy. We showed you who's boss, and it ain't a bunch of pine trees. We're done with you. So long, sucker." He and Tommy shared a spiteful laugh as they dragged their conquests.

. . .

I heard the details during Christmas vacation. Parents can actually come in handy sometimes. Dad always read the paper cover to cover, and Mom met a lot of ladies while shopping and doing errands, including a visit to her hairdresser.

Even when the two small pines were standing, we all noticed the odd sweet-smelling aroma coming from them as opposed to the *pine needle* smell you usually get. Turns out at Tommy Ozolinth's house, 'sweet' meant 'good to eat.' Tommy's dog, cat, and little sister ate some of the irresistible-smelling needles that were falling at an alarming rate the second it was taken inside. Apparently they tasted as good as they smelled. But they weren't

exactly digestible or compatible with their insides.
Tommy's family spent the Christmas holidays in the
emergency room, the vet's, and the hospital. Even though
everyone recovered, Tommy's dad was so pissed that he
took all his presents away and told him he wasn't getting
them back. Ouch.

As for Joseph, *his* tree, which he had put up in his
bedroom, somehow caught fire Christmas afternoon while
the family was out visiting. A neighbor saw the smoke and
called the fire department. Luckily, the fire was confined
to Joseph's bedroom, but smoke damage permeated the
entire house. The only things destroyed were the contents
of Joseph's bedroom, among which were all his newly-
opened presents.

Best Christmas ever.

. . .

Not much more to tell. Those two incidents in 1958
were probably the pinnacle of my association with the
Ghost Pines.

I managed to outlive my unpopularity from fifth
grade, and from then on I had a normal life both in and out
of school. I even had a steady girlfriend during my senior
year.

Joseph LaFrance and Tommy Ozolinth seemed to
fade into the background. They no longer tormented or
picked on anyone. I think they got the meanness and
whatever evil they had knocked out of them that Christmas
so long ago.

After eighth grade, I seldom went to see the Ghost
Pines. I had a full, happy life. They had filled an important
void for me as a young child. After all, what kid can resist
a spooky mystery? Shortly before high school graduation I
paid them a final visit before I went off to college. They
had moved a few feet forward and to the left, and I

immediately thought of Grandpa Claude. The Chief was now twelve feet tall again. The stumps of the two little pines Joseph and Tommy cut down seven years earlier did not exist. I just wanted to say a farewell and thank you to them. So I said just that: "Farewell and thank you."

The word 'good' floated in my mind somewhere.

During my college years I would sometimes run into an old classmate, and after we caught up I could never resist the temptation of asking about LaFrance and Ozolinth. They turned out okay, I guess. They were still close and ended up working for a big logging company downstate. Joseph cut down trees for a living. I wonder if that day at the pines planted some irresistible urge in him. Tommy was a driver for the same company. Neither of them married. They had *each other.*

Shortly before his death in 2002, I was visiting my dad in the nursing home and told him the two strange episodes from 1958; the pants incident and the Christmas tree incident. I asked his interpretation of them, as he had always been a man who saw things for what they really were.

Dad had long since lost his *intellect,* but not his *clarity.* He thought a bit, then said, "Rudy, there are a lot of backwoods tales around these parts. Some things in nature are *un*natural.

That's all I needed to hear.

. . .

One last thing. In 1975 I married my high-school sweetheart, Diana Bushey, the one girl who had always been nice to me in fifth grade. We had a simple ceremony with immediate family and friends and a Justice of the Peace, held in front of the Ghost Pines on a beautiful spring day. As the JP pronounced us husband and wife, I was hoping for some last "message" from my long-time friends.

I looked up at them. I'm sure I was the only one who saw it.

There was no wind, but all thirty-seven (?) of them had their treetops bowed forward.

"CRUISERS"
2014

Yankee blood still flowed in Highland Point, Connecticut, two miles from the Massachusetts border. And with it, the old Yankee ways still flourished. The teenagers and pre-teens had their computers, internet, I-pods, and fancy cell phones. But the driving force was still old-fashioned New England self-reliance, hard work, and an austere outlook on life and the land.

Russell Poe was one such New Englander. Born and raised on the family farm, he continued working the land well into his sixty-second year. Leading out the back of one of his fields was a dirt road, which meandered half a mile in thick woods until it came out on Lawrence Lane, a newly-developed cul-de-sac.

Poe never allowed himself to believe that his work was done. He constantly found new projects on his house, barn, farmland and the old farm road which connected his land to the "new age" residents on Lawrence Lane.

He took pride in keeping the old farm trail passable, and from spring through late fall would occasionally hack at the underbrush which constantly threatened to turn it into a tangle of weeds, bushes, and trees struggling to take root.

On one of these trail-blazing expeditions in late October he first noticed a huge mass of thick brush, bushes, and vines in a peculiar shape. It was at least thirty-five feet off the trail, but it was an annoyance to him all the same. How had he missed it in the past, he wondered. Now that he *had* noticed it, he could not let such an unruly mess continue to exist, even *near* the old trail, of which he had legal right-of-way. Russell Poe, like his father before him, liked things neat and orderly, even nature's "things."

He hauled some brush-clearing implements in a metal pull-cart he often used. When he got down to his intended target he found trees, brush, brambles, vines, fallen logs, and a few healthy-sized boulders populating an area approximately fifteen by twenty feet. It was as if a piccc of the Amazon's deepest jungle growth had found its way to Connecticut.

He hadn't worked on the recalcitrant patch of nature very long before he realized that it was camouflaging a large object in its center. At first Russell assumed it was a moss-covered boulder, but it wasn't. There was a large metallic object hiding in there. His first thought was a rusted hulk of farm machinery, once belonging to his grandfather, the original tenant of this farm. An old plow or tractor, perhaps abandoned by Jonas Poe during the Depression.

This was stimulating to Russell, coming in contact with a once-important part of the history of his land. He worked with machete, loppers, sickle, and axe for the better part of forty-five minutes. At that point, he had torn down enough of the growth that he could push the rest of it aside.

The remains of a gold-colored 1949 Mercury Monterey lay inside the cocoon nature had created. Russell *did* have a certain appreciation for the car. After all, it was two years older than he, but it was not part of the farm's history. Someone had left it out here to rust, as was often done in these parts in the 1950's and 1960's.

Russell usually spoke his thoughts when he was alone. "Don't think anybody's been at this old girl. Everything's still here."

Although the tires had long-since flattened and rotted, the doors, hood, and trunk were intact, as were the seats, steering wheel, and everything else inside that normally would have been cannibalized. Out of curiosity, he found the latch for the hood, popped it and lifted. At first reluctant to budge, he gave it a mighty upward thrust and it opened, then sheared off its hinges on one side and broke free, its weight causing the other hinge to give way. The rusted gold hood slid off onto the ground.

"New England winters for ya. Kill anything that's not took care of proper." He attempted to open the driver's side door, but couldn't get it open more than a few inches before it refused to budge further.

"Well, this is a fool's errand if there ever was one." He gathered his tools and prepared to leave. As he walked around the front of the car he took a last look and noticed that the VIN number, once visible on the driver's side dash, had been filed away to nothing, and the license plates were gone.

"Car thieves for ya. Steal anything that's not locked up proper."

A car stolen more than fifty years ago and no longer driveable was not something Russell would have given a second thought, even if it *was* near his property. He did not need police poking around on a matter that in his estimation, was of no consequence.

Whoever had the car stolen had reported it long ago, and whoever stole it was long gone. With all the obstacles between the trail and the Mercury, how would a tow truck even get down there to haul it away?

He *had* made one observation, however. There were several boulders near enough to the car to theorize that it could not have been driven between them. In his mind, someone had placed them there *after* the abandonment of the vehicle. And a good deal of the debris closest to and on top of the car seemed to have been *placed* there in a deliberate attempt to conceal it. It was just car thieves doing a thorough job of covering their tracks.

One nagging question remained if he chose to consider it: why had someone bothered to steal it in the first place? Russell thought about it, then moved on to other things. There was his pumpkin crop to harvest for Halloween.

. . .

Lawrence Lane was a kid's paradise. Several teens lived on the street and the immediate neighborhood, along with a healthy dose of pre-teens and young children.

A few days before Halloween, Brock Folsom and twins Teddy and Eddie Richardson made their way through the woods behind Lawrence Lane on their way to the Poe farm to buy pumpkins for themselves and Brock's younger brother Harry. They, along with friends Paul Landon and Will Esterling were starting to frequent the woods just behind their houses to sneak cigarettes, whatever alcohol could be snuck out of the house, and "girly" magazines. Brock, 16, and the Richardson twins, 15, usually went just far enough into the woods to avoid being seen or heard by any nearby adults.

So it was not their usual custom to tromp all the way down the trail to the Poe farm. About seventy yards from the end of the trail, which came out on Poe's back field, they stopped dead.

"Guys," called Brock, "look, a car. An old car!"

All three rushed toward towards the metal hulk, now stripped of most of its usual camouflage.

"Was this here before?" asked Teddy. "How come we never saw this?"

"We don't usually come down this far," commented Brock. "But the times we did, we couldn't have missed it completely."

"Wait a minute," said Eddie. "Wasn't there a shitload of trees and vines here?"

"That's why," said Brock. "I wonder if old man Poe found it and chopped all that crap down."

"Maybe it was *his* car when he was a kid," offered Teddy.

"I doubt it, Teddy," replied Brock. "This old Merc' must be from the 40's. He was too young to have a car then. Probably his father's."

"Think there's anything on it we can use?" Eddie asked, tripping over the hidden edge of the hood.

Brock and Teddy let out a laugh. All three walked around the Mercury, inspecting it thoroughly. Eddie tugged at the partially-open driver's side door, which would not budge, even as he exerted more energy on it.

"Careful, Eddie," called Brock. "That door might give on you and you'll trip over the hood …*again.*"

"Wise ass."

After a few more minutes of inspection, Teddy said, "There's nothin' on here we could use, right?"

"Not a chance," said Brock. He looked at the hulk and smiled. "Back in her day this was one sweet machine."

"How do you know?" asked Teddy.

"Look it up. I bet the internet has some pictures of these from collectors. What a beauty she must have been."

"C'mon, guys," called Teddy. "Let's get down to Poe's and buy the damn pumpkins."

Ten minutes later, they were handing their money to Russell Poe. The twins kept shooting odd looks at Brock. He finally figured out what they wanted.

"Say, Mr. Poe," said Brock, "on the way here we passed an old Mercury just off the trail."

"Ayup."

"Was it your father's?"

"Nope. He never owned a car. Needed a pickup for the farm."

"Do you know how it got there?"

"Nope. Just found it last week. Cut down most of the brush and whatnot what was keepin' it out of eyesight."

"Is it any good for anything?" asked Eddie.

"Scrap metal, maybe. And probably not worth it to hire someone to come get it, so I would say 'nope' to that, too." Poe fixed the boys with a calculating look. "For the right price I would be willin' to sell it to you if'n you got somebody to haul it away."

"No offense, Mr. Poe, but it's not even yours to sell," said Teddy.

Russell Poe exhaled. He put the money in his pocket and headed for his front door. "Enjoy your pumpkins, boys."

. . .

So began the spell the abandoned Mercury would cast over not one, but two peer groups of Lawrence Lane.

At first it was Brock, the Richardson twins, Paul Landon and Will Easterling. There was something alluring about the old Mercury that drew them there. They would smoke, drink and look at magazines there; the same things they did several hundred yards closer to their houses. Brock in particular seemed to have some unidentified *affinity* for the car.

"They don't make cars with this color gold any more," he stated.

"Yeah, because it's ugly as hell," stated Will.

On one occasion Paul Landon invited two girls from his homeroom who he liked. The girls, Margaret Lafferty and Claire Deisi, went over to the car, but seemed almost repulsed by it.

"What's the big deal about an old junk car?" protested Claire.

"For one thing," began Brock.

"Don't even start," said Will, cutting him off.

"This thing gives me the creeps," stated Margaret.

"What fun," said Claire. "C'mon, Margaret, let's go over to your house. Thanks for a great time, Paul." They quickly walked back to the trail and towards Lawrence Lane.

"Nice goin,' Brock," said Paul.

"Me? What did *I* do?"

"They caught this crazy vibe you got with this hunk of junk."

Neither the girls nor Brock and his friends, now in a debate over the merits of an abandoned car attracting girls, noticed two eleven-year-old boys fifty feet away, concealed by a large maple tree. Brock Folsom had not realized how much his actions were scrutinized by his brother Harry.

Harry had been trailing Brock and his friends secretly since Halloween. He had seen the unlikely, tantalizing sight of the derelict Mercury a week ago, and had told his closest friend, Mark Delaine. They were only vaguely aware of the argument going on concerning the car's merits as a "chick magnet." They were in pre-teen heaven at the very sight of it, and how their still-childlike imaginations could avail themselves of *an actual car.*

After dinner that evening, Harry found Brock studying in his room.

"Hey, Brock."

"I got a test tomorrow. Waddaya want?"

"Uh, Mark and I were up on the old farm road today."

Brock's head popped up from his biology book. "And?"

"And we saw you and the other guys and those girls." Harry was treading carefully, trying to gauge the chances of him and *his* friends being included in the communing with the magical Mercury.

"You were *spying* on us?"

"I already know what you guys do in the woods. I would never tell. I just wondered why you guys went way up there lately."

"Then you saw the car, right?"

"Yeah. Whose is it, old man Poe's?"

"No, somebody abandoned it years ago. Nobody even knew it was there until Poe cut down all the stuff that was covering it. It's a 1949 Mercury Monterey." Brock suddenly realized what his younger brother was getting at. "You should stay away from it. You could get hurt near that thing. You don't know if something's gonna come tearing off. It could collapse while you and your friends were screwing around."

"We would be careful."

Brock suddenly seemed disinterested in the topic. "Do what you want, then. The guys don't want to hang out there any more, so I'm done with it. If something bad happens, it's your own fault."

Harry, on the verge of scoring a social victory for himself and his friends, said elatedly, "What could possibly happen?"

Brock shrugged. "I don't know. Scram, now, I gotta study."

. . .

Harry Folsom and Mark Delaine had their hands tightly gripped on the partially-open door while Travis Willliams and Billy Clonsett had each one of them by the waist.

"Ready?" called Harry. "Pull!"

Inch by inch, the door surrendered, finally opening to its full width. Harry jumped inside, his face recoiling. "God, the smell!" He jumped from the vehicle. "This thing needs to be aired out something fierce."

"Let's open the other door," said Billy.

With the other door fully closed, Harry and Mark grabbed the door handle and depressed the button, while the other two positioned themselves as before, holding tight to their waists.

"Okay," said Harry. "Just like before. Ready? Pull!"

The door flew open as though it had been rigged on a spring device. The four boys landed in a pile, looking like a goal-line stand in a football game. They arose, looking at each other in astonishment.

"Let's get in," called Mark. "Shotgun!"

Harry ran around to the driver's side. "I got the wheel!" The front seat bent forward to let Travis and Billy into the back. "Pull the seat up!" yelled Billy. "We're getting crushed. And leave the doors open. We need air."

Harry found the seat adjustment lever and pulled it. The seat dutifully moved forward. "This old girl is just full of surprises."

"This old girl?" chided Mark. "You sound like your brother, Harry. Cars aren't alive, you know."

"No, but they have … personality."

For the next half hour, they took turns "driving," riding shotgun, and manning the back seat. Each "driver" had his own scenario, from stock car races in upstate New York, to navigating the route from Lawrence Lane to the consolidated school they attended. Each had his own driving "style," ranging from Travis steering with his feet, to the more conventional hands on the wheel at 'ten' and 'two.'

When Billy Clonsett's turn came, he grabbed the wheel at 'nine' and 'twelve,' a unique style that did not go unnoticed.

"That is one strange way to steer a car," said Mark.

Billy seemed miles away, so to speak. "Heading down Peacable Hill Road, Route 53. Down to Route 6, gettin' on Main Street. Gonna take a half right here, onto Oak Street."

There was something about this narrative that caught the attention of the car's three "passengers." There was no veneer of "just pretending."

"Billy," said Harry, punching him in the shoulder, "what the hell you doing?"

Billy let go of the wheel, looked over at Harry. "Nothing. Just pretending to drive."

"You named all these streets and Routes we never heard of," said Travis. "And you looked a little loopy."

Billy seemed to resemble himself again. He gave a smirk and said, "Hey, drivin' a hot car will do that to you."

. . .

The boys knew that they only had a few weeks before snow and cold would put the kibosh on their "driving sessions" in the old Mercury. They got together one day after school at Billy's house at the bottom of Lawrence Lane. They wanted to come up with a name for themselves. Billy's father had a collection of LP's from the 60's and 70's, and they scoured them for ideas.

They were fascinated with pictures of a California group, *The Beach Boys*. Several of their early albums featured "hot rods," as they were called then, and other expensive sports cars.

"Hey, I got it," said Harry. "When we get behind the wheel, it's like we're *cruising*. We can be "The Cruisers.""

"How about just "Cruisers"?" said Billy. "Makes it sound tougher."

Everyone agreed to meet at the Mercury as often as possible before the cold and deep snow would make the experience more an ordeal than fun.

They knew enough not to tell anyone or broadcast anything on social media about the car, and their fantasy driving sessions. The consensus was that it would attract all the wrong boys, and scare away all the right girls.

On one Saturday Billy convinced everyone they should neaten up the area. Tools were "borrowed" from garages, and an entire morning was spent cutting, chopping, and hauling away everything deemed "messy" near the car. Several large boulders were rolled away.

Travis looked up from one of the rock-rolling efforts, and said, "How the hell did the car even *get here* with those rocks in the way?"

The car's hood, which everyone had tripped and fallen over several times, was hefted up and put back, more or less in place.

And every time Billy sat behind the wheel, "cruising," his itinerary was a litany of streets that none of them had ever heard of.

A sampling: Wells Street intersected Center Street, then wound down to Prospect and High Streets before emptying out on Railroad Avenue, which was also Route 6. You could ride along the river on East Branch Avenue until it hit the intersection of Route 6, then shoot down until you came to Stone Ridge Road, a dead end.

Billy's travelogue and spaced-out demeanor were now accepted by the others as just his way of living the experience.

Officially, it was Mark Delaine's idea to use the Mercury's hood as a toboggan. By December 10th, there was enough accumulated snow for sledding. School had been cancelled that day, and after all four Cruisers had done their assigned shoveling, they met at the top of Lawrence Lane and tromped up the old farm road.

"You sure this is gonna work?" asked Billy.

"Where we goin' again?" asked Travis.

"Jesus, you guys," complained Mark. "For the last time, where the farm road meets Poe's back field, you go left. There's a huge bank that empties out into the far end of that field. It'll be like sliding down a mountain."

Carrying the heavy hood through the deep snow was quite a task, as it turned out. The total distance of the "portage" amounted to over two-hundred yards.

They piled in, and suddenly realized that their combined weight kept the hood from moving. Travis volunteered to get out and push before jumping on, but it was still overloaded. Billy got out next, and now, the slightest movement caused the hood to move towards the edge. On the count of three, Travis and Billy pushed, the hood careened over the edge, and they jumped on.

The sudden jolt caused the hood to flip, and all four were thrown into the snow. Two attempts later, they got it right. The ride down was as scary as it was exhilarating.

"We're going too fast!"

"You see a brake pedal, idiot?"

"Hey, you're gonna push me out!"

"You're choking me, dammit."

"Stop leaning on me. I'm gonna fall out!"

"Then stop choking me!"

. . .

It was a long, cold winter, but whenever possible, the Cruisers plodded their way to the top of the hill, where they left the gold "toboggan."

Harry spent a lot of time that winter on the family computer. Although they all had gotten used to Billy's spaced-out travel narratives, there was something about it that Harry always thought was eerie. Billy had mostly named streets that could exist anywhere, but on a couple occasions, he had made references that Harry was now trying to track down.

The names "Brewster" and "Brewster Hill" had been mentioned, along with "Interstate 84," and signs saying "Danbury, CT. 5 miles." Harry knew that Danbury was over an hour downstate. He had an uncle who had gone to college there. So he looked up "towns named Brewster," and got two locations. One was in Massachusetts. The other was just across the

Connecticut/New York border, *just five miles from Danbury, Connecticut.*

Harry wondered if Billy had visited relatives there as a small child. He then found a street map for Brewster, New York. Just about every readable street name had been mentioned by Billy in his "travels." Lifelong friends, Harry had no problem telling this to him. Billy seemed surprised, but not freaked out. "I must have seen it on a map, and it stuck in my subconscious."

"But *specific* street names? And you should see your face when you're "cruising." It's like you're another person."

"There you go again."

"Would you be willing to go up there, just the two of us?"

"And do what?"

"Cruise. Just say whatever comes into your head behind the wheel."

"This is screwy."

Harry talked him into it. On a Saturday late in February they went to the Mercury, brushed accumulated snow from it, and sat in the front seat, Billy behind the wheel.

It was the usual, Billy naming street that Harry now knew were in Brewster, New York, some sixty miles away. As Billy described going down Riverside Drive, he said, "Going by Vera's house now."

Harry grabbed him. "Billy, stop." Billy dropped his hands and looked over at him. "You just said you were going by Vera's house. Who's Vera?"

Billy's eyes were wide. "I don't know."

"But you just *said* you were driving by her house."

"Honest, I don't know. This stuff just comes to me."

"No! Dammit. You aren't *you* when you're cruising. What's different?" He thought a moment. "Switch places."

They traded places and Harry grabbed the wheel. "Okay, I've got the wheel and I'm looking out the windshield. All I see are trees and bushes. What do *you* see?"

I imagine streets. I can see their names when I'm driving."

"And all those streets are in Brewster, New York! And I don't think you are *imagining* them. They're *real* for you at that moment!"

"Hey, maybe I'm physic."

"Psychic, idiot." Harry pounded the steering wheel. "Damn it, I want to see this stuff, too."

"Then stop holding the wheel like a scared little girl, and do it the cool way, like me."

"Yeah, *that's* the secret," Harry said sarcastically. He repositioned his hands on the wheel to the 'nine' and 'twelve' position, something only Billy did. He looked in front of him. There were no trees or bushes. He was on Hillside Park, passing the intersection of Hillside Terrace, and coming up on Carmel Avenue. "Let's get down to Putnam Avenue," he said.

It was Billy's turn to grab Harry. "Harry, you did it. You were driving in that place you said, Brewster."

"I *was* there that time." He looked out the windshield to fine snow-covered trees and bushes, then looked at Billy in dismay. "Same old *shit!*" Billy was staring at his hands on the wheel.

"Your hands, Harry. Put them back at 'nine' and 'twelve' like before."

Harry did as Billy ordered. "Just turned off Putnam Avenue onto Lincoln Road. A bunch of little streets I never saw before. Four of them. They all—"

Billy grabbed Harry's hands and repositioned them at 'ten' and 'two' on the wheel.

Harry looked over at Billy, his eyes wide as saucers. "Nothing."

"Only at 'nine' and 'twelve,'" whispered Billy.

"That weird girl in school," Harry said.

"Which weird girl?"

"Sonia. The foreign one."

"What about her?"

"I heard her telling one of her friends about how somebody dead could live through somebody who was alive."

"I don't think we ought to mention something like that to *anybody.*"

"We should tell Travis and Mark, right?"

"Just them. Nobody else."

. . .

Travis and Mark were both told and shown the incredible discovery, and over the next two weeks, took their turn holding the Mercury's wheel at 'nine' and 'twelve' and taking a tour of Brewster, New York. It was agreed that no one go anywhere near Sonia Ihasz.

Harry felt that Vera, the girl Billy mentioned, was the key. He got busy on the computer and put in a search for "Vera; Brewster, New York." It was a huge longshot, but it was as specific as he could get.

His search results included the *Vera Bradley* handbag line, and ads for Aloe Vera lotion. About halfway down the first page he saw it, and nearly forgot to breathe. A newspaper headline from the Brewster, New York daily paper read, *Teenage Couple Missing.*

Peter Wolchik, 18, and Vera Canizarro, 16, were reported missing on Saturday, May 8th, 1954. They had gone on a date the previous night to see *On the Waterfront,* starring Marlon Brando. None of their friends had seen them after the movie. An all-out search was under way for Peter's car, *a gold 1949 Mercury Monterey, New York license plates AW9-670.*

Harry printed out the article. They had been *playing* in the missing car. He did follow-up searches on the computer to make sure that this had not played itself out to a logical conclusion. After all, what if the couple had gone off somewhere to elope, or had stayed somewhere else that night? But there were additional articles in his search verifying that this was indeed serious, and had not resolved itself. He called the others immediately and told them of his findings, and that they must all meet at the car and decide what to do.

· · ·

At the Mercury they all sat behind the wheel one last time. They retrieved the car's hood from the hilltop and replaced it as best they could.

Among the information Harry had printed out was the name of the lead detective on the case in 1954, Carlson Everett.

"He's gotta be dead or retired by now," said Travis.

"I want to try to call him. If I can't find him, then we'll call the Brewster Police Department," said Harry.

On a day when his parents weren't home, Harry gathered the Cruisers at his house. The only phone listing in Brewster for 'Everett' was a William Everett. Maybe he was a relative. It was their only hope. Harry put the phone on 'speaker' mode and made the call.

"Hello," a male voice answered.

"Hello. I was trying to contact a Carlson Everett, please."

"That's my father. Hold on. Dad!"

After a short pause, an older man's voice was on the line. "This is Carlson Everett. Who's calling?"

Travis and Mark were gesturing at Harry not to give his name.

"This is Harry Folsom of Highland Point, Connecticut. My friends and I discovered an old Mercury in the woods near our house." Harry gulped. "We are sure it's the car from the Peter Wolchik and Vera Canizarro disappearance." Harry was positive he heard a gasp from the other end of the line.

"What color?" the voice managed to say.

"A metallic gold."

"License plates and VIN number?"

"Plates are gone, and the VIN number filed off."

"Listen son, I'm retired. Obviously you looked me up somewhere. That case was never solved. Those two teenagers were never found. Give me your phone number, and I'll get someone at our police department to call you and get more information."

"That would be great."

"And don't go near the car or touch anything, all right?"

Too late now, Harry thought. "Yes, sir."

"You know, young man," said Everett, "every detective has one case that haunts them till the end of their days. This was mine."

"Nobody knows what happened to them?"

"Well, someone kidnapped and killed them, most likely. Who or why, we'll probably never know. What a waste of two human lives what never got to reach their potential." He sniffed loudly. "I'm eighty-seven. At least now I know what happened to the car."

"Yes, sir."

"I gotta ask, son. Why would you think an old car in the woods would have anything to do with an unsolved crime?"

Harry looked at the others. Travis shrugged. Mark put his finger to his lips, and Billy shook his head. "I'm not really sure. I think it was just a … vibe we got from it. Like … it was trying to tell us something." The others were looking at the floor or rolling their eyes.

"You know, young fella, I been at crime scenes where I got the same feeling. Maybe someday you would make a pretty good detective."

"Thanks, sir."

"So you give me your number and I'll have someone call you as soon as possible. It would give me a little closure to be the one to tell our department that Peter Wolchik's car was found." Another pause. "And son?"

"Yes?"

"Thank you. A little closure is better than none."

. . .

A few minutes later the Folsom's phone rang. It was Lieutenant Roger Terriault of the Brewster Detective Bureau.

Harry thought it best to tell the complete truth. There were no objections from the three eavesdroppers nearby. He informed Terriault that a local farmer had originally found the car in October, and he and his friends had opened the door and sat inside.

"And how is it again," asked Terriault, "that you thought to investigate online? Where would you even start? Mr. Everett told me there was no VIN number or license plates."

Harry looked at his three friends. "Well, Detective, you can believe this or not, but whichever of us was behind the wheel was getting definite vibes about where the car was from. And we got a vibe about the name 'Vera.' So I did a computer search from there and eventually found a news article from 1954 about the missing kids, and the gold Mercury. Mr. Everett told me everything else."

"I guess that's gonna have to do," Terriault said. "This job gets more unbelievable every day. By the way, you and your friends should *never* have gone inside that car. What little evidence of whoever abducted and probably killed those two teens may be gone, now."

"We feel terrible about that, sir."

"Well, you didn't know that it was a crime scene. We'll be up there tomorrow morning to investigate, and we'll make sure that your local and state police are informed. They will contact the press, so be prepared for reporters on your doorstep."

The next morning there were, indeed, local and Connecticut State Police and a crime scene unit from Brewster at the top of Lawrence Lane, led by Lieutenant Terriault. A flatbed truck with a winch wound its way up the farm road. All four Cruisers had told their parents the entire story, or as much of it as they deemed necessary. They had been allowed to miss school that Wednesday, March 19th.

Lieutenant Terriault had met the four at Harry's house had told them no press would be informed until after the initial investigation. The boys would be allowed to watch the crime scene unit from a distance, in appreciation of their help. When everyone got to the road section adjacent to the car, Terriault came over to them and asked in a low voice, "You fellas didn't think to open the trunk, did you?"

They all looked at each other, mouths open. "No, sir," said Harry.

"Oh, God. If my hunch is correct, you boys are going to have to leave."

Technicians with a pair of special crowbars were able to get the trunk open with surprisingly little effort. "Two sets of human remains, here," called one of them.

"You boys head back to your street," said Terriault. "I'll be in touch with you before we leave here."

They waited in Harry's house, checking the window every few minutes. It was over three hours before vehicles descended the trail and out onto Lawrence Lane. All four boys ran out for one last look at the Mercury, resting on a flatbed, its trunk ajar. No one said a word.

Lieutenant Terriault stopped to say goodbye and thank them, and have them and their parents sign a statement.

"Kind of ironic," he said. "Today is the exact day Peter Wolchik bought that car off a lot in Brewster." They all watched as a police van descended onto Lawrence Lane. The boys knew that inside were Peter Wolchik and Vera Canizarro. They were going home at last.

. . .

Fame is fleeting, at least the kind earned by the Cruisers. A flurry of phone calls, interviews, and notoriety, some of it national, as newspapers and wire services picked up the story, faded almost as quickly as it had appeared. By March 26th, only a week later, the four boys noticed that the only people who paid them any attention were the same people as before. Winter was melting away, and people's minds turned to other things.

Shortly after dinner one evening, the phone rang at the Folsom residence. Brock answered it, and called Harry over. "Grandpa wants to talk to you, big shot."

"Grandpa, hi."

"Harry, I got a story I want you to hear. It has to do with that car?"

"Really?"

"Yes, so just listen. I had a brother who died twenty years ago; he didn't take very good care of himself."

"Oh, sorry."

"Anyway, he was not a good man. Got in a lot of trouble with the law; burglary, forgery, that kind of thing. Well, he did some crime, and it involved crossing a state line, so he ended up doing five years in Danbury Federal Penitentiary."

"Geez, I didn't know any of that."

"He's not a popular family topic. While he was in prison, he and another inmate became close friends. A couple years after they got out, he gets a call from this guy asking a big favor."

"Yeah?"

"His old friend wants him to get rid of a car for him. His friend and this other guy wanted my brother Art to meet them up here and ditch the car."

The hair on Harry Folsom's neck and arms was standing by now.

"So they drive up here in two cars, the friend's and one other car. I'm sure you know what car that was."

"Yeah." Harry's mouth was wide open, but he wasn't breathing.

"They drove up to where Lawrence Lane is now. It was just a hunting trail then, and connected to that farm road by your house. They bring the car up there, and my brother drove it up the farm road, piled stuff on it, rolled some big rocks near it, and took off. And that's how that old Mercury got there back in 1954."

"Grandpa," Harry asked tentatively, "how do you know about this?"

"My brother had a big mouth. He told me that a few times he ditched stolen cars for people for a price. They gave him a hundred bucks and took off, not knowing where he would stash it. He had no idea this one had two dead kids in it. When he told me, it must have been ten years later."

There was a slight pause. " He was trying to come clean before he died. Had throat cancer."

"Grandpa, shouldn't you tell all this to the police in Brewster?"

"I did. The day your story hit the news. They're checking prison records from the 40's and 50's to see who my brother's friend might have been. Kind of like looking for a needle in a haystack, now."

"Wouldn't some of those guys be dead, now?"

"Probably half of them, at least. Why?"

"I was just thinking, if the guys that killed them are dead, then they got away with it, didn't they?"

Paul Folsom let out a short sign. "In *this* life, maybe, but not in the *next* one, Harry.

. . .

Peter Wolchik's remains were turned over to his brother. Calvin Wolchik fondly remembered his older brother, who thought he was so "hip" with his gold Mercury, driving with his hands at 'nine' and 'twelve' on the wheel.

Members of the class of 1956 of Brewster High School took up a collection to help pay for Vera Canizarro's funeral. On May 7th, 2014, the sixtieth anniversary of their disappearance, the couple was buried in adjoining gravesites, paid for by citizens of Brewster, New York. Members of the Police Department served as pallbearers.

Former detective Carlson Everett died in July of that year.

Despite an exhaustive search, which involved interviewing over eighty former inmates of the Danbury Federal Penitentiary, Brewster police were unable to solve the murders of Peter Wolchik and Vera Canizarro. The case remains open.

"HOOLIGANS"
2014

According to Mrs. Costello of 20 Pratt Hill, my friends and I were a bunch of "hooligans." We just laughed. Not at *her*. We laughed at the word itself. It sounded so *ridiculous*. We enjoyed a good laugh more than anything, and Mrs. Costello was our biggest source of entertainment.

She had *six* kids and a husband who worked long hours, so it was her against them most of the time. Her husband Alvin worked in the meat department of a supermarket, and came home dead tired. He left the raising of those kids, and whatever went with it, to his wife.

The two oldest, Allan and Barbara, a year apart, were a year or two younger than us, and were busy most of the time as caregivers-in-training. We just called them 'A' and 'B.' The two middle ones, twins, were Charlie and Carrie, the 'C's. They might have been somewhere around seven or eight. They were too young for us, and were kind of self-contained, stayed in their yard most of the time, and seemed to be each other's best friend.

Mr. and Mrs. Costello, working their way through the alphabet, named the other twins Dustin and Destiny, the 'D's. *These* were the two who provided the cause for all the entertaining effects on their mother.

. . .

It was 1980, in Richardson, Oregon, just on the Idaho border. Routes 130 and 28 intersected in our town of 4,357, with Interstate 84 running just north of us. You could *walk* to Payette, Idaho from our neighborhood. We didn't, though. We rode our bikes. We had a "bike gang." There were six of us.

Vinnie Beverly was my best friend, and didn't mind when we ragged on him and called him "Beverly," like he was a girl. Adam Oliver was the smartest one in our group. He actually *liked* teachers, and got all A's. I never even saw him open a book. Willie D'Erlon was okay most of the time, except when he got on one of his bragging kicks, telling us an ancestor of his was one of Napoleon's Field Marshalls. We didn't know what that even was, so we ragged on him and asked if that was a lawman that stood out in a field all day. Willie told us that a Field Marshall was like a four-star general. We still didn't care.

The two girls, yes *girls,* were Gina Fortin and Janie Markoff. Gina had bushy, blond hair and was like one of the guys, only kind-hearted and generous. We were always bumming money off her. We seldom ragged on her, since she cried easily. Janie had short black hair, and was as tough as they come. She didn't have it easy at home, and sometimes took out her frustrations on the rest of us. But when we had a destination to get to with our bikes, she was right there was right there with us. I sometimes thought that we were the only fun she had.

My name is Tony Ross, and I'm going to tell this story and try to be as truthful as I can.

The thing is, we noticed many unhappy adults in our daily lives. It was like they reached a certain age and *forgot* how to have fun. We decided that we were going to get our money's worth out of being kids, just in case it happened to us, too.

It wasn't just riding our bikes that gave us a rush. It was *how* we rode. We often screamed at the top of our lungs while we tore ass down hills, through people's yards, (that was when Mrs. Costello started calling us hooligans) and out to the cliffs, even though we had been told not to go near there.

Out on Unterdeld Road where the paved part ends there's a dirt road, and where *that* ends there's a wooden fence and an eighty foot drop off a sheer cliff. There's no way to get down there, with other steep drop-offs and the West Robena River. As little kids, we were all told the story about a boy who was exploring out there by himself and fell off. He wasn't found until the next day. That was in 1968, the year before we were all born. The kid's name was Michael Heath. After hearing that story, we were asked what lesson we learned. To most of us, it was *don't go out to the cliffs **alone,*** but the adults were trying to scare us into not going out there at all.

Fat chance once we had friends and bikes. We regularly rode right up to the edge where the fence is, sitting on it, *standing* on it, and throwing rocks at targets we picked out at the bottom.

Years before, that was where a lot of teenagers went to smoke, drink, and according to my older brother Rob, "do some other stuff." But after Michael Heath got killed, the police started regular patrols there after dusk. We had no problem, though, because we rode there during the day.

One of our favorite rides was called an "orchard raid." We're in kind of a semi-rural area here, and there are some sheep and livestock farms north of town, and even potato fields. But our favorite place is Hito's Orchard, owned by this little Japanese guy. If someone happens to touch a blade of grass that's on his property, he yells and chases us, cursing us out in Japanese.

Since he was such an ass, we made it a point to raid his orchard at least once a week. He grew the best apples I ever tasted, and that includes Washington apples.

On one occasion, one of our teachers, Mrs. Rowley, took Vinnie and I aside and scolded us for riding our bikes with "reckless abandon." Adults, right? We looked down and pretended we were sorry, but after that, "reckless abandon" was our battle cry.

Adam eventually looked up the word 'hooligan.' When he informed us it was a "tough or aggressive youth," we were quite flattered. Willie had thought it was a last name, and that Mrs. Costello thought we were all from the same family! We ragged on him but good for that one.

I don't know if it's the same for everybody, but in my experience there are days you just stop and realize that something in your world has changed. You can't be sure *when,* but you are positive that it *did.*

It was the two girls in our bike gang, mostly, but girls in general. They *looked* different to me, or *seemed* different. Gina especially. She had been my friend since I'd *had* friends. But it was the same with Janie, to an extent, and even girls that I never saw outside of school.

That's where having an older brother came in handy. Maybe this girl thing was something all boys went through. My brother Rob was fifteen, a sophomore, and I constantly heard him on the phone talking to girls or about girls, but up until now I just tuned it out. One night after supper I asked if I could talk to him in my room privately.

I explained my problem, mainly my new feelings and *perceptions* about girls in general, Gina and Janie in particular.

He looked down, smiling, shaking his head. "Well, well, the day has finally come, little brother."

"What day?" I still took things literally.

"The day you start seeing girls as members of the opposite sex, instead of just people."

"I *know* they're the opposite sex, Rob."

"Scientifically you do. But now it has finally triggered a hormonal reaction in you."

"What the hell are you—"

He put his hand on my shoulder the way an adult might. "Tony, Tony, Tony." He laughed softly. "You reached the age where you're *attracted* to girls; the way they look, the way they talk, the things they do. Everything about them is *exciting* to you now."

"Oh, Christ," I said softly.

"It's a good thing. Hey, every person is the result of a man and a woman who—"

"Please stop talking!"

"I know it's hard to understand at first. But I guarantee you all your friends are going through the same thing."

"Then how come nobody has ever mentioned it?"

"Did *you* mention it?" he asked, as though he knew the answer.

"Of course not. It's too embarrassing."

"There you are, little brother. You suffer in silence at first. But sooner or later somebody will either say something, or act differently, and then the rush is on."

"What rush?"

"The rush to be part of the new social order."

"Jesus, Rob, will you please just—"

"Tony, once boys and girls start getting together, nobody wants to be left out. Get it?"

"Yeah, I guess so. So when does all this start?"

"Next *Wednesday!* I don't know. But it's gonna happen soon, you'll see."

"Oh, man. Why can't things just stay the way they are?"

He laughed. I considered everything he had told me. "Okay, Rob, thanks. So I guess I'm normal, right?"

He punched me in the shoulder. "You? Normal? That's pushin' it." He was almost out of the room, then came back and sat next to me on the bed. "Hey, one more thing. Very important."

My eyes got wide. "What is it?"

"Those two girls, Gina and the other one."

"Janie."

"Yeah, forget about them as girlfriends. Get to know some other girls. Don't pick one of those two."

"What's wrong with Gina?" I said, a bit defensive.

"Nothing. But she's your *friend.*"

"Wouldn't that make her perfect to have as a girlfriend?"

"Just the opposite, Tony boy. Eventually you'll break up, and then your friendship is ruined. If you pick a different girl, Gina can *always* be your friend. You have her as a girlfriend, it'll ruin everything." He jabbed his finger at me for emphasis. "Don't shit in your own nest, little brother."

He left without further explanation, and I wasn't sure if I understood. I took most things literally, as I said. He couldn't possibly have known about the time I snuck into Gina's house and used her bathroom.

. . .

I guess Vinnie, Adam, and Willie didn't get the memo on not shitting in your own nest. It wasn't long after my talk with Rob that I sensed a gradual shift in the way those guys acted around Gina and Janie.

One time Adam had all his old report cards with him, showing them to Gina, making sure to mention that there was not a single grade below A-. Then Willie starts bragging about how he can do a handstand and walk at the same time, which he did. He also had an article from some military journal telling about a battle where his supposed ancestor, Jean Baptiste D'Erlon was a hero. Gina seemed impressed. I started wondering if Rob had given me good advice.

But the capper was when damn Vinnie actually started *flirting* with Janie, telling her she had big, puppy-dog eyes. I seriously thought I was gonna puke. I was hoping Janie would just slug him one, but she smiled shyly and said, "Shutup, asshole."

Janie had a rough upbringing, like I said, and she called all four of us boys either 'shithead' or 'asshole.' It was a term of friendship with her. It led to a lot of confusion at times. Janie would call out, "Hey asshole," and we would all look, which would lead to, "Not you, the *other* asshole," and finally, "Not *you,* shithead over there."

There were sporadic outbursts of this new "social order." I was hoping for the law of averages to kick in, and that eventually those guys would embarrass themselves with all this nonsense. But one time in the midst of all this, Gina gave me a look as if to say, 'Your turn, now.'

I just looked at her and said, "I'm sorry, I don't have anything prepared."

Then came another change. The girls insisted on playing basketball with us guys, so the two-on-two became three-on-three, with one girl on each team. They had never shown an interest in this before. Were they trying to get our approval, earn our admiration?

Playing street basketball with girls was like walking on eggs, at least for me. We play a pretty physical game. What were we supposed to do now? We agreed that we would dial it down when the girls had the ball. Gina and Janie played like girls who had *watched* basketball, but not actually played it.

Janie had older brothers, so she held her own, but with Gina, it was almost comical. She would dribble towards the basket, *walk* a few steps, dribble some more, *run* with the ball, and then wave everybody away while she took a shot that usually hit the bottom of the rim.

I was sure the girls now perceived *us* differently as well.

And all the while, we rode our bikes, yelling "reckless abandon," raising hell, getting called 'hooligans' by Mrs. Costello, and still managing to have a good time being a kid. And our main source of fun still was watching what the two little Costellos, Dustin and Destiny, managed to do to drive their beleaguered mother batty.

. . .

Dustin and Destiny were two of the most out-of-control kids I ever saw. They were around five or six. I swear they were borderline psychotic.

They were notorious wanderers, often found several houses away, in someone's back yard, torturing a cat or throwing rocks at some other little kid. Mrs. Costello had no concept of *watching* them when Allan and Barbara were in school. She tried to keep them inside, but they snuck out. She locked the doors, but they went out their cellar and came out the hatchway door. She locked *that,* but they went out their bedroom window, etc.

When they did stay in their yard, they found a million ways to cause havoc. There was a garage in their back yard they somehow got on top of from a large branch on their mulberry tree.

Their father finally got around to sawing it off, but they continued to climb the tree, often getting so far up they were too scared to come down. Fire Department rescue units came over several times.

On one occasion they wandered so far that some kids found them in the woods half a mile away, playing by a stream that was nearly overflowing from spring rains. The kids took them to their house where their mother tried to find out who they were, but couldn't get them to say their names. (I think they were stupid as well as reckless.) Finally, a neighbor lady recognized them, and drove them home. It was 1980, so the woman was thanked instead of arrested.

If wandering and neighborhood cats weren't enough temptations, older brother Allan had a pigeon coop. So there was a week or two one May when the neighborhood was on "pigeon alert," trying to round up the dozen or so birds that Dustin and Destiny had let loose, minus the one that died when those two little hellions fed it something undetermined. They used crayons on one of the others, trying to make it into an Easter chick. We discovered the hard way that a pigeon's first impulse upon being grabbed is to shit. Good times.

My personal favorite was when they found some paint cans and brushes in their cellar. Mrs. Costello, in a rare moment of vigilance, intercepted them and put the stuff back on a shelf. But she forgot about the small stepladder down there. So the 'D's ended up with the paint and brushes after all. They had just been told by their wacky mother that they were *not* to paint the house or garage. Obedient little bastards that they were, they opted instead to paint *each other.*

Dustin painted Destiny leaf green, while Destiny returned the favor, painting Dustin fire engine red. Not on their clothes, mind you, since they seldom wore anything other than underpants outside, (one of Mrs. Costello's feeble attempts to keep them from ruining their clothes) but on their actual skin, faces and hair included.

I remember asking if I could borrow the camera to get a picture, but Mom told me those people had enough trouble already; they didn't need their kids turned into a tourist attraction. It was weeks before all the paint was gone, and I heard the Costello's bathtub was ruined in the process.

. . .

Now we come to the part of this tale that shames me to this day. As I said, the social vibe had shifted in our group, but I was still trying to follow my brother's advice of not getting involved with Gina or Janie in a way other than friendship. But Adam, Vinnie, and Willie continued to make inroads with them. Of course, the other half of my brother's advice was to get to know some other girls in school, but that was not going well at all.

So I was at the bottom of the heap in the "new social order." I even asked Rob about it, but I think I caught him at a bad time. He didn't seem as interested as he had been a few weeks earlier.

"Just keep plugging away," he said. "Even you're bound to get lucky."

Well, that was no help. I pretty much gave up at that point. But it occurred to me that there were two girls right under my nose who knew me and liked me (I supposed) whom I saw every day outside of school. It was time to shit in my own nest and see how that worked.

I had always been the "idea guy." The orchard raids, the rides out to the cliffs, riding into Idaho, the suicide runs down West Robena Hill were all my ideas, as well as the almost daily forays through the Costello's back yard, yelling "reckless abandon" at the top of our lungs.

It was Thursday, June 19th, the first day of summer vacation. We usually celebrated with an orchard raid, followed by a ride out to the cliffs. We gathered in front of my house, as usual. Vinnie was bumping the front tire of Janie's bike with his own front tire, like some freaky mating ritual. "Knock it off, shithead," was her response. After a few more bumps she started bumping *his* front tire, looking at the ground with a slight smile.

I guess it was the sight of my best friend and one of my two girl friends "bike flirting" that caused me to say what I did. Ideas were my strong suit, and my thought was that *I* would impress the girls with something truly imaginative and daring. The words coming out of my stupid mouth were, "Hey, let's have "Rag On Mrs. Costello Week.""

Janie smiled an evil smile, Gina giggled, and the three guys were wide-eyed in anticipation.

"What are we gonna do, asshole?"

"We're in," said Vinnie, looking at Adam and Willie, who nodded eagerly.

"What drives Mrs. Costello nuts the most?" I asked, stalling for an idea.

"Us riding through her yard," said Adam.

Everyone nodded in agreement, except Gina. "Her two little brats, Dustin and Destiny," she said, smiling at me.

"That's right, Gina," I said, hoping to gain favor with her.

"So what you gonna do?" asked Willie.

Think fast, Tony. "We come up with something really *outrageous,* and get those two little shits to do it. Then we watch the fun when Mrs. Costello catches them."

"That's actually pretty funny," said Vinnie, laughing a little.

Adam was looking up, head tilted, the way he did when he analyzed a situation. This was crucial. If there was something wrong with my idea, he would be the first to identify it.

He smiled slyly. "With those two, the possibilities are almost endless. We just have to come up with the right idea to plant in their insane little heads."

And there it was. Big smiles on everyone's faces, Vinnie pounding his handlebars in anticipation, Janie vibrating with soft laughter, and Gina with her cute giggle.

So we started the short ride down to 20 Pratt Hill. I rode slowly to buy some time to think. It was critical that I start "Rag On Mrs. Costello Week" with a bang. As we rode by Mr. Cox's house, one house up from the Costellos, I noticed something I had overlooked for the better part of a year. He had constructed a stone wall separating his property from the Costellos. It was about two feet high, fashioned with small rounded stones, rather than the huge flat ones most walls have. There had to have been hundreds of stones that comprised that wall.

We didn't know much about Archie Cox. Like every other man in our neighborhood, he went to work every morning in his old car, carrying a lunch pail. When I thought back on it, there were many late afternoons and Saturdays when I had seen him painstakingly building that wall. With the Costello devils next door, I guess it was a necessity.

We got down to Costello's back yard, and instead of tearing through, I held up a hand, like a cavalry officer halting his troopers. The 'D's were in the road, killing ants.

"Hey, Dustin and Destiny," I said, going up to them. "Where's your mommy?"

"She takes her vitamins, then goes to sleep," Destiny answered.

Obviously some medication. I thought there would be a window of time where I could pull off a really bodacious prank, with a little help from the 'D's.

Rest periods included it took those two only ninety minutes to *disassemble* Archie Cox's stone wall and bring all the stones into their own yard. Laughing hysterically, we went back to my house and waited. A short time later, the shrieking, screaming, and yelling started, courtesy of Mrs. Costello. I knew we would never get blamed for it, as Dustin and Destiny were not really adept at explaining things, and didn't really know who we were.

The tumult continued through the day. When Allan and Barbara got home from wherever they had been, we could see them carrying stones back to Archie Cox's property line, attempting to rebuild the wall, I sent Adam on a recon mission to see how things were going down there, and he returned, laughing as he spoke.

"It doesn't look *anything* like a wall, and it's about five feet farther up. They'll never come close to finishing it in time."

We took turns riding down there to see for ourselves, then went off to the cliff, so as not to be too conspicuous. By the end of the day, all the stones were back in Mr. Cox's yard, in several ragged piles. He had torn down the "wall" that Allan and Barbara attempted to rebuild.

It was a cruel, heartless thing I had done. I know that now, but at the time I felt I had gained big-time status with the gang, especially Gina and Janie. I knew I had to keep it going. The next day the gang met in front of my house, expectant looks on their faces. I was in control, and it felt good. "Let's go, guys. It continues."

The 'D's were in the road again, sitting on a beachball. I took two chocolate coins from my pocket and gave each of them one, mentioning that I found them by digging in *their* yard. By noon their yard looked as though there had been an invasion of ants on steroids. Once again, Allan and Barbara had gone to the YMCA, and Mrs. Costello was sleeping off the effects of her "vitamins."

The aftermath played out almost exactly the same, except Allan and Barbara made the two little snots help them fill in all the holes. Mrs. Costello hit 'E' above high 'C' with her shrill, sustained diatribe against her two youngest. "Ran On Mrs. Costello Week" was now a huge hit. Again, we got away without suspicion.

Archie Cox spent the weekend rebuilding his wall. I thought about it, but decided that a repeat performance would not play well in the originality department.

Most of us were stuck doing "family fun" things that weekend, so the torture of Mrs. Costello was put on hold.

On both Monday and Tuesday I came up with "chores" that Dustin and Destiny could do to "help out" around the Costello residence, and made sure they got paid in advance with bubble gum and some shiny, useless trinkets I found in a junk drawer at home. The chores included "cleaning out" their garage, and "helping mommy take in the clothes from the clothesline." They seemed eager to do this and possibly atone for their previous misdeeds. But who really knows with those two. Anyway, you can imagine how wrong these latest endeavors went.

I was now regarded as the genius of our group. Sure, Adam was the brain, but that was with knowledge. Creativity and resourcefulness are different aspects of brilliance, and I was the uncontested champion.

On Wednesday I went into the woods near my house and caught two medium-sized garter snakes. There were tons of them there. I had them in a jar, and when the gang gathered in front of my house, I could *feel* the intrigue.

A short bike ride later, I had convinced Dustin and Destiny that these were great pets and that they should take the jar inside and let them loose. "Be careful," I warned. "Don't drop it."

I was surprised when Destiny asked me, "Where?"

I thought a moment. "Your back porch." It was closed in, and the snakes would be contained. Inside the house they would find hiding places and probably never be seen.

We knew by now that Allan and Barbara would be coming up the hill from the YMCA within twenty minutes, but Mrs. Costello was good for another hour of sleep. What the hell medication was she on, anyways?

We didn't want to be seen when the snakes were discovered on the Costello's porch, so we killed some time with an orchard raid and a ride out to the cliffs. Adam mentioned that it would probably be Barbara or Allen who would discover the new family "pets," but it didn't make any difference. I told him Barbara would probably scream bloody murder and wake her mother up. Then the real fun would start.

Mr. Hito was nowhere to be seen, so we just lay on the edge of his property, munching some of his scrumptious apples, then went out to the cliffs. While we were there, looking at the scenery below, Gina walked her bike over to me. My senses tingled in anticipation.

"You are *so* clever, Tony."

"Thanks. That's what they tell me." Smooth, huh?

"Do you like Joanne?"

"Joanne from our class?"

"Yeah. Do you like her?"

"She's okay, I guess. I don't know. I mean, I don't *like* her, like her."

Gina nodded and smiled, looking down. So my time had come after all. I was reminding myself to tell Rob that his 'don't shit in your own nest' theory was wrong. I couldn't picture ever breaking up with Gina. She had been the right one all along.

"Gina! Shithead! Let's get going!"

I looked up to find everyone heading back. Gina and I caught up to them, and we rode at a brisk pace, anticipating the pandemonium we might witness at the Costello house.

We were a good half mile down the dirt section of Unterfeld Road when we heard a car approaching from around one of the blind corners.

"Car!' I called out. I instinctively put myself between Gina and the road.

It happened so fast, or so *slowly,* I can't decide which. To this day, I remember every detail. A bronze-colored Plymouth Duster passed us, doing all of twenty miles per hour. A woman was driving, her mouth opening and her head turning as she yelled at the two passengers in the back seat, a little boy and girl, who waved at us as they drove past.

Adam was the first to recognize it. "It's Mrs. Costello, guys, with Dustin and Destiny in the back."

"What's she doing way the hell out here?" somebody asked.

"Oh, my God!" yelled Adam. "She finally flipped! She's gonna throw those two off the cliff!"

I still couldn't put ideas and words together, but it *seemed* alarming. We all turned and rode after the bronze Plymouth, which had sped up. It was soon out of sight.

"Hurry, guys!" someone yelled.

In the back of my mind I was putting cause and effect elements together, and the one which terrified me was that the snakes on the back porch had pushed the unstable Mrs. Costello over the edge, and she was going to kill those two little kids. ***Because of me.***

A couple of minutes of frantic pedaling brought us near the end of the paved section of the road. The Plymouth was up ahead, about eighty yards away, stopped, its brake lights showing.

"I can see the kids in the back seat!" yelled Vinnie. "Let's go!"

Dustin and Destiny were waving frantically. It was obvious now they were calling for help. We were close enough now that there was no way she could have done anything to them.

Twenty yards away, Vinnie jumped off his bike, letting it drop. I could hear his feet pounding the gravel.

Mrs. Costello gunned the Duster's engine, throwing sand and stones in our faces as the car sped the final thirty-five yards, hitting the wooden fence at perhaps forty miles per hour.

Gina let out a piercing scream while the rest of us watched in muted horror. We had seen so many cars go off cliffs in movies and on TV that it seemed strangely like we were on a Hollywood set. Gina's scream was just fading when we heard the metallic smash, followed by two more as the car bounced. Mercifully, it did not burst into flames. Nobody wanted to look down at it, because that meant going to the edge of the cliff, with the fence now gone.

(How easily we could have met the same fate with some of the moronic things we did on that fence.)

Finally, Vinnie crawled on his stomach to the edge and looked down. "Oh, my God," he said softly. The rest of us boys did the same. Adam told us to listen for sounds of someone calling out. There was nothing but the sounds of birds, and Gina sobbing behind us. Janie covered her face and shook silently.

"We gotta get back and tell someone," Adam said. "They could still be alive down there."

We rode back to town at the fastest clip ever. We rode with reckless abandon, only the fun element was gone.

. . .

It was sadly ironic. The Fire Rescue unit, which had gotten Dustin and Destiny *down* from the mulberry tree was now bringing them *up* from the bottom of the cliff. No one survived.

The six of us *needed* to be together, so we parked in front of my house and just sat there and talked. Or said nothing. We could see cars parked beside the Costello house in both front and back yard. Police and relatives.

Adam had the most useful suggestion. "Lay low and listen to everything your parents say about this. Eavesdrop if you have to. We can meet here and share info."

And that's what we all did. We found out stuff, especially after the wake and funeral, which most of our parents attended.

First off, and very important, my asinine prank with the snakes had *no* bearing on what happened. Allan and Barbara came home from the YMCA, Barbara spotted one of the snakes hiding behind a wastebasket and got a broom and swept them both off the porch like a nine-year-old female St. Patrick. No one even *told* their mother they had been there.

Mrs. Costello awoke from her deep sleep an hour later, made everyone lunch, then returned upstairs. My parents were having a hushed conversation about this in their bedroom. I was in *my* bedroom with a glass pressed against the wall. (That works, by the way.) Mr. Costello said at the wake that his wife had been treated for depression for years. Her medications put her to sleep, but were not much help beyond that.

He knew things with his wife were very fragile. He had even got rid of his shotgun and extra clothesline they had, and kept knives and such out of sight. He feared something like this *could* happen; he was just doing the best he could so that it wouldn't.

Poor Mrs. Costello usually awoke to something outrageous that Dustin and Destiny had gotten into. It really wasn't their fault. Allan and Barbara were much older, and Carrie and Charlie were in their own little world. It was only natural that Dustin and Destiny would make a fun world for themselves as well, unfortunately without any stable adult influence.

From what we also found out, there were things going on that made "Rag On Mrs. Costello Week" almost superfluous. We came to the conclusion that this would have happened without any of the things we had added to the simmering cauldron inside Ann Costello, age 36.

She was, essentially, a tragedy waiting to happen. I think each one of us felt some measure of guilt, anyway. Me, especially.

1985

In time, we outgrew the bike thing. Even before we did, we never rode with "reckless abandon" again. And **never** through Costello's yard.

After eighth grade, Janie's mom remarried, and her stepfather moved the family to Maine, where he was from originally. Gina attended a private girl's school way over in Portland, so we only saw her on school vacations. She was now very different from the fun-loving, sweet kid we had grown up with. She was polite and friendly, but you could tell she lived in a different world. Even in the summer, she was seldom around.

Adam began ninth grade in a school for gifted children fifty miles away. We still saw him on weekends and vacations, but he didn't seem interested in us or anything we were into.

So it ended up with Vinnie, Willie, and me still friends. We do lots of stuff together, hanging out, going to the mall one town over, playing sports, etc. We don't even *have* bikes any more, but sometimes we drive out to Hito's Orchard and *buy* half a bushel of apples. I don't think he knows that we were the 'hooligans' who raided his orchard years ago.

Allan Costello is a sophomore at the tri-town high school, but I seldom see him. Barbara is a freshman, and I see her all the time, walking hand in hand with whatever boy she currently likes. She turned into a real beautiful girl, and always says hello to me. I return her greeting quickly and look away.

As for me, I still haven't found that special girl yet, but I know it will come in time.

One other thing. These days, I rag on *no one*.

DUE OUT IN LATE 2019

SUNDOWN SERENADE

The gang from Lilac Lane is featured in two selections in Dave Lopardo's latest collection. They share the pages with an eclectic array of short fiction which includes mystery, drama, crime, a touch of humor, and a few of the most bizarre tales ever devised by the unpredictable and overactive imagination of the author.